First Wave

NORTHWEST COUNTER-TERRORISM TASKFORCE BOOK 1

Lisa Phillips

Chapter 1

Tonight wasn't the first night Dakota had spent alone in the woods. Last time had been years ago, long enough she'd almost convinced herself she didn't remember.

She hadn't forgotten the cold, though. The way her ears numbed because she'd pulled her dark hair back in a ponytail. Then and now.

Tucked in her pocket, Dakota's phone vibrated. She lifted a hand and used her slender fingers to answer the call on Bluetooth headphones.

"Pierce." Her quiet voice sounded far too loud in the stillness of after midnight.

"Here I thought you might be doing something interesting this late on a Friday night for once." The director's voice was void of any kind of tone. She never gave anything away. "And yet, when I locate your phone it seems that you're sitting on the side of a mountain, fifteen miles from the Canadian border."

Dakota said nothing.

"It's thirty-eight degrees. It'll get to twenty-seven by morning."

She let her eyes drift across the tops of the trees in the valley below. The fence that bordered the apple orchard, along with a dusting of snow.

Director Bramlyn sighed. "I suppose it was too much to assume you'd wait until Monday. Look into this then—in the company of one of your team members. You know, the three people who are supposed to *have your back*."

She didn't include herself in that count. Just the two other agents on the team, and their tech person. The director's support came in a different way that was no less effective.

Dakota said, "Case'll be closed by then."

"You found something?"

"Not yet," Dakota replied. All they had so far was chatter that'd been picked up. Movement from here to the border. A park ranger who'd been paid off, then disappeared. The local sheriff was next on her list of people to track down. Hopefully he'd still be breathing when she found him.

"Keep me apprised."

"Will do." Dakota pressed her lips together. "And I'll call Special Agent O'Caran if I need some help."

"I guess I can't argue with that." The director sighed.

Needing help had different definitions for different people. Dakota knew how to spend a night in the woods by herself. Predators came in all shapes and sizes, and she hadn't met one yet that she couldn't handle with the knife or one of the two guns she carried. Occasionally she only had to utilize a well-placed knee to subdue an aggressor.

"So long as you actually do lean on the resources available to you when you need them," the director said. "After all, it's why I pay my taxes."

The corner of Dakota's mouth crept up. "I thought you had some under-the-table deal so you don't have to pay in."

"I wish." Victoria laughed. The director sounded like a classy matron—minus the British accent—from one of the TV shows Dakota would *never* let on to the team that she actually watched. She sighed. "Are you sure you're good?"

She was really worried? Dakota said, "My nose is cold and I think one of my feet went to sleep."

"Don't freeze to death," Victoria said. "We'll have to hike in there and carry you out."

"Nah, just leave me for the animals."

Victoria choked. "For goodness sake, just be careful."

Dakota said, "You know I will." Her capability wasn't in question. Victoria knew her history—all of it. That was the deal they'd struck when

Dakota came on board. Neither of them wanted secrets. She also had no intention of being babied just because Victoria didn't want this place to mess with her head. So she said, "I'm good."

"Try to at least *sound* convincing when you say stuff like that."

"I always sound convincing."

"Maybe to all the other people you lie to." But not Victoria.

"Just...mark me down as camping for the weekend, or something."

"Did you even take a tent with you?"

Dakota waited a second, then said, "I think my phone battery is dying." She even reached up and touched the mute button a couple of times, and said a few random words so it sounded like she was cutting out.

"If you don't call me in twelve hours, I will send the entire team with backup from the state police to look for you."

Dakota lowered her hand. "Deal."

Plenty of time for surveillance here. If nothing happened she would pay the sheriff a visit. Flash her badge and watch him squirm.

They all squirmed.

"I'm going to regret this." Victoria sighed, and the call ended.

A rustle in the brush to her left cut through the silence. Dakota blew out a breath, slow enough that there was no cloud of white. She shifted her weight and lifted her left foot, rotating the ankle. It clicked every time. Had ever since...

She didn't finish that thought.

The past was something she didn't remember. And whether that meant she'd strived to forget, or was still convincing herself she didn't remember, the outcome was the same. Dakota was alive *now*. That was all that mattered.

Grass under her feet. Cold night air in her lungs. Mountains behind her, and the lights of civilization in the distance.

One eye on the rustling brush, Dakota lowered her foot back down. Her gun hand was free, but she didn't reach for the weapon holstered under her arm. Her other hand held a thin flashlight not much larger than a pen, her thumb steady on the button so she could turn it on when needed.

Dakota crept between trees, as silent as the night. She made her way down the slope toward the orchard, where rows of apple trees lined the outermost field. The property was huge, the house a hundred acres to the west of where she stood, over the slope. Chatter had specifically mentioned the road that led to this end of the outfit.

Movement accompanied a low rustle. Dakota froze, her right shoulder and hip pressed against a tree trunk.

A dog raced between apple trees, nose to the ground. One of those police dog types, black and brown coloring. It even had a vest on. No markings, though. There was little as far as a breeze tonight, but she had no idea if she was upwind or downwind of the animal. The last thing she needed was to be scented.

Twenty feet behind the dog, a man followed in a half-run. Tracking with the dog's progress but giving it space. He moved like a man trained, his stance alert even with his focus on the animal. Military maybe, or some kind of federal agency.

There wasn't an operation here tonight. If there had been, Victoria would have passed that information on. Most of the time the exchange of information between federal agencies worked. Not always. So she didn't write this off as random.

Dakota tracked their progress as she made her way to the base of the hill and hopped the fence. She skirted the edge of the orchard, making sure she stayed out of the way.

Was this one of them? The man and his dog seemed like they were looking for something, but it was possible this guy was a scout and whoever had sparked the chatter about a new "weapon" moving through here intended to show up.

Fifty feet to the west she stopped.

Where was…

"Following me?" The man's voice was low. Not deadly. She knew what that sounded like. This had a ring of authority but without a layer of intent to do her harm.

Like *she* was the one who shouldn't be here.

Dakota reached for her weapon. She heard the unmistakable snick of a gun being drawn from its holster and froze.

"Drop what you're holding and put your hands up."

• • •

What was probably a flashlight dropped to the dirt. The woman lifted her gloved hands. She'd been reaching for something, he just didn't know what. Josh heard the familiar sound of Neema's panting as she padded closer to his left leg. They were a team, and the dog was an asset—considering she'd realized someone else was there before Josh had.

Who was this woman?

Josh clicked on his flashlight. "Turn around slowly."

As she turned, he shone the light on the darkest of brown hair, almost black, that hung down to the middle of her back. Her mouth was set at an unhappy slant. The frown that marred her features drew her dark eyebrows together. With the lack of light, her eyes looked as black as her hair. Her skin was smooth and flawless.

She quite literally took his breath away. The sight of her distracted him enough that he forgot what he was doing for a second.

"You wanna get that light out of my face?" The lift of her hands splayed her jacket wide enough he saw the gun in its holster.

"Tell me why you're following me, and I will."

"How about you tell me why *you're* here." She reacted like he was an annoyance, nothing more or less. Like she had as much right to be here as he did? Maybe more?

Josh said, "I show you mine, and you'll show me yours?" before he thought it through.

She made a dismissive noise with her mouth. "Hardly."

"Guess not, then. Sorry." For politeness sake. "My mouth runs away from me sometimes."

"I'm glad you have better control of your dog."

His favorite subject. Josh smiled, though the woman couldn't see it considering his light was in her face. He would've pet Neema's head but he didn't have a free hand, so he leaned his weight left. She braced her weight against his leg in response. Shared comfort, a united front. "This is Neema."

"Okay."

"Your enthusiasm is overwhelming." Josh gave the command to release Neema, so she could move around if she wanted to. The woman's body shifted. A small movement he thought might've been a start. Was she really nervous about his dog?

"She won't bother you."

Neema didn't move to the side to do her business, though. She wandered toward the woman, and he could hear her nose working. The woman took a step back.

"Unless there's a hot dog in your pocket."

The woman chuckled, but it gave away her nervousness. She still held her hands up but stood motionless while the dog learned her scent.

"Neema, leave it." Sure, he could've given the command a few seconds ago, but where was the fun in that? He might need his dog to know her smell. Neema turned away and wandered to the edge of where he could see her.

There was no reason why she couldn't sniff around a little.

The woman held herself as though she was in complete control—apart from the fact she was uneasy around the dog. It was debatable, between Neema and the woman, as to who had more presence. The gun won out, though. Neema could be vicious, but she didn't have weapons to utilize.

"So who are you?"

She shook her head, a slight movement. "Lower the flashlight, and I'll show you my badge."

So she was here in an official capacity. "All right." He shifted it down and to the side while he tried to figure out what he was going to tell her. Caught red-handed in the middle of the night. Josh said, "Let's see it."

She reached back, which he allowed considering her gun was under one arm. A move like that always made him tense though. Anyone given the opportunity to reach for something out of sight could mean the difference between life and death in a second. He'd had far too much training to ever relax in a situation like this.

But she didn't know what Neema was capable of.

The woman pulled out a leather wallet and flipped it open. Badge and ID. "Homeland Security."

But she didn't tell him her name.

"Nice to meet you." He figured she might appreciate the irony in that. "On a case?"

"You could say that. You?"

"Something like that." Ish. Okay, not really at all. This was his weekend off, but what he was doing here was his business and not the business of this stranger who hadn't identified herself.

"What is your dog looking for?"

Josh glanced around to see where Neema had gone. When he didn't find her, he called out, "Yellow!"

From his left, not far, Neema's bark replied to him.

"Yellow?"

He shrugged once. "It just means bark. But no one else knows that except the two of us." She raised her left brow. He gave an almost-smile. "And, well, now you. I use it like Marco Polo normally." And if the dog kept looking for what he was here to find, then it saved him time.

The woman bent down and picked up her flashlight, which she slid into her jacket pocket. "Well, it was nice meeting you and all..."

She let that trail off. Josh got the feeling it wasn't all that nice to meet him.

The woman continued, "But you're going to have to tell me who you are, and what you're doing here." Her stance was loose. Still, he could see her readiness in the flex of her fingers. She could pull that gun in seconds, and he'd guess she was fast.

"I'm Josh," he said. "Josh Weber." He didn't give more detail than that, since he wasn't here in an official capacity. What he did with his free time was his business.

Would Neema find what they were looking for? He wanted the answer to be yes, but had to face the fact he might return home with no news at all. The lead that had pointed to this apple orchard was slim. Maggie might have only stuck around here long enough to post that selfie to Instagram. Or she could've been driving through on the way to somewhere else.

Maybe he would never find her.

Neema let out a bark. One short, sharp alert.

Josh broke from his conversation with the Homeland Security agent and raced between the rows of apple trees toward the source of the sound. On the way, he gave her the command to bark again.

The female agent chased him the whole way there. He heard the shuffle of her clothing and the intake of breath as she inhaled and wondered if she would tackle him. Or give up and shoot him in the back.

Neema sat beside a body, laid out on the grass. A trail of tire ruts stretched from the woman lying there and off to the northwest.

Josh pulled up short. His stomach sank, but he said, "Good girl," and scratched Neema's neck.

"Move the dog away from her." The Homeland agent's voice was sharp. She crouched beside the body. It was turned awkwardly so that one shoulder was up but her hips were flat on the ground. Face down. Arms spread. Hair wrapped around her head.

The woman agent shifted hair aside and touched the neck.

After a second of silence she glanced up at him, a dark look on her face. "She's dead."

Chapter 2

Dakota let out a sigh. She could feel the cold of the skin even with her gloves on.

A dead young woman was not the way she wanted to spend her weekend. Yes, she'd opted to come out here and do surveillance. But that didn't mean she hadn't expected to be on her couch on Sunday with her thick socks on, binge watching season five of her favorite show. With caramel popcorn.

She pulled her gun, stood up and turned in one move, then stepped toward the man. "Gun on the ground, hands on your head."

His eyes flared. "I didn't do this."

Now that the flashlight wasn't in her face, her eyes had adjusted. The guy was a pretty cute murderer, but still a murderer. Or at least involved in this somehow. She wasn't going to quibble about his level of involvement. "Hands on your head," she repeated.

"But—"

She cut him off. "Now."

The dog barked, body braced in a forward lean that pointed her toward Dakota. Like she was about to lunge.

"You keep that animal back, and do as I said." His hands were raised, one still holding the gun, but she didn't like this inaction. Who was he?

He bent his knees and lowered the gun to the grass. "Okay. Fine." When he stood he said, "But I didn't do this. In fact—" He motioned to the dog, then the body. "—if that's who I think it is, we're here *looking* for her."

"You knew this body would be here?"

"Not the way you think." He sighed, palms out. She didn't believe this man would be subdued, though. Not until he was in cuffs, which she hadn't brought with her. He said, "Look…it's complicated, okay?"

"Then explain it." But not right now. Dakota shifted and had to pull off her glove so she could use her free hand to slide out her phone and dial Victoria's number.

It rang once and then the director answered, her voice sharp through the earbud still in Dakota's left ear. "You found something?"

"I'll take you up on that offer now." She wasn't about to let this guy know she was out here alone with no backup. "I've got a body drop."

"Anyone I know?"

"Unknown. She's been strangled." At her words, the man winced. "By the look of how she was dumped, I'd say tossed here. Killed somewhere else."

"Give me an hour."

Dakota wasn't sure that was possible, unless the team was closer than she knew. Victoria was resourceful, though.

The director said, "I know a guy in Life Flight. If they're not busy I'll have the team in the chopper and at your location ASAP."

"Copy that."

"Forensics?"

"And I've got a witness." One who was possibly a suspect.

Victoria said, "Who?"

Dakota watched him, giving back that intense study he was doing of her in equal measure. "Unknown. So far."

He *was* going to tell her who he was, or they were going to have a big problem. Given all the people Victoria knew, and the number of people in the federal government who owed her a favor, they could collectively make this guy's life a nightmare.

He must have seen something of her intent in her eyes, because his brows lifted. But he said nothing.

"Be careful."

"Oh, I will." Dakota let him make of her tone whatever he wanted.

Victoria hung up chuckling, though it sounded uneasy. Dakota put her phone back in her pocket and gave the man an assessing look. "Military?"

"At one point."

"Tell me what your name is." Not a question, a command. "Better yet, show me your wallet."

He lifted his chin. "Driver's license, or badge?" A clear challenge, but there was something there.

Was he on an operation? She couldn't help but wonder if this guy was here in an official capacity. She waved to the body. "Friend of yours?"

That wince came again.

"Name." She put every ounce of authority she possessed into it.

"Josh Weber, as I've already told you," he said. "But I'd rather my name was left *off* the official Homeland Security report."

Ah-ha. "Not supposed to be here?" Maybe she took a little too much satisfaction in that. This wasn't a competition, and neither was the authority here in question. Obviously she was in charge. He just didn't seem to have wholly recognized that yet. Or wasn't willing to submit to it.

He shrugged and glanced over at his dog. No less alert than before, but not baring teeth at Dakota either.

"Why don't you just tell me why, and I'll see what I can do?" She could be nice. Sometimes.

He scratched at his hair. To buy time so he could figure out what to say? "Can I look at the body? See if it really is who I think it might be?"

She took a step back and to the side, so she'd be able to see whatever he did and still keep him in her sights. "Don't touch anything. And don't get too close."

He crouched and bent to look at the woman's face. "I'm going to pull out my phone."

Dakota nodded.

He slid it from the front pocket of his jeans and swiped the screen. Despite the sweater and heavy jacket, he was probably as cold as she was and she wore gloves. When he'd swiped to what he wanted, he showed her the screen, a grim look on his face.

Dakota nodded again, still holding her gun in front. A loose aim on him. She'd drop him if he tried anything. "Why do you have a dead woman's picture on your phone?"

"She's my neighbor's granddaughter. Her name is Maggie." He paused for a second. "She's nineteen."

"Okay," Dakota said. "I'll tell the medical examiner when he shows up. Any idea of the last name?"

His frown was back. Almost like he'd given her some test she hadn't studied for, and she'd failed. What was up with that? He said, "Detweiler."

"Okay," she repeated. Why choose a different word when the same one worked? It wasn't redundant, it was efficient. "Now back up."

"I want to lay my coat over her."

"What? No."

He straightened. "It's respectful."

"It's also cold as all get out." Dakota motioned to the dead young woman with a sweep of her hand. "She doesn't need it."

A car engine revved to Dakota's left. Headlights cut across this field in the orchard. The dog let out one short, sharp bark. Like it wasn't obvious to them all that someone was here?

Dakota glanced toward the truck, taking her attention off the man for just a second.

She heard the rustle and realized what he'd done.

Half expecting him to barrel into her, she shifted back. Fighting stance. Ready for whatever came. Then it registered that the sound grew quieter, now gone over the noise of that truck.

He was running *away from her.*

"Hey!"

She raced after him, mad at herself that he got a head start. Rookie mistake. One that grated against her. She wasn't naïve, far from it. The admittedly cute murderer was going to have to face the consequences when she caught up with him.

At the truck?

He was getting picked up. That had to be it.

Dakota ducked between two trees, and with the dark, she missed the branch. Not because she was distracted by being angry at this guy, it was just the lack of light and the fact he'd *ruined* her night vision with that flashlight.

She slammed into it with the corner of her forehead and went down. Flat on her back.

Out cold.

. . .

Josh ran toward the truck. He skirted around to the left so he would come up on the passenger side. But not close. He had no intention of doing anything but observe. He was here to find out what had happened to Maggie. If it involved these people, then he needed to know. Like he needed to know if this truck was dark blue. The color of her boyfriend's half ton rig.

Neema kept pace beside him. He ducked between two trees, and a branch whipped at his face. *Ouch.* The sting radiated across his cheek.

He glanced back to look for the Homeland agent. No one on his heels, and no sound of someone either. But that truck roared through the field. Headlights dipped and rose as it traversed ruts in the ground. Pretty soon it would knock down an apple tree.

Brakes squealed. Josh winced at the sound, more for what it would do to Neema's sensitive hearing than his own. He gave a command and they slowed, Josh angling both of them in the same semi-circle so they came up on the passenger side. He padded through trees and kept low.

The engine shut off.

A door slammed…two.

Three.

Outnumbered, even with Neema's help.

He got close enough to spot two figures cross the beam of the headlights. Tall, bulky men. They were accompanied by one shorter and thinner. Wiry like a teenage boy. Was one of the men Maggie's boyfriend? Her killer?

If so, why return to the place she was dumped? That made no sense. He'd want to keep himself as far from the situation as possible. Not risk being seen here.

"Where?" One man barked.

The teen lifted his arm. "Over there." His voice shook as badly as his extended limb. Josh watched him lower it back by his side.

The man who'd spoken first grasped him on the back of the neck and shoved his body forward. "I mean, show me. Idiot."

The young one stumbled. "O-kay."

Josh watched them walk across the field, through rows of apple trees toward Maggie's dead body. Neema stood completely still and silent by his side. Ready for whatever command he would give.

He followed the men, hanging back so they wouldn't hear him. The homeland security agent had seemed in command, capable. Was she watching the same way he did? Surely she'd have caught up to him by now.

One of the men swore loudly, fast and short as a gunshot.

Josh frowned. The men had stopped suddenly.

"What…oh." The first man, the one who seemed to be in charge. Of at least the teen. "She's out cold."

"She's hot." That was the teen. There was a shuffle, and he said, "Ow. What'd you do that for?"

"You don't get dibs." A third voice, one Josh hadn't heard yet.

The teen said, "Fine. I see how it is."

"And don't forget it."

The first man spoke again. "Dakota Pierce. This says, 'Homeland Security Investigations.'" He swore again. "What's she doing out here?"

The third man said, "She's got a nasty gash on her forehead. She dead?"

Josh's entire body felt like it turned to stone. Neema shifted closer, sensing the change in him. He wanted to yell. Or throw up.

"Nah," the man answered. "Just out cold."

The teen said, "Was she looking for Maggie, too?"

"You mean the girl you decided to just *dump out here in the open*?"

"I said I was sorry," the teen whined.

"Take her gun. And don't shoot your foot off."

"Do we have time for this?" one of the taller men asked.

"Depends on what you had in mind."

Josh didn't like the tenor of their conversation at all. Whatever they wanted to do with Dakota, it wasn't going to be good. Had she been conscious she'd probably have shot them already. She hadn't seemed like a woman who would accept a whole lot of that kind of thing, and maybe that was an understatement. As for him, he would be right there beside her, adding his own bullets to the mix.

Except for the fact the rounds would be extracted from these men by the local coroner. Then he'd have to answer a bunch of uncomfortable questions about why his slugs were found in dead lowlifes at a spot he wasn't exactly supposed to be.

It should've been his weekend off. Josh was already skating on thin ice with his boss, an assistant director at the DEA. And with the senior agent he'd been assigned to.

He hadn't realized how badly he would grate against the procedure. He'd figured there would be a whole lot more hands-on work alongside the paperwork he accepted as necessary. What he hadn't anticipated was being paired with one of those agents just clocking in and out every day, biding his time until retirement. The man only wanted to do computer work.

Josh had been "boots on the ground" for as long as he could remember. And he had a sealed juvenile record to prove it. Always wading into the fight when there was someone to protect. Something to fix. Or save. There was no way he'd let this agent face three men alone. Especially when she was unconscious. He wanted his life to count for something even if that meant he got messy in the process, or if he risked his job.

He had to help this woman.

The three men were still talking. So graphic, it was getting pretty gross.

"And when we're done?" the teen asked, his voice animated now.

"We kill her," the first man said. "You're the expert at dumping bodies. Guess that makes it your job." Bitterness laced his tone.

"I said I was sorry. What more do you want from me?"

Number three said, "How about a little respect for your brother?" He paused. "Now pick her up. Let's go."

Josh moved in closer, gun out in front, and called out, "Hold up."

Two of them whipped around, guns drawn. The teen dropped Dakota's arm.

"No one is taking her anywhere."

Dakota started to stir, letting out a moan.

Neema growled. Josh said, "You boys best move on."

He wanted to arrest them all, but had no backup and wasn't out here with any of the authority his own badge held.

One of them lifted his weapon higher. The other's attention was on Josh's dog. She had Kevlar strapped around her, but she could still get seriously hurt if they managed to hit her.

Josh took a half step left to cover her.

He saw the movement as it began. Knew the man's intention immediately. He'd been in too many firefights not to recognize that glint in someone's eyes. Murder looked the same the world over.

Even at home.

Bullets flew. He dove to the side. Rolled.

And came up shooting.

Chapter 3

Clothing brushed her face. Someone stepped on her hand with their boot—thank you, gloves. Still hurt, though. Dakota couldn't help the moan that escaped her lips with her next exhale.

She blinked at the sky. Her head reverberated pain from a spot on her temple to the back of her neck, where her pulse throbbed with every heartbeat.

A gunshot blasted.

Two shots answered it. Then a third.

Pause.

"You wanna go down for killing two feds," someone called out, "then keep this up." Her mystery man. Where was his dog?

A gunshot answered him.

"That's some heat you'll have on you. Until you're locked up for life." He went quiet and a shot rang out. "I wouldn't want that much attention."

Dakota's ears rang. She tried to lift her head, but everything rotated. Her. The ground underneath her. She rolled and vomited onto the dirt.

Voices called out. She couldn't make out the words, or who it was.

"…go!"

"What about—"

"Just go!"

The truck? She remembered that, but not much else. What was going on? Dakota pressed her hands onto the ground and tried to do a push up, get her feet under her. She managed knees. When she lifted her head the world swam again. She forced herself to wait, to get steady in her balance, and then she stood. Swayed. Leaned against a tree.

A tree. That was it.

She reached up and touched her forehead. Pain stabbed like a knife, but she couldn't feel much with her gloves on and couldn't see what that wet stuff was. Blood. She wiped at the injury with the back of her hand.

A truck engine revved. Dakota turned her body first, letting her head move at the same time as her shoulders. Headlights swept over the trees, and she flinched. Too bright.

Not her first concussion. And on a scale of one to *bad*. This was…probably a seven. But only because of the blood.

Now, what did she have to do first? She couldn't think against the nausea.

Something nudged her hand, low by her hip. She looked down and saw the dog. Couldn't remember her name. She lifted her hand to touch its head…

"There you are."

She turned and tried to speak, but that sick feeling clogged her throat.

"Shhh." He reached up to touch her forehead. Dakota sent a weak palm strike into his chest. He barely moved but dropped his hand. "Point taken. No touching. But you're hurt."

Dakota took a slow breath, then exhaled. Cold air. *No more hurling.* "I'm okay."

His look told her what he thought of that. "They're gone. It's just us again."

"And the dead girl."

He nodded. "I think they might've been here to find her."

"Huh." She couldn't nod right now, and she didn't know what else to say.

"Did they hurt you?"

"Ran into a tree. Chasing you." She should've brought cuffs with her. It would be eminently satisfying if she could slap those bad boys on him—to get him back for leaving out some key information. He'd told her nothing. She didn't want to admit to a desire to pay him back for her injury too, but…

Okay, she should at least be honest with herself, even if the truth was ugly. Even if it meant she was someone she wouldn't even want to be mixed up with.

He had the decency to wince at least. Good. It was basically his fault.

"Can I see?" He turned on his flashlight.

Dakota waved it away. "Who are you?" It had been his voice, saying those guys would be killing two feds. She had a whole lot of questions about what'd happened while she'd been unconscious, but still.

"Is that really the point right now?"

"You're a fed."

"Okay," he said. "But this isn't an official investigation, so it's not like that's relevant."

"It is."

"I'm not here as a fed."

"Just a man with a dog," she said, "looking for a body. Josh Weber." She was pretty proud of herself for remembering that.

"You really don't look good." He reached for her elbow. "Can you walk, or do you want to sit down?"

Dakota pulled out her phone instead. "Backup will be here in a minute." The team would descend, and she'd have to have her act together. At least enough to fight past the sickness and do her job. "I need a bandage."

He shone the light at her face. "You need more than that."

"No, I don't." She gritted her teeth at the light against her eyelids. He moved the beam away, and she opened her eyes. "I just have to clean up."

"So you're one of *those* people."

She stared at him.

"Stoic. Don't let anyone know you're hurt." He studied her. "I'm not saying it's a bad thing. It's just that—"

She brushed past him. "Whatever."

Unfortunately, her equilibrium wasn't up to par, and she'd moved too fast. Dakota swayed. Josh caught her. One strong arm slid around her back, the other grasped her under the elbow. Just enough to steady her. Nothing more.

"Who are you?" The question came out as a whisper, giving away entirely too much. Not just curiosity, but also interest. Because yes, he intrigued her. More than any man had in a long time.

He'd held his own against more than one man with a gun. Enough to warn the shooters off. To save them both.

"Just Josh." He walked with her, but she didn't know where they were going. "What about you? What's your name?"

"Dakota." She got her balance enough to shift away from him. He got the message and let go. The dog kept pace with them.

"Just Dakota?"

She smiled, but couldn't glance at him right now or she would hurl again. It was for the best. She didn't need distractions in her life. He was one of her people, and that was good enough. More than that wasn't even on the table. She didn't do relationships.

If he turned out to be lying, then she would either arrest him or shoot him.

Those were the facts. They'd keep her in good stead and meant she didn't lose focus on her work. When the job was done she'd go home to her quiet house, a place she loved. Her retreat. The sanctuary she'd never had, but which she'd forged for herself.

The pounding in her head grew louder, until she realized it wasn't coming from inside her head.

"Helicopter."

She wanted to look up but figured that wasn't a good idea. "Cavalry." Too bad she hadn't been able to mop up the blood on her face before they got here. She waved one arm above her head, then moved to the open area at the edge of the orchard. It wouldn't be good if they landed by the body and blew away key pieces of evidence.

The chopper lowered to the ground. Dakota leaned against the fence and covered her ears. Josh stood beside her, and she took a moment to study him.

He'd been in a gunfight and didn't look any worse for wear. He knew how to handle life when it got crazy, which made her wonder again about that military bearing he had.

"You okay, Pierce?"

She blinked and realized Special Agent O'Caran was watching her. Oops. "Fine," she called out over the helicopter rotors. Another man walked behind him.

They were both here?

O'Caran's baby face features made him look to be in his early twenties. Bright blue eyes and blond hair. He could be the heartbreaker doctor on a TV show. "Victoria said you had a case."

Behind O'Caran was a taller, thinner man. Salvarez. Hispanic heritage. There was no better hunter she'd ever met. His deadly gaze flicked between her and Josh Weber, then took in her injury. Then he barked, "Explain."

. . .

The look she gave him when Josh suggested she let the EMTs check her out almost made him take a step back. Almost.

The taller of the two men walked past him, intentionally clipping Josh with the duffel bag he carried. Evidence collection, probably. "You heard the man, Cupcake. Go see the EMTs."

The combination of both the bump and the nickname caught Josh's attention enough to make him turn and follow the guy. Cupcake? The younger of the two shot Josh a look, and then went with her instead of Josh and the tall one.

"Show me this body."

"You aren't going to arrest me, or lock me down as a witness?" Clearly these guys were feds as well. Homeland agents, just like the woman.

The Hispanic man glanced at him with a long look. "Should I?"

"Just a question."

The man squared off with him. "She tried to arrest you, right?"

"Actually, I was going to arrest *her*. Maybe."

"But you didn't." He pointed at Josh. "Smart move." They trudged across the field of trees all the way to where Maggie lay. "Anyone touch anything?"

"Dakota checked for a pulse." Josh hung back. The man crouched to look over every inch of the young woman. "Her name was Maggie."

"And you know this how?"

Josh figured there wasn't any reason to keep it a secret. "She's my neighbor's granddaughter. Eden asked me to see if Neema and I could find her."

The man straightened. He eyed the dog as she wandered around the edge of the tree line sniffing everything. "Why'd your neighbor ask you?"

Josh paused. "You guys are Homeland Security, right? Does Maggie have something to do with one of your cases?"

He studied Josh, then pulled out his phone. "Full name."

Josh figured there wasn't any reason to lie, or not tell him.

"You live local?"

"Coeur d'Alene." Not like his address was a secret. "But I work in Spokane."

The man nodded. Josh might've been fooled into thinking the guy was distracted, typing on his phone. He wasn't.

Assuming otherwise would've been a mistake, especially considering how his attention never shifted when the other two wandered over.

Before they emerged from the trees, the tall man with Josh called out, "How's your head?"

Without even looking up from his phone.

Dakota stepped into view. "Fine." But the bandage on her temple said otherwise.

The associate who'd gone with her said, "She has a concussion."

She frowned at him. "He said *probable*. That doesn't mean it's definitive."

The man with Josh said, "You throw up?"

She made a face. Across the other end of the field the helicopter lifted from the ground, momentarily cutting off any conversation.

Josh folded his arms and waited out the whomp of rotors as the chopper moved away. "So what does Homeland Security want with this apple orchard?" It was only a guess that their presence here didn't have anything to do with Maggie.

The younger of the two men pointed at the woman. "Dakota is Homeland." He stepped forward, right hand stretched out. "Niall O'Caran, NCIS."

A Navy cop?

They shook, and then Niall pointed to the taller man. "Salvador Alvarez, US Marshal."

Josh frowned. Dakota chuckled, then said, "Yeah. That's pretty much most people's reaction." She pushed out a breath. "Northwest Counter-Terrorism Task Force."

"Never heard of it."

She folded her arms. "That means we're doing our jobs. You see, people think federal agencies can't work together, and for the most part they're correct. FBI and some other agencies work great with local law enforcement one-to-one, on a smaller scale. We work the cases that cross state lines, as well as the jurisdictions of multiple federal agencies—those that would normally leave the FBI and the DEA squabbling over who is lead on the case. We're fighting the same war. We're on the same side. It isn't perfect, but we're in a unique position to focus on specific cases, using our individual skills without the bureaucracy."

"Investigating without red tape?"

That sounded like the best parts of the job he'd wanted. And a whole lot more interesting. But Josh had to squash that thought, otherwise his attempt at contentment would go out the window.

The marshal cracked a smile that looked scary more than anything else. Salvador Alvarez, the younger guy, had said. "We don't have carte blanche. What we have is the understanding that we can piece things together that otherwise wouldn't be connected, and a boss with a serious amount of pull."

Dakota took a step away. "You got this, right Sal?" She wandered to a tree and lowered herself to sit, her back against it.

The thin man frowned. "Yeah, Cupcake. I got it."

The dichotomy between a Marshal who was admittedly pretty scary looking, and his use of the word "cupcake," made Josh wonder if there was something between them. Something other than the respect of teammates. The very thought of something more between the two made him feel strangely disappointed.

Alvarez tossed the younger man a pair of gloves from his duffel bag, and they got to work processing the body.

Josh glanced at Dakota. Maybe she should've gone back in the chopper to get seen by a doctor. Neema wandered over to her then. She sniffed the hand Dakota had placed in her lap, then laid down beside her.

The woman agent stiffened.

Didn't like dogs? Or wasn't used to them.

Plenty of people didn't know what to do with a dog, especially one who could be imposing. Too many owners failed to train their animals, or didn't recognize how easily dogs could develop psychological problems. Neema wasn't his child. She was a trained marine asset, an animal, and they weren't a family. They were a pack.

A pack that needed to let this team get to work. He could report back to Eden with the sad news about her granddaughter. He wasn't even supposed to be here. Josh should be at the YMCA, playing basketball with the youth group kids. The last thing he needed was to insert himself into someone else's case.

He'd tried to respect the agent the DEA had assigned him as a mentor. But how could he when all the guy wanted to do was watch surveillance video and file reports? They'd visited a bank once. That was the only time they'd left the office in four months of working together—except to get lunch. The guy was like a cop who only wanted to write traffic citations instead of responding to actual calls. He just couldn't understand it.

"You guys have a lot to do, so Neema and I will get out of your hair." He clicked his fingers. His dog got up and wandered toward him, stretching out her back legs one by one as she came over. He scratched her head and nodded to the agents.

US Marshal.

NCIS.

Homeland Security.

This wasn't his life. It was theirs. Maybe one day he could find out more about them. See if they had an open spot on the team.

"Alvarez."

Josh glanced at him and saw the glow of his phone screen up against the man's cheek.

"Yeah." Pause.

Josh waved, ready to get out of there.

"Maybe." Another pause. "Yes, Ma'am." He hung up the phone. "How about you don't leave just yet, *Special Agent Weber*."

Dakota gasped. "What?"

"You heard me," the Marshal said. "He's a fed. Josh here is an agent with the DEA."

Chapter 4

Dakota gaped. "DEA? I heard you say you were a fed but I didn't believe it." Part of her had assumed it was just a bluff. "Why didn't you say something?"

Sal turned away to bag evidence while Niall took a million pictures. She didn't miss the satisfied look on his face. He took entirely too much pleasure in putting Josh on the spot.

The relentless click of the camera didn't feel good with her head pounding like this, but she was alive.

Josh ran a gloved hand over his hair.

"Maybe I should call your boss and ask them that question." She didn't have to like sitting here with the mother of all headaches while they did the work. She could've done it herself if she hadn't run into a tree branch.

She pulled out her phone, not necessarily intending to use it. More to let this guy know she wasn't going to be swayed, even if he talked a good game. She'd learned the hard way what manipulation did. Dakota didn't rely on her feelings anymore. She used logic and reason to make decisions.

"I'd rather you didn't do that." Josh took a couple of steps toward her. The dog wandered some more.

Was the animal going to sniff her again? Dakota shifted her wary glance to look at the DEA agent. "I've known a few DEA agents. You don't want to hear my opinion of most of them."

He shrugged. "I'm new. The reputation is that they're a bunch of rule-breakers and partiers, right? It's true of some, but the DEA higher-ups are actively trying to bring in new blood. To shake up the agency and get things running efficiently again."

"So why don't you want them to know you're here?"

"Because I'm doing a favor for my neighbor, trying to find Maggie."

"By trespassing on private land."

He shot her a pointed look. Yes, that was exactly what she'd been doing as well. She hastily changed the subject. "Who was in the vehicle?"

"Two guys, late thirties. Forties, maybe. The third was a teen."

"Looks like you'll be spending your Saturday looking at mugshots."

He groaned. "Just as long as I'm back at my desk on Monday."

"With your name conveniently absent from any official record?"

He said, "I'm not going to ask for that. It would be unethical."

"Okay." She wasn't approving of his statement, just gauging what kind of man he was.

"However, if we could refrain from calling my office before then..." He let that hang. "My supervisor will find out eventually. He'll rap my knuckles and we'll go back to shipping manifests and quarterly reports."

She made a face.

He barked a laugh. "Now you feel my pain."

"Not quite what I thought the DEA was about, but okay."

Josh shook his head. The hint of a smile curled his mouth. "It would be funny if it wasn't incredibly frustrating. He's just biding his time until retirement, doing busy work."

Dakota did a slow nod. She was so glad Victoria didn't work that way. Nor had anyone at Homeland Security been like that, for that matter. Not when she'd trained with them, or those first few years before Victoria found her and snapped her up for her own team.

Sal glanced at her again. The twitch in his eye indicated amusement. She didn't know what was so funny. "Almost done?"

"Not hardly." Sal straightened to his full height and pulled out the cell phone he kept in his inside coat pocket. She didn't think he'd ever worn a suit in his life. Except maybe at his mom's funeral. Right now he had on insulated jeans, work boots, a thick shirt and several layers beneath that coat.

Similar to what Josh wore. Working man clothes. Clothes that said, "I'm outside and it's cold. If I'm going to get dirty, I may as well be warm and comfortable doing it." They were men who cared first about doing a job the right way. Not about appearance.

Her butt was cold from sitting on the ground. Her ears were numb. She could use a hot cup of decaf coffee, but aside from that—and the headache— she was all right. Her clothes were keeping her warm enough.

Not like the stuff she'd worn growing up.

Threadbare clothes were something she'd stuffed down into her mind, forgotten like the rest of those years. Not that being poor was something to be ashamed of. Plenty of good people had little to their name. Money didn't make you a better person, it just showed your true character. For Dakota, a steady paycheck had proven to her that she could be the kind of person she wanted to be, regardless of the income.

Someone who gave plenty of her time and money. Someone who didn't have to live what she'd lived as a child. She'd moved on. Made a life. Found good things, good people. Faith that was just as logical and reasonable as she was. Her life made sense now. At least as much as she figured it ever would.

"Are you up for a walk?"

Sal's question jogged her out of her own head. Good thing. She didn't want to get lost in there. "What?"

He motioned with his head. "Go meet the coroner out front of the house. Show him where we are and then talk to the residents."

Dakota wanted to nod. That wasn't a good idea. "Sure." Better than sitting around here.

Josh even wandered over and stuck out his hand. She didn't actually need help to stand but if it made him feel useful, that was fine. She clasped his wrist and he hauled her to her feet.

"Take Niall with you. Leave *Special Agent Weber*."

The NCIS agent handed Sal his camera and came over to her. He held out his elbow and used the worst British accent ever to say, "Fancy a stroll, milady?"

"Don't ever do that again." Rolling her eyes, she took his elbow and they ambled past Josh.

Niall laughed. "Yes, ma'am." He opted for a southern drawl that time.

"And don't call me ma'am."

They set off through the trees to the main house, about a mile to the north. Niall said, "Do you think he just wants to grill that Josh guy more, or is he actually worried you'll, like, pass out?"

"It's Sal. Who knows?"

He nodded, as if she'd dispensed great wisdom. "Did that shot they gave you kick in yet?"

"I don't feel like I'm going to hurl up a meal I haven't eaten anymore, but my bell definitely got rung. Like a gong that goes on and on, you know?"

"Um…sure."

She huffed out a laugh. "Tell Sal I'm fine."

"And that DEA agent? What about him?"

"Why would I care about him?"

Niall looked down at her as they walked.

"What?"

"Huh. Okay." He was quiet for a moment. "Don't say I didn't warn you."

"Warn me about what? Bell got rung, remember. Not exactly firing on all cylinders."

"The DEA agent could've walked with you. I'm sure Sal would've let him do that instead of me."

"I doubt it," she said. "He's probably deep in interrogation mode already. Really tightening the screws, you know? Maybe we'll even hear him scream."

Niall laughed aloud. "Sal isn't that bad. Is he?"

Dakota let his question hang in the air. "Just promise me you'll never agree to go camping with him." She did an exaggerated shiver. "I still have the scar I got last time."

· · ·

"How much of that was the concussion?"

The US Marshal, Sal Alvarez, tipped his head to one side, eyes on the body. "Dakota is…Dakota."

"Does she have Native American in her?"

"Probably." He glanced over. "Though, I'd advise against asking her any questions about her past, prior to her joining the task force four years ago. Or anything about her personal life at all."

Josh glanced over at Neema, who had stayed away from the body so far. She'd never been trained as a cadaver dog, so he had figured she might at least be curious. He called her over, pulled off his gloves and ran his hands down her sides. Over her hips. Her expertise ran more in the direction of sniffing out Afghani heroin. She wasn't an official DEA asset and likely would never be with her hip the way it had healed. But she was still his dog.

"She cold?"

Josh nodded. "I should get her inside pretty soon. She's already been out longer than she's comfortable with. Her hip will lock up."

"Injury?"

"She was retired from the Marine Corps when she got hit by a ricochet sniper round. Shattered her hip joint." He watched her walk, assessing her gait. She was either okay, or she was determined not to let on that she hurt—and it could be either. "Three surgeries."

"That why you got out?"

Josh shrugged one shoulder. It figured the man knew about his military service, the same way he'd known Josh was an agent for the DEA. "I lost the drive for it. Didn't see much point being out there without Neema, so I finished up and came home."

"And her?" Sal pointed to the deceased woman on the ground between them. The man wasn't interested in an in depth conversation on how Josh was doing, acclimating to life outside of the military. He had a job to do and Josh was a witness—if not an actual suspect in the murder.

"My neighbor's granddaughter." He figured he'd have to say that several more times before he was released to go home. "Margaret Detweiler. She's nineteen. Enrolled in some classes at Spokane Falls community college but mostly floated around, driving her grandmother crazy with worry about what she was up to."

"So this is just a good deed?"

"I'd rather it was showing up to find her and have a chat," Josh said. "Maybe scare some sense into her about how she was living her life."

"What's she doing all the way out here?"

Josh said, "Eden told me recently that she had a new boyfriend. I think he's local. I showed Eden how to find an iPhone on her Verizon account online. That's how I knew she was in this area. The phone's been off for a few days though."

"You know who the boyfriend is?"

"Eden thought his name might be Terry, but that was all she knew. Maggie never showed her a picture of him or told her much. It was early, maybe only a few weeks into their relationship."

He glanced at the dead woman then, standing in silence while the grief washed over him. Josh didn't even know her, though he'd met her once. She'd been so young. All that "full of promise" stuff was pointless if a person didn't seize it. By all accounts this woman hadn't seized anything but her right to do whatever she wanted. As though her actions had no impact on anyone else.

Now she was gone, and he'd have to tell Eden what happened. At least, Josh wanted to be the one to tell her. It shouldn't come from some faceless badge who didn't care. Eden's health was precarious at best. This wasn't going to be good for her.

Josh hung his head, long enough to ask God why this had happened. It wasn't a blow to his faith. It wouldn't be a blow to Eden's either. They'd had many conversations about God's will, and man's part in that. Enough to know she would lean on Him through this, despite how hard it would be.

"And the orchard?"

Josh opened his eyes. "She posted a picture on Instagram. This place was in the background."

"That's some solid detective work, Weber." Sal grinned. "We'll make an investigator out of you yet."

It was probably supposed to have been a compliment, but all Josh could think was that this guy was insinuating he wasn't an investigator *yet*. Maybe just that he wasn't a marshal like Sal or a part of this task force like the rest of them. Insulting either way.

Did they have some kind of "better than everyone else" mentality? He hoped not. A group of people who'd managed to mesh different fields and different methods, who got along with each other just fine. It would be a shame if it was the rest of the world they had a problem with. Josh had never liked that "us vs. them" mentality. Life wasn't so cut and dry, but he couldn't explain because they wouldn't see his point with that kind of thought process. He mentally corrected himself. *If* that's what they were even thinking.

Neema made a quiet "woof." He went over to where she'd sat, close to a tree. Josh crouched and saw a phone lying in the dirt. "Sal, right?"

"Alvarez."

Josh ignored that. If the man wanted to be professional here then that was fine by him. "A cell. Maybe hers?"

He stepped back. Sal retrieved it from the grass with his gloved hand and slipped it into a plastic bag. He clicked the home button. "Fingerprint."

He used the dead woman's thumb and unlocked the phone. Swiped through screens. Josh didn't get close enough to see or he'd be looking over the man's shoulder, and some people didn't like that. Alvarez turned the phone so Josh could see the screen. "This guy?"

The image was of a living and happy—in a bleary-eyed, cigarette in hand kind of way—Maggie. She stood beside a bigger man. A man Josh had seen.

"That's one of the guys who was here." *He* was her boyfriend? Certainly hadn't acted like a grief-stricken lover when he'd been cuffing the younger man over the back of the head. Or when he'd blatantly stated what he planned to do with the unconscious Dakota. "He seemed to be the one in charge."

Alvarez nodded. He got out his own phone and did something on both, holding them side by side.

"How long until you know who he is?"

Alvarez frowned at him. "Depends on what you plan to do with the information."

Josh lifted both hands. "I'm not interested in interfering. I've already gotten more involved than I'd planned. I can go home and tell Eden what I found. You guys figure out who murdered her."

Somehow he didn't think it had been done by the teen, though it seemed he had dumped the body—which he explained to the marshal.

Maybe the kid was strong enough to have made those strangulation marks on her neck, but did he have the temperament? More like he'd been assigned the task of depositing her here. Where her body would be found. The man in charge—her boyfriend—hadn't even known about it. He'd wanted to find her, but he hadn't seemed overwhelmed with the loss, either.

"What are you thinking?"

"He didn't care about her," Josh said.

"And that makes you angry?"

"More like frustrated. It complicates things."

"In what way?"

Josh thought for a second, knowing full well this was a test. "He didn't do it—the boyfriend. Maybe he knows who did, maybe not. The teen was the one who dumped her here. That's at least three people, with the killer added in. So who actually murdered her? And why?"

"Good."

"Because I could reason that out?"

"No. Because you're going to stay here, and we're going to figure out why."

The only reason their counter terrorism task force would investigate a murder was if…

Josh gaped. "You think Maggie was mixed up with terrorists?"

Chapter 5

Dakota scanned the pdf on her laptop screen. A copy of Josh's military service file, followed by everything the DEA had compiled on him. Test scores. Assessments. Psychological evaluations. The phrase *doesn't play well with others* came to mind, but she couldn't fault him for it. There was nothing wrong with working better alone.

At least, that was what she told herself.

The rap of knuckles sounded on the door to her motel room. She looked at the time on her screen. 8:07 AM. She closed the lid of the laptop and grabbed her weapon. "Who is it?"

"Josh."

She pulled the door open.

He saw her gun right away and lifted both hands. One held a white paper bag. The other held a drink carrier with two paper cups. "Peace offering?"

She motioned him in with her head. "Do you need to bring me a peace offering?"

"I don't know." He set the stuff on the dresser and eyed her. "It's hard to tell. Isn't that a woman thing—like I should know why you're mad?"

"Maybe if I was actually mad."

"Good." He held out a cup. "Americano, right? That's what Alvarez said."

She accepted it and took a sip. "Whatever else he said, he's lying."

Josh grinned. "Really?"

"Salvarez says a lot. Most of it's just to throw you off. That's why he's so good." She took another sip and sank onto the edge of the bed so Josh could have the chair. "And he's the best hunter I've ever met. Never met an animal, man, or beast he couldn't track."

"Okay, wait. *Salvarez*? What am I missing?"

"Salvador Alvarez," she said. "I tried Alvie, but he *really* didn't like that. So we settled on Salvarez."

Josh shook his head. "I heard him call you 'Cupcake.'"

She groaned. "Don't remind me. He thinks he's funny. I just ignore it."

"Ah." He handed her a blueberry muffin.

"You didn't bring Neema with you?" She glanced around. Like the dog would jump out at any second? That was ridiculous. She was being ridiculous.

"I let her out on the grass across the street this morning. When I suggested we go out in the truck, she wandered back to her crate and laid down. So I left her in the room."

"And when housekeeping comes to clean?"

"I told them not to." His eyes shone with humor as he took a sip of his own drink.

How did he take his coffee? Seemed to her that since he knew her preference, she should know his. They might end up friends after this weekend. She wasn't interested in romance; her life didn't have room for it. She wasn't home much. Work took her all over Washington, Oregon, Idaho and Montana. Sometimes even up into Canada and Alaska.

Weeks on the road, working cases. Hardly the scenario where she'd pause for an evening out. Like that even sounded enjoyable.

Josh frowned. "How's your head?"

"Annoying. So much so that my brain is trying to distract me by coming up with random thoughts," she said. "You got anything?"

"I talked to the lady behind the counter at the bakery for a minute," he said. "There was a line. I guess they don't open until the snow melts, and then not all the time until it gets warmer."

"Small town."

He nodded. "I showed her the picture of Maggie and her boyfriend that was found on Maggie's phone. She said his name is Terrence Crampton." He took a sip. "After that, the conversation was hurried along. Seemed like she was afraid of him, actually. Like speaking his name would summon him to her bakery."

Dakota grabbed her phone and told Victoria in a quick email. "That was a good idea. Now we can run a complete check on him."

"Find out all his dirty secrets?"

She shrugged.

"But he could be a terrorist, right? That's what this is about. Why you guys are here." He took a sip. "*Salvarez* didn't say much after the coroner showed up."

Dakota set her cup aside. "We received a report of chatter related to this area. Movement between here and the Canadian border. Someone paid off a park ranger, and later they killed him. We think the money he received was the half upfront, because I found him dead behind his cabin. Next on my list is the sheriff."

Josh shook his head. "It's hard to believe Maggie would be involved with possible terrorism. I guess I only really know her grandmother, not her."

"Truthfully, we have no idea what it is. Could be drugs, could be weapons. Could be something else entirely." She paused a second. "Can you think of anywhere else that might be worth visiting today, to find out more about Maggie and her boyfriend?"

"Is this a test?" He didn't seem too happy about that fact.

"If it was," Dakota said, "would your answer be any different?"

"Good point." He tossed the wrapper from his muffin into the trash can, then dug out two fritters from the paper bag next to him. He handed one to her. "What about the local bar? Seems like that's a place people go. Get loose lipped, and maybe say more than they'd planned about what they're up to."

"Agreed."

"Didn't you and that NCIS guy go to the house last night?"

She nodded. "O'Caran. They answered the door, said they'd heard the helicopter. Apparently, unless it directly affects the apples, Mr. and Mrs. Johnson aren't all that concerned about what happens on their property."

"And Maggie?"

"Said they'd never heard of her."

"Did you believe them?"

She shrugged. "We'll see."

"So you wait for evidence and that has to back up what someone says? *Then* you'll believe them?"

"Well, otherwise you don't know if they're lying. Actions prove more than words, right?" That was the only way you knew whether someone was trustworthy. She'd been working with Niall and Sal for years. Victoria and Talia, as well. Trust took time to build, but they were there now. "I don't like liars, but everyone lies. Most people are hiding what they really think, or what they're really doing. At least what they don't want you to know about."

"I'm not sure if I think that's sad, or incredibly wise."

Dakota shrugged and crossed the room to her boots. "It just is. Don't read more into it than that."

She pulled her shoes on, then holstered her gun under her arm and tugged her jacket over it. "Ready to go?"

"Sheriff first?"

She nodded. "Might as well get a jump on this. Sooner or later he's going to hear that a body was found at that orchard, and then his undies are going to be in a twist because we didn't go to him first."

"But you guys have jurisdiction, right?"

"Doesn't mean he isn't going to be bent out of shape, thinking it should have been his case to solve."

Josh said, "Maggie isn't a local. The victim is from Idaho, and this is Washington. It's hardly his jurisdiction."

Dakota nodded. "That's good. I'm going to use that if he kicks up a fuss about her."

"In that case, you're welcome." He crossed to the door and held it open for her.

Dakota didn't step through it. "You can go first."

"I was being polite."

"I know."

He frowned.

"Just go. I'll be there in a second."

Josh shrugged. She wasn't sure if she believed he wasn't bothered. Maybe, maybe not. Time would tell, if they were actually working together. As it was, they weren't going to have time to develop trust before Monday morning, when he returned to work. They would just have to figure out how to work together before then.

And if they couldn't, she would send him on his way.

• • •

Josh leaned on the bar and shifted his foot. The sole of his boot stuck for a second to the floor. The bartender looked up from the phone Josh held out and sniffed. "They come in here sometimes. Play pool."

Dakota stood sideways next to him. He didn't think for one second she was so focused on watching the room that she wasn't listening.

The visit to the sheriff's office had been a waste of time. He wasn't in. Wasn't likely to be in all weekend, given he was visiting his sister the next town over and doing his grocery shopping while he was there. None of the deputies were on duty, except one, and he was tied up dealing with a downed tree.

Dakota had left her card with the receptionist anyway, but Josh didn't figure she'd be getting a call anytime soon. Guess that meant they didn't need to worry about the local cops trying to take over the murder investigation.

Josh said, "What about friends of theirs?"

The bartender looked over at the pool table. "Kinda early for their crowd."

Probably, but Josh had no intention of returning later to flash his badge around a bunch of drunk people. Especially when most would be packing guns of their own.

"What about where I can find them?"

The bartender made a face. "You wanna go up there, that's your funeral."

Josh waited.

"There's a compound. It's off Highway 16, north of town. But I wouldn't go there." The bartender leaned forward. "It's members only, if you get what I mean."

"Bikers?"

"And then some."

Whatever that meant. Bikers, plus more? Josh didn't know what to make of it. "What about Terry Crampton? Anything else you can tell me about him?"

"So he can hear I was talking to you, and I get my legs broke and my bar torn up?"

"Okay." Josh didn't want to be responsible for a man losing his livelihood—or his ability to walk. It said enough that they would retaliate like that just for information given.

The bartender had only spoken in a low voice. Didn't want to be overheard. Even the old guy at the end of the bar had turned away, not wanting to be a party to this conversation.

It was a risky way to live, skirting the knife edge between safety and danger. Bikers alone could incite that fear in the people who lived in their town. Could they be transporting drugs or weapons? Maybe Josh should bite the bullet and call in to his office. See if they had any information on bikers in this area. But wouldn't Dakota have been able to find the same information? If this team of hers was as good as they seemed to be—and as connected—they'd have access to what his office did.

He also figured they'd fully vetted him between last night and this morning.

Josh glanced at Dakota as they left the bar. This time he didn't hold the door for her. Outside a fresh dusting of snow covered everything in a thin layer. Huge piles of unmelted snow, plowed into mounds, had turned brown. Exhaust fumes and dirt. Mud. Snow was great when it first fell, but that was short lived. Eventually it turned nasty.

They walked to his truck. "When y'all ran your check on me, did anyone alert the DEA that you were asking?"

"Worried about being called into the principal's office on Monday morning?"

"Maybe." It wasn't exactly like that, but still. "Just wanted a head's up. So I know what I'm walking into."

"So far we've kept it below the radar. That's Victoria's specialty."

"Your boss?"

"Victoria Bramlyn. Officially she works directly for the DOJ, but that's just so we have the pull to do what we need to. She came over from the state department. No one knows what she did before, but she has contacts everywhere."

Josh figured that meant he had to trust the woman. He'd take Dakota's word for it—especially considering how earnest she seemed. Unlike her tactic of waiting to see people's actions before she'd offer trust, Josh had found that most people showed their true colors straight away. And if he couldn't get a read on a person, Neema usually could. He was a pretty good judge of character, generally able to tell when someone was trying to hide something.

Dakota didn't like to rely on anyone. She had something in her life that had given her reason to hold herself separate from other people. Naturally distrusting, she chose to rely on herself.

Josh was curious enough he wanted to ask her about it. But she wasn't going to open up until her conditions were met—until she knew she could trust *him*.

There wasn't enough time for that. Not when, right now, they had until tomorrow night to figure out who killed Maggie and what it had to do with shipments.

They had to focus.

"So what do you think?" he asked her. "Bikers?"

Dakota shrugged. "Maybe. We can find the compound and then run the information. See what we get back."

"Want to drive over and look? Maybe do some surveillance?"

"Sure."

"How's your head?" Maybe she shouldn't be traipsing around snowy mountainsides when she had a concussion.

"I'll let you know if I need a break."

That was something, at least. She'd sat down last night as well. Maybe she wasn't the kind of stubborn woman who pushed herself to breaking just to make a point. *Good to know.*

"All right." Josh held the passenger door open for her.

"Are you going to keep doing that?"

"Probably."

"Who taught you to be a gentleman? Maggie's grandmother? Your mother?"

Josh tried to figure out the answer to that. "My mom, probably."

"What's she like?"

"She was amazing."

Her brow crinkled. "Was?"

"Cancer. I was fifteen. It was awful, but she was a great mom. It's easy to remember the good things. All the stuff moms do like make cookies and sew Halloween costumes. You know?"

"Sure." The word sounded choked.

Josh said, "But I also remember the way she'd get on me if my room stank. Or if I left my stuff all over the hallway when I got home from school." He grinned. "Because we're all human, and no one is perfect. She said that was why she needed Jesus in her life so much. Because she'd get overwhelmed trying to do it all herself."

It was a risk. A feeler, to see how Dakota viewed faith.

She nodded. "God is there when I need Him."

"Like that song, right? *I need Thee every hour.* She used to sing that while she was cleaning." He smiled at the memory. "I haven't thought of that in a long time."

Dakota's smile didn't quite meet her eyes. She opened her mouth to say something.

The roar of a truck engine cut her off.

Josh spun around to see. Dakota grabbed him. He kept spinning, taking her with him, going down to the ground. Instinct fired even before he could discern what the problem was.

Then he saw it. Flying through the air.

Grenade.

Chapter 6

They rolled across the ground as the truck exploded behind them. The front end lifted up in a fireball that nearly flipped it over completely.

Dakota didn't quite scream, but the noise she made wasn't far from it.

The sound was like thunder. Like the boom of a rocket launcher tearing apart a metal building. They rolled to a stop, and Josh groaned in her ear. His truck.

The truck that had pulled up alongside them was gunning it away from them. She noted the license plate.

"Dark blue truck." She glanced at him. "Same one as last night?"

"Maybe. It was dark." He nudged her. "Get off me."

Dakota rolled to sit beside him. Squishing him with her enormousness? Didn't matter what size a woman was, she figured they always felt two sizes bigger than they really were. At least, she usually did.

"Not because you're crushing me."

She narrowed her eyes. Behind him, flames licked the truck. The black smoke rising from the front end stank badly enough her nose wrinkled.

He said, "I just want to get up off the ground."

"I'm going to wait a minute before I do that." She pulled out her phone and called Talia.

The woman answered before the first ring had sounded in Dakota's ear. "Hello, IT—"

Dakota spoke over her. "Blue truck. Washington plates." She rattled off the letters and numbers. "Find out who it belongs to. I want their address. Now."

"Backup?"

"Yeah, send the boys." Salvarez and Niall could help her navigate the local cop, who was surely done dealing with that tree. Explosions probably didn't happen much in this town. She figured someone from the bar, one of the crowd now gathered outside, had already called the deputy.

She hung up on Talia and watched the bartender come over with a fire extinguisher. He handed it to Josh, who used it on the flames. Dakota's backside was numb from sitting on the ground. She gritted her teeth and stood, pulled out the hairband holding her ponytail in and redid it. Her head pounded. Enough she thought about being sick but swallowed the sensation down and took a few deep breaths.

Josh gave the fire extinguisher a few short bursts, then said, "Who'd you call?"

"Technical support."

He handed the fire extinguisher off and came to stand beside her. His eyes surveyed her head. "Did you hit it again?"

She said, "No," instead of shaking her head.

"Technical support?"

"Talia Matrice. She's on loan from the NSA. Probably already knows everything about you, including the time you failed a math test in the sixth grade. And what you had for dinner last night."

Josh's eyebrows lifted.

She said, "It isn't just that she's good. She's also incredibly nosy. She says social media killed it though, because everyone posts all the time about every single detail of their lives. Still, the juicy stuff is always buried."

His eyes turned interested. "What juicy stuff is there about you?"

"Plenty buried. Not really juicy, though." And that was all she was going to say about that. He hardly needed to know the ins and outs of her history, but she could at least acknowledge she had one. He'd figured that much out, and she wasn't going to insult his intelligence by denying it.

Before he could dig farther, she said, "Sorry about your truck."

"I have insurance."

"O-kay." Weren't most guys all about their vehicle? She'd figured he would be mad about the fact it had just been destroyed.

"The point is you're okay, I'm okay. No one got hurt."

There was an edge to his words. One she didn't understand. He seemed almost frustrated—because of her concussion? That wasn't his fault. "The fact they did this means we're on to something. If there was nothing to find, then they wouldn't have reacted to us digging into their business like this."

"So we're on the right track?"

"Something we did, or said, got back to them and they retaliated."

He worked his mouth back and forth. "I told them we're feds."

"Could be that. Or it could just be us coming here." She indicated the bar with a sweep of her hand. "Maybe one of them called the owner of that truck, and they paid us a visit."

A car pulled into the lot. Salvarez was at the wheel, Niall beside him. The two had been canvassing town and visiting again with the owners of the apple orchard. She was interested to know if they'd discovered anything. A destroyed truck was hardly a win, unless Talia got the name of the owner of the fleeing truck. And that was assuming it wasn't a stolen vehicle that had sped away.

Following the car was a fire truck, and then a sheriff's department vehicle. If they'd intended to stay under the radar, it wasn't working. So much for an incognito investigation. Everyone in town would know they were feds by the end of the day—not just those guys from the orchard.

Salvarez shut off the car. Both guys came straight to her, but Sal in particular took in the vehicle. "You guys okay?"

Josh said, "We're good."

Dakota nodded as much as she could without pain reverberating through her skull. She could use another dose of Ibuprofen, but always forgot to note what time she'd taken the last dose. How long had it been?

"Pierce?"

She snapped out of her thoughts. "What?"

"You okay?"

Dakota said, "I'm okay."

Salvarez didn't look convinced, but he let it go. "Bomb?"

"Grenade."

Josh said, "Military."

Dakota turned to him.

"I'm just pointing out that it isn't easy to get a grenade unless you're in the service and you stole it. Or they could've bought one from someone who is. They don't exactly sell them on the open market, right?"

"That jives with what we found this morning," Niall said. "The military connection. Or at least a military-style of operating."

Dakota frowned. She had to wonder if this was going where she had a feeling it might. It was like a ghost suddenly appearing at the corner of her vision. That otherworldly specter of the past reared its head, mouth open, ready to chomp down and devour her.

Salvarez's eyes were dark when he said, "This morning we found out there's a local group holed up outside of town, living off the land. Recruiting local guys who don't want to pay taxes."

"A militia?" Two words, but it sounded choked coming from her mouth. She cleared her throat and then asked it again.

Salvarez nodded, his eyes knowing.

Josh said, "You think that's who is transporting drugs, or guns, or whatever through the orchard?"

"Could be." Sal shrugged one shoulder, his attention still on her. "Niall and I are going to go check it out."

Because he was trying to save her from having to do it? "This is my case." She got to town first, that meant she took point. The only agent with seniority here was Victoria. Salvarez didn't have the authority to bench her. "Josh and I will go."

She saw him glance at her out the corner of her eye.

"I have to go check on Neema."

"Fine. We can do that on the way." Why did he sound like he didn't want to come with her?

The sheriff's deputy who'd shown up wandered over. Dakota figured she'd continue making her point and strode between the guys toward the deputy. She stuck her hand out and introduced herself. Watched that flare in his eyes when she mentioned Homeland Security, and the task force.

Just another day on the job.

• • •

Josh shook the deputy's hand.

"Thanks for speaking with me. I appreciate your time."

"No problem." Like Josh was one of these task force agents, some high-up federal guy who deigned to speak with the small town sheriff's deputy.

Instead of what he actually was—a rookie entirely too worried about what would happen when his name ended up on a report. Or when someone called his office and it got back to the assistant director that he was here, wrapped up in a murder investigation.

Dakota stood with her fellow task force agents. The conversation was intense as indicated by all the frowns and gesturing.

The sheriff's deputy wandered off, and Josh looked over his truck. It was a wreck. No way could he salvage that. It would have to be towed away and scrapped.

He sighed. That sweater on the back seat was his favorite. Or, it *had* been his favorite. Now it was a charred mess. Other than that he didn't keep much in there, but he'd have to figure out a new way to get home. After he called his insurance guy.

Josh turned away from the crowd gathered, the agents and first responders, and started walking toward the center of town. The air was crisp. Thankfully the side of the road wasn't lined with a curb of mounded brown snow. Most of that had melted. April was coming.

His boots splashed the puddles as he walked, and cars passed him with a gust of wind that numbed the back of his neck.

His phone was going to ring at any moment. He knew it. He'd get fired or called back to the office and reprimanded. Then fired.

It could've been a whole lot worse. When he'd confronted the two men and the teen, they could've killed both him and Dakota. Josh had forced the situation. And he thanked God it hadn't been worse. She could so easily be dead right now, because he'd put her in danger just trying to save her life.

The reason didn't matter. Not when he should've thought through the outcome more. Instead, he'd just reacted. Gone on instinct.

Josh stuffed down the urge to kick a mound of crunchy snow.

The quicker he got back to Neema, the quicker he could find a way to get out of here. Get back to his life. He didn't need to hang around Dakota and her team, not when doing so just reminded him of everything his career as a federal agent wasn't. Yet. Maybe it never would be. And what was the point in longing for something that hadn't happened and might not ever?

When the truck exploded, he'd protected her. That made up for putting her in danger in the first place, right? They were square. He could leave right now, with his conscience—and career—intact.

A car pulled up alongside him. Josh waited for it to pass, but it just slowed. Like they were trying to keep pace with him.

His hand shifted toward his weapon.

After a second the engine revved and the vehicle pulled directly ahead of him. The front window rolled down. Dakota said, "Need a ride?"

"I'm fine walking." He was halfway to town already.

"It's cold."

"I like walking. It's my time to think."

Usually he did it with Neema beside him and earbuds in. Not that he was actually listening to anything, but people were less inclined to stop and talk if they thought you couldn't hear. Together they hiked mountains. Ran along forest trails. They even walked the neighborhood around his house. Didn't matter, so long as it was quiet and they were moving.

Dakota said, "Get in the car, Weber."

Behind her, in the driver's seat, that Alvarez guy snorted. Was the third one, the guy Niall, in the back?

This was about reminding him he *wasn't* part of their team. Maybe getting a ride wasn't that big of a deal, but it also wouldn't help that much.

"Do you want me to tell you that we need your help?"

"You don't," he pointed out.

"Maybe we do and none of us know it yet," she said. "I'll at least admit to that much."

He'd have figured she was mostly serious, except for that gleam of humor in her eyes. He didn't need to be placated. "I don't mind getting a ride." It was cold, and he didn't have his gloves.

"Then get in."

He'd been right that the other guy—Niall—was in the back seat. He nodded to Josh and then went back to his phone.

Alvarez glanced over his shoulder once before he pulled back onto the road, and they headed for the motel. "Don't forget you still have to look at mugshots."

"Did you get anything back from the license plate?"

Dakota was the one who answered that. "Nothing yet."

"How's your head?"

"Fine."

He said, "You expect any of us to believe that's true?"

The guys reacted to his words. Shifted. Glanced at him. Josh just sat there. The three of them were in agreement about that, at least. Dakota was one stubborn woman. But despite it, he didn't think she would endanger anyone just to prove she was fine when she wasn't. Josh didn't have enough experience with her to know when to push the situation and when to hang back.

Dakota said, "Whether it is or not doesn't matter. What matters is finding who killed Maggie Detweiler and what the source of that chatter was. That's where you come in."

"Mugshots?"

"Yes." She paused. "We know who Terrence Crampton is, but we need to ID those other two guys."

"You think Terry and his buddies are the ones who tossed a grenade under my truck?"

Alvarez said, "Pretty definitive way of saying back off."

"Except that it strands me in town, and now I have a grudge as well. How does that help them cover up what they've done and keep me off their tails when they've no doubt got more nefarious things to do?"

Someone snorted, he wasn't sure.

Dakota twisted in her seat and said, "Nefarious?"

He shrugged. "Don't hurt yourself."

"I'm—"

Alvarez and O'Caran both said, "*Fine*," dragging the word out far longer than she would have done.

Josh nearly laughed.

"Maybe I wanna walk," she told them. "Did you think about that? No, because you only think about *yourselves*."

"You don't want to walk, Cupcake."

"I *like* walking."

Alvarez said, "You do?"

"Yes, *gumdrop*." She leaned closer, firing the word at him like a cannon blast over the deck of a warship.

Josh said, "Do you guys ever get along?"

Sal said, "Yes."

Dakota said, "Of course."

Beside Josh, O'Caran glanced over, shook his head and mouthed the word, *No*. Josh smiled, and the young NCIS agent returned it. Then he glanced at his phone. Seemed like this guy felt his pain, because he said, "If you guys are done bickering, Talia got a license plate."

The NSA person?

"The truck that fled the scene belongs to Terrence Crampton."

"Sounds familiar," Josh said. "Maggie's boyfriend is the one who threw a grenade at us?"

"He threw it at your truck." Dakota pointed out.

Like it made a difference? They could have been seriously hurt, even if Terry hadn't been aiming at them.

"Meet Terrence Crampton." O'Caran held out his phone so Josh could see the screen. "This the guy?"

Josh looked at the screen. "Yep. Confirmed. That's the guy on Maggie's phone, and that's one of the guys I saw standing over Dakota last night."

Alvarez's grip tightened on the wheel until his knuckles whitened. O'Caran didn't look much happier. Dakota stared straight out the front window.

"But he wasn't the man who killed Maggie."

They had no idea who the killer was.

Chapter 7

Dakota sipped water, trying to keep her lunch down. She needed to push away the nagging ache that made her head thump. The smell of dog breath on her cheek wasn't helping. Why did she always get the slice of pie? She really should've stopped after the sandwich, but diner pie was the best. Plus, she was a sucker for whipped cream.

Josh sat in the driver's seat, the engine off. She was beside him. They were across the parking lot, watching the entrance to a fitness center.

The front door swung open and a group of three teen boys strode out. Shorts and tennis shoes, hoodies. Red cheeks and sweat.

"Him?" She glanced at Josh to see what his answer would be.

She waited while he studied the three. Once they'd discovered the name of the truck's owner, it hadn't taken long to discover he had a teenage brother—with his own driver's license. The vehicle used to dump Maggie's body?

Salvarez and O'Caran were getting a warrant to pull Terrence Crampton in for questioning concerning Maggie's death *and* the attempted murder of two federal agents. Dakota and Josh's job was to find the teen.

His brow crinkled. "I think so."

"That won't hold up in court."

"Okay then, that's the person whose image is on Austin Crampton's driver's license. And that's his pickup." Josh glanced aside at her. "Will *that* hold up in court?"

He knew the answer. He could read it on her face. Dakota said, "He's pulling out."

Josh turned on the engine of Dakota's rental and followed Austin out of the lot. Neema's tags jingled as she shifted to put her nose to the cracked back window. Josh said, "Think he's going home?"

She studied the back of Austin's rusted pickup. "Guess we'll find out."

He pulled onto the highway and headed out of town. Was home the compound? She didn't want him to get there and hunker down behind locked gates. They'd lose their lead.

Dakota bit her lip, then reached in the backseat ignoring how much twisting hurt and got what she needed out of her duffel of supplies.

She flipped the switch on the bottom and set the flashing blue and red light on the dash. Right where Mr. Austin Crampton would see it. And then pull over.

"You carry one of those with you?"

She shrugged. "Comes in handy sometimes. Like now." She motioned out the front window, where Austin's brake lights had come on. He slowed and pulled over.

Dakota sent a quick text to Talia so their NSA computer specialist could mark their location and an update of what they were doing. Maybe she already knew, but it was procedure.

They both climbed out.

Josh met her at the hood of her rental. "You want to take the lead on this?"

She nodded. He'd probably never pulled anyone over before. Dakota wandered to the driver's door and rapped on the window, one hand on the butt of her holstered weapon. "Get out of the car, please."

The door cracked. Austin Crampton didn't look nervous and neither did he look belligerent in the face of authority.

She shifted to flash the badge clipped to her belt. Just to see his reaction. "Special Agent Pierce, Homeland Security. Get out of the car, please."

When he straightened to stand, she backed up a step and said, "This is Special Agent Weber, DEA."

Josh nodded.

The kid looked curious. Cautious. Like he'd been taught to stay calm, find out what the law wanted before he said or did anything.

Dakota had been taught the same thing.

"Was I speeding?"

"This isn't about that." Dakota shifted her stance. "This is about last night. A dead woman and an apple orchard."

"Sounds like a bad movie." And the kid didn't think it was a comedy.

"Maybe, but right now my colleagues are out getting an arrest warrant. We're going to bring in the person who dumped Maggie Detweiler in that orchard."

Austin's nose flared.

"Maybe find out what else has been going on at the orchard, under the noses of hardworking people."

That got her a lip curl.

"Don't think much of people who pay their taxes?"

Austin said, "No, I don't think much of them."

He was good. Or he'd been trained well, at least. Taught not to give away anything, to use her own words to formulate his answer. She said, "Sheep, right? That's what y'all call them. Mindless animals working day in and day out, for pittance. It's like *you've* woken up. Seen the light, or whatever." She watched him for a reaction. "You're the only free ones."

He shrugged, but didn't disagree with her.

He'd been told that. But did he believe it? Was Austin Crampton looking for a way out, a normal life?

"So y'all live off the land. Screw the government, right?" She shifted closer to him. Nose to nose, but he'd have no way of getting to her gun before she could stop him. Being disarmed was the kiss of death for a federal agent's career.

Dakota said, "Well, guess what. You're a citizen, and that means you're subject to the same laws. You didn't kill that girl? Great. But you dumped the body in that orchard."

His eyes flickered.

"No matter what you think is going to happen right now, there's one thing you gotta consider. You don't know me, Austin Crampton. You don't know the world of hurt I can bring on you. You wanna breathe free anytime in the next thirty years, that's up to you. You want to rot in jail for her murder? We can make that happen, too."

"So I talk?" He folded his arms. "I'm not gonna do that."

"They taught you well, I'll give them that. But even they can't keep you from going down for this. Not with all the evidence I'm going to bring against you."

"I'll get a lawyer."

"You think they're going to foot the bill? Where's the money gonna come from? I'll make sure you end up with the most useless public defender in the state of Washington." She let her lips curl up at the corners. "You'll have no chance."

"I *didn't* kill her."

"Maybe. But I can still prove you were there. You touched her, right? Not so much of a stretch between that and you being the one who strangled her." Dakota shrugged and glanced away. "Won't be that hard."

"No—" He stopped. Cut himself off.

Enough restraint that it impressed her.

She glanced around, like she didn't care one way or the other what happened to Austin.

Josh's face was hard. Dakota didn't have time to explain what she was doing. Not if it was only to make him feel better. She just hoped he didn't butt in on the conversation and try to soothe the kid.

Austin let out a frustrated sound. "I don't wanna go to jail."

That was the most honest thing he'd said so far. "Tell me who killed her."

He pressed his lips into a thin line. "I'm done talking." The teen shifted, so she had to step back, and he went to his door. "You wanna arrest me? Do it."

Or what? Dakota wondered if he had a loaded weapon in that truck. Probably. She didn't figure it would take much for him to pull it out and use it.

Austin climbed in and gunned his engine. The back wheels fought for traction and it fishtailed for a second before it caught, and he sped off down the highway.

"You want to burn that kid just to get a result on this case?"

He said that like it was a bad thing.

Josh spoke again. "He didn't kill Maggie. He knows who did, and you're going to make him shut down if you push too hard."

Dakota walked to the passenger door, wishing she felt okay enough to drive. "It's called 'food for thought.' So when I hit him up again, he's more amenable to the suggestion of talking to me versus jail time."

"Because you're the resident expert on teens?"

As if Dakota was going to explain her resume to him. "Kids like that? Yes, I am."

. . .

Josh leaned across the restaurant table. "Is she always like this?"

Dakota was in the restroom, so he wanted this conversation done before she got back. That meant either Alvarez, or O'Caran, needed to talk fast.

"Yes." Alvarez sipped his drink.

O'Caran said nothing.

Josh glanced between them. "That's it?"

O'Caran picked up where his partner had left off. "If you want to know Dakota, maybe you should ask her."

Josh sat back in his seat. The two of them were on the opposite side of the booth. Dakota hadn't protested much over the fact she'd been sat beside Josh. Alvarez had just given her a look, and she'd sat down. Josh figured her head hurt too much to argue.

"Fine," Josh said. Dakota had been hard with that kid. Threatening to lock him up. Josh would probably have taken a more "youth pastor" approach. Try to befriend the teen. Then, when the rapport was established, he'd bring in the truth. She'd gone in fast and smacked him with a reality he hadn't wanted to face.

Who would want to acknowledge the fact that they were facing jail time? Especially when it was only a threat. All because Josh didn't want his name in the report. There was no way he could get away with testifying as an unnamed witness just because he hadn't wanted to get in trouble on Monday.

Ugh. This whole thing was becoming a tangled mess.

The kid seemed to have known what his rights were. Enough he'd walked away when he was done talking. Dakota had pushed Austin to talk. Now she had to follow up with another conversation to see if the "food for thought" she'd given him to chew on had accomplished anything.

He'd have offered to buy the kid a milkshake, or something.

"We typically work different angles of a case alone and then collaborate when necessary. Or if we need backup," Alvarez said. "She's used to taking care of stuff like this on her own terms."

"Doesn't that just breed a culture where no one relies on anyone else and everyone does their own thing?" Josh shrugged. "Doesn't sound like you'd end up with an effective team that way."

"We're a team that solves cases," O'Caran said. "We put together pieces that no one else does. We know our strengths. And we'll hand things off to each other when someone else is better qualified to follow the lead." He paused. "Does that sound unhealthy to you?"

Maybe not. "So Dakota is the most qualified to follow up with a teen?"

Alvarez shrugged.

"This teen, yes." Dakota stood beside the table. "Scoot over."

Josh did so, and she settled beside him on the bench seat at the booth. Their steaks were delivered, his with the extra mushrooms and onions on top. They were quiet while they ate, and then he asked, "Anything interesting on Terrence?"

Near as they could figure, the third man had been a friend of Terrence's.

Alvarez shrugged one shoulder. "Drove by his house. The truck was out of sight, but we hung out long enough we saw a guy leave. Followed *him* to the compound and took a look around as best we could without being spotted."

Josh said, "There really is a compound?"

"And they're all linked to it." Alvarez glanced at Dakota, a look Josh couldn't read. "Bunch of militia guys holed up there doing who knows what."

Dakota said, "And that's who taught our teenage boy what to say when he's pulled over by two federal agents. Our retaliation for them blowing up Josh's car."

A dark feeling settled in his stomach. "That was just payback?"

"No. But it's what they're going to think."

"And you really think he was coached?" Josh wasn't sure how she could know that. Unless she'd seen it before.

"No doubt. He knew what to say, what not to do. And that he could leave at any time."

Josh stuck a chunk of steak in his mouth, giving himself time to think while he chewed. If the kid was a part of what went on at the compound, then it meant he'd been taken under someone's wing. Was Terrence part of some kind of backwoods group who hated the government—one that involved younger siblings?

And what did that have to do with the chatter Dakota had been following up with?

His last thought had to be said aloud. "So how does Maggie's murder tie in to all this?"

O'Caran shrugged one shoulder. "Heard something she shouldn't have. Or stuck her nose in something she wasn't supposed to know."

That made sense. "She got too close."

Dakota said, "Which means there's something to get close *to*. Otherwise they're risking way too much attention. No one was supposed to find that body. At least not this soon."

She tapped her foot under the table, then shifted her leg beside his. "The owners at the orchard know who they are. I think they look the other way, maybe for the money. Maybe so they aren't threatened."

"So the militia people need the orchard."

"Or their facilities. They could be putting supplies in the apple transports."

Josh let that all percolate. Maggie's death had spiraled into them investigating the activities of a group of people who could be up to any number of nefarious things.

"What about that dog of yours?" Alvarez said. "Think she can sniff out what they're transporting?"

"She can't tell you what it is she smelled." Neema could sniff out a handful of explosives made from specific components. Her skill set was extremely specific. It wouldn't help them here unless that was exactly what was being moved through the orchard.

"Might be enough for a warrant."

Josh pressed his lips into a thin line. It didn't work that way, and he could see Alvarez and the others knew that. "What about surveillance?"

"That could take weeks," Alvarez said. "And I doubt we'd get much, considering the armed sentries they have. We'll be spotted."

"What about getting a bug inside?" Maybe if Dakota really did get the teen talking, she could persuade him to plant something in one of the buildings.

"There's a residence and a barn. A building that looks like a Quonset hut, probably barracks or supplies." Alvarez paused. "We'd have to know where the sensitive conversations take place, and get something planted in there. And that's assuming they don't regularly check for bugs."

"Sleep on it." Dakota glanced at all of them. "Over breakfast we can talk again, see if anyone has had any ideas."

Josh nodded. Alvarez finished his steak. O'Caran had his phone out, typing.

They headed back to the hotel, and he let Neema out to pee and wandered around close by her. A shower would be good, along with about twelve hours of sleep. Josh prayed they'd come up with something before breakfast. A way to figure this out. Get a break in the case.

He had to leave in twenty-four hours, and that was pushing it for him to get to work on Monday morning. Whichever way he figured it, he was going to be exhausted.

Nose to the ground, Neema circled a tree and headed for the dumpster. Josh wandered after her, not looking forward to what she was going to find.

A truck pulled into the lot. He heard the engine and his instincts tweaked like they'd been doing every time a truck showed up lately. He forced himself to not pay much attention. Neema could easily find something that might injure her.

He was around the side of the motel when the first thud sounded. Josh gave the dog the command to come, and then heel. He circled the front corner of the building and saw two men carrying Dakota. Her body was limp, her head hanging down between them.

"Hey!"

Shouting was a reflex. He had no weapon.

But they did. One man swung around. He dropped Dakota's leg as he brought his arm up. She lifted her head.

He saw a glimpse of her face.

Then the muzzle flash was gone before Josh realized what it was. Fire hit his shoulder, and he fell to the ground. Rolled with the momentum and almost blacked out at the pain. His body stopped and he blinked up at the stars.

Neema whined. Licked his face.

Someone shouted.

Tires squealed. He managed to shift far enough to see the truck peel out of the parking lot.

Dakota was gone.

Chapter 8

US Marshal Salvador Alvarez heard the gunshot as he emerged from the bathroom in his room. The roar of a truck engine followed.

He swiped his gun off the bedside table and flung the door open. Weber was flat on his back in the middle of the parking lot. That dog of his stood over him, barking at the fleeing truck.

Niall barreled out of his own room, gun raised. Sal moved past him and down the stairs, fighting the growing ache in his bones. Forty years hunting was catching up with him.

Sal went over to him. Josh started to sit up, pushing back the shoulder of his jacket.

"You got shot?"

Josh gritted his teeth. The kid was tough. He didn't even look fazed. "I think it went through my shoulder."

Sal knelt on the asphalt and checked Weber's back. The wound was high up on the man's torso, above his collar bone. Not much more than a scratch between his neck and shoulder.

"A graze." Sal replaced the jacket over the man's shoulder. "You're lucky, it missed everything important." Like his giant head…and ears.

He didn't want to dislike the kid, but—okay, yes. He wanted to dislike the kid. Dakota wasn't part of Sal's personal life, but that didn't mean he liked the idea that someone else might be.

He'd seen Weber look at her when she wasn't looking. Just like he'd seen her look at him.

The dog bounded back over to them and barked at Sal.

He stared it down. "Sit."

Weber chuckled. "Nice try." He raised his voice a little and said, "Neema, sietz."

Ah. German commands. The dog planted her butt on the asphalt, ears up. Complete one hundred percent focus.

"It was worth a try, at least."

She barked at him.

Weber chuckled again, then groaned.

O'Caran trotted over. "Ambulance is on its way." He glanced around. "Where's Pierce?"

"The truck," Weber said. "They took her."

"Terrence Crampton?"

"I think it was the same truck." Weber glanced over at an ambulance pulling into the parking lot, followed by a sheriff's department Jeep. "They grabbed her out of her motel room and stuffed her in the truck before I could catch up and stop them."

And Josh had been shot for his trouble, for trying to save Dakota's life.

"All right." Sal nodded.

The woman might enjoy telling everyone who would listen that she was perfectly capable of taking care of herself, but they weren't just words. It was the truth. Sal had seen her do it many times. He'd been with her on operations that took the whole team working together to get the job done. Sal knew what she was capable of. "She'll hold her own until we find her."

"They're after revenge, remember?" Weber's face had paled. Worried, or in pain? Or both? "They blew up my truck. We talked to Austin and now she gets kidnapped? It's that retaliation she was talking about."

Sal said, "If they wanted her dead they'd have killed her inside the room or on the street. Why take her with them only to put a bullet in her somewhere else?"

Josh closed his mouth, fire in his eyes. So he didn't like what Sal said. Did Sal care? Not especially.

"She'll hold her own," he repeated.

Josh looked away. The kid needed to not forget that Sal knew Dakota a whole lot better than he did after one day. The EMTs came over and helped him into their ambulance.

"No."

Sal turned back to see Josh shake his head.

"Just patch me up. I'm not going to the hospital."

"He's really worried." O'Caran came to stand beside Sal. "He cares about her."

"She got under his skin."

"But...Pierce?"

Sal grinned. "I've heard that can happen sometimes."

"But not to you." O'Caran returned his smile. "Because you're Mr. Stone Cold US Marshal."

Sal shrugged. It wasn't untrue. Niall could think what he wanted.

O'Caran shook his head. "Whatever."

Sal's phone rang. He swiped to answer and said, "I was just about to call you."

"Explain." Just one word. Victoria didn't use more when few would suffice.

Sal told her everything he knew. Then he said, "Just tell me she'll be okay."

It didn't matter that he'd told Josh she could hold her own. The kid needed to believe they knew her better than anyone. Not just because they'd worked together for years. It was more than that. She'd let them in first. They had become family to her. Josh had to trust that.

It grated against everything Sal was, but he actually cared about Dakota. He was worried.

None of them had a good track record with their actual families. For one reason or another they'd all needed, and found, what was missing in their lives with Victoria's team.

Though, if that were true, he wasn't sure why he still felt...empty.

Victoria said, "If these people are who we think they are?"

Sal said, "They are, and Terrence Crampton is one of them. His woman is dead, and Dakota was snooping around asking questions about what they're up to. The grenade was overkill, but I figure they're protecting their *assets*."

"Good. Dakota will find out what they're doing."

Too bad this wasn't a re-con mission. They'd kidnapped her.

Now Sal and Niall had a man with a gunshot wound on their hands. Dakota had a concussion. Added to the kind of people these were, and the fact it was a hot button with Dakota, he was worried.

Sal wanted to hope this would work out for the best. Enough it almost made him want to pray for help. But that would be admitting he couldn't do this himself, and his entire life had been about proving to everyone—including God—that he didn't need help.

"What do you want me to do about Weber?"

Victoria was quiet for a second. "You think he's in danger?"

"They shot him, but Dakota is the one they took." If these people thought she was the weak link, he'd feel sorry for them when they discovered the truth. "He can help us. Probably." Sal glanced over at Josh, sitting in the back of the ambulance. "He wants to."

"I'll submit the paperwork."

"Copy that."

Victoria hung up.

"Weber!" Sal let his voice ring across the parking lot. Josh looked up. The dog barked. "When you're done getting your owies kissed all better, you're with me."

The man's face was priceless. At least Niall didn't start laughing. Sal didn't need that. And he didn't need arguments from a rookie, even one that was a fed.

With some animals, you had to establish the alpha from the outset. Otherwise they'd get ideas that maybe they could be in charge, and you'd end up in a fight for who was on top. Like Josh could find Dakota better, or faster, than Sal? Just the idea amused him, though he didn't laugh.

As if.

• • •

"Where are we going?"

Sal headed for Dakota's motel room. Josh entered after him. *Here, I guess.* Neema waited by the door for his command.

Neither Sal nor the other guy, Niall O'Caran, glanced at him. Not feeling the need to explain much? He'd been trained by the DEA, and before that, the marines. Still, it seemed like Neema might be of more use to them than he was.

Josh rolled his shoulders to try and discard the feeling. *Ouch.* He glanced around, looking for some evidence. "This is a waste of time."

They knew who had Dakota—same truck, same guy. Terrence had a lot to answer for.

Militia, Sal had said. Like a homegrown army, determined to fight the federal government. Dakota was the enemy to them. The embodiment of the very thing they lived their lives in defiance of.

Sal didn't acknowledge him. Josh might as well have been invisible.

He said, "What are you guys even looking for? It isn't like they left something behind that'll tell you where they have her."

Niall straightened on the far side of the bed. "We know where they have her."

"So what are you looking for? Because maybe she doesn't want you two going through her things. Maybe she wants you to *go get her.*"

"You're new," Sal said, his words measured. His tone flat, like he was placating Josh. He lifted Dakota's computer and tucked it into her backpack, then continued, "So I'm going to do you a solid, and explain. Don't get used to it."

Josh said nothing.

"We take what she doesn't want looked at, and what doesn't need to get tied up as evidence for the next however many days the sheriff's department will hold it."

"That isn't legal. Plus it's your case, right?" He almost said, "our case" but was glad he'd held back.

"We don't need their questions about who we are. The lengthy explanations about why we're here. Or about how we all ended up working together when we're from completely different federal agencies."

They'd barely explained it to him. "So you clean up here, and then we go get her?"

"Yes."

Josh fisted his hands, then shifted his weight from one foot to the other.

"That dog of yours going to need to pee before it gets in my car?"

"She." Josh didn't answer the question, which was insulting. Neema wasn't a toddler that needed a training diaper.

"I'm done." That came from Niall.

Josh nearly threw his hands up in relief, but didn't. That would have sent a searing pain down his shoulder. Yep, good choice.

He saw the look that passed between them, but who cared when they were gearing up to go get Dakota. She was all that mattered. In a completely platonic, I-just-met-you-and-we're-colleagues kind of way, with a side of, "I got shot trying to help you" thrown in for good measure.

She seemed like a good woman. One whose heart was in the right place, even if she was a little gruff. Maybe even rough around the edges. He'd never liked those women who wanted to be all prissy and objected to camping. What was that about?

There was something about Dakota Pierce that drew him to her. Maybe he would never figure out exactly what it was, and maybe didn't have time to, but that wasn't the point right now. She was in danger and their job was to help her. At least, it was Niall and Sal's job—and the other two, Victoria and Talia. Dakota needed him and he was glad he was on this job—granted, only until tomorrow night. But still glad to be able to help get her back to safety.

For now, he was part of this. It didn't matter if it fit with his plans, or not.

And he was going to do whatever it took.

Determined to push through that flash he'd seen, the look on her face. She'd been...not scared. There was far more to it than that. Angry. Frustrated. They bested her. She was on her way to being incapacitated. The thread of possibility that they would use her and then dump her somewhere. All of it had been there on her face. That split second flash he'd seen before the gun exploded.

Josh wanted to get her back. To replace the bad with the relief of being found. Safe with her team again.

He wasn't going anywhere until he made that happen.

"Car."

Josh climbed in the back, and Neema hopped up beside him. She lay across the backseat with her head in his lap.

Sal shot her a resigned look and started the car. He navigated to the highway fast enough Josh's eyebrows lifted, but he said nothing. Apparently Sal thought he was on a California freeway. Or he was as determined to get to Dakota as the rest of them.

"So what's the plan?"

Niall shifted in his seat, then handed Josh a tablet. "This is the layout of the compound. We think she'll be held here." He pointed to the center building, roofed like a house on the satellite image. "But the reality is, we have no idea. We have no surveillance set up and no intel."

"Call Talia." Sal's order was clipped. "She can get us a location."

"She was wearing her watch? I didn't see it in the room, I figured it was tucked in a bag." Niall glanced between them.

"Josh, was Dakota wearing her watch?"

He frowned, trying to spawn the image in his own mind. The memory of her being taken. He'd been looking at her face, not her hand. They'd had ahold of her.

Then the gun went off, and he'd been on his back.

"I didn't see."

Sal sighed, like Josh now had another strike against him.

"What's with the watch?"

Niall said, "GPS."

Sal pulled out his phone and made a call. "Yeah, it's me." He was quiet for a minute and Josh could make out someone talking on the other end, just not what they were saying. It was a woman. Victoria, or this Talia person?

Sal said, "Copy that, red leader." He hung up.

Cupcake? Red leader? The man seemed to have a thing for comedy nicknames. Cute, but was that going to get Dakota back?

Josh quit holding back his frustration. "Tell me you got something."

• • •

His fist reared back. Dakota could barely make it out through the swollen skin around her eyes.

…that all men are created equal, that they are endowed by their Creator with certain unalienable rights.

He hit her again. She'd lost count how many times, but he seemed determined.

This was her second time through the Declaration of Independence.

A whimper escaped her mouth. But then, there was no point holding it back, was there? He had to at least *think* he was making progress.

…it is their right, it is their duty, to throw off such Government.

Terrence Crampton flexed his fingers and shook out his hand. Dakota took a second to tug against the tape securing her hands behind her back. They hadn't taped her to the chair. Just dumped her here and started in, determined to break the federal agent.

Was he going to ask her a question at some point?

Terrence glanced at the teen, who he'd shoved in the corner to watch. "Go get her."

Austin scurried out. Terrence's gaze roved over her. She felt it like an oily touch, head to toes and back up. All over her skin.

The history of the present King of Great Britain…

Terrence moved to stand between her knees and braced his weight, his palms on her thighs. He leaned his face close to hers, their cheeks touching. He inhaled, deep through his nose.

...the most wholesome and necessary for the public good.

It was like counting backwards from one hundred. Just a distraction technique, trying to get all the words and phrases correct. She'd been using the technique for years. Since she'd first read the Declaration of Independence in grade school.

Dakota didn't like that she had to employ it again now. But life was funny like that and things seemed to have a habit of coming back around in circles.

He made a noise in his throat. Approval she didn't need, or want. Dakota thought about bringing up her leg. Maybe she could smash her foot against something sensitive. They hadn't given her any time to pull her boots on before they hauled her out of her motel room.

Inconsiderate, really. Now that she thought about it.

Who did stuff like that?

Someone about to get her face smashed into his if he didn't back up, that was who. It was tempting. *So tempting.* She'd never in her life wanted to lose her cool more than she did right then. And with her history, that was saying something.

The door opened.

"What are you doing?" The woman's voice was throaty, like a long time smoker. Or someone with strep.

Terrence straightened and stepped away. Dakota lifted her gaze to look at the woman. She remained in the shadows of the yellow glow of the bulb that hung from the ceiling.

"That's what I thought." The woman flicked her hand from Terrence to the door. "You've screwed up enough."

She stepped into the shed, shifting sideways slightly so she could fit her frame in the door. Checkered shirt. Dirty beige work pants. Huge boots. Flat hair, and an expression not unlike a pug.

She stared at Dakota with black eyes. "Do you know what we do to nosy government agents?"

...a right inestimable to them and formidable to tyrants only.

Dakota said, "I guess I'm going to find out."

Chapter 9

Josh stopped between two trees, crouching behind the cover of a downed tree that was now overgrown. Neema panted against his ear. He gave her the hand signal to lay down. She settled her belly to the grass with a grunt.

He pulled out his binoculars, the infrared kind. It was so dark out here he couldn't see much of anything. Lights at the compound were sparse.

Josh spotted sentries. He keyed his radio. "I've got two on roving patrol between me and the entrance."

"Two on my end doing the same," was Sal's reply.

"One at the south end." That was Niall.

"Copy that. Five total." The woman's voice had the edge of an accent he thought might be South African. Later he would ask about that. For now all he'd needed to know was that this was the famous Talia, and she was running comms for the operation.

Fear walked with cold fingers up his spine. That whisper in his ear, telling him this was futile. Dakota was already dead.

Josh gritted his teeth and studied the compound through his binoculars. He had taken up position on the west side. Sal was across, east, about a mile from Josh. Niall had the rear, to the south of them, where there was a small exit in the chain link fence. The north edge was where patrols were focused, guarding the wide opening. Where they'd be spotted if they approached.

Neema shifted. He glanced back and saw her ears were perked. Her nose twitched.

He scratched under her chin and kept looking through the binoculars. There. Two dogs jumped and tussled with each other, big German Shepherds with heavy fur and equally heavy bellies. They seemed more interested in the bone they were wrestling over, but Josh wasn't going to take for granted those powerful bites. Especially not when they could get Neema between them and overpower her.

She'd faced enough through two tours. She didn't need to get jumped by a couple of bullies in back country Washington State.

Sal's voice invaded his thoughts. "Lot of activity around the central house."

Josh moved the binoculars and saw two men in front of a shed, both smoking. The glow of cigarettes illuminated their faces. He thought it might be Terrence and the other guy—not the teen, the friend—but couldn't be sure without getting closer.

Talia said, "Rookie, you're gonna get an email."

Josh felt his phone vibrate in his pocket before she'd even finished talking. He said, "Copy that," and shifted to pull it out. The email was from Victoria Bramlyn, State Department. Director of Domestic Security. He read through it, eyebrows lifting as he got further and further down.

Talia said, "Do as instructed with the attachment and get it back to me, or you're flying solo. And none of us can help you out of *that* mess."

"Copy that." Josh opened the document. It took him a minute or so to navigate the attachment, sign it as instructed, and send it back.

A request to the DEA from Victoria Bramlyn that Special Agent Josh Weber assist her on a case he was uniquely qualified for.

Didn't say what the case was. Or what his "unique qualifications" were. But his boss had signed it. They'd dragged the assistant director out of bed? That wasn't going to go down well when he got back to work. Though given the document he'd just returned to Victoria there might not be much the man could say.

These people had pull.

He said, "Done," over the radio.

Sal's voice came back at him through his earpiece. "Welcome aboard."

"It's been a dream for so long," Josh drawled, heavy on the sarcasm.

Niall chimed in. "I'd like to thank the Academy…"

Josh cracked a smile.

Talia came on again. "While you bozo's have been performing your comedy routine, I've been redirecting satellites. Two heat signatures in that shed."

Heat was good.

Heat meant she was still alive.

Sal said, "Our girl in there?"

Even if she was, there was little they could do that wouldn't start an all-out war between them and double their number of armed men willing to die.

Josh said, "How do we get her out?"

• • •

"What time is it?"

The woman started, halting her long-winded speech about freedom and something or other. "What…who cares? That isn't why I came in here."

"Okay," Dakota said. "I was just curious what time it was." She shrugged one shoulder, but not much. She didn't want the woman to think she wasn't all that secure. The last thing she needed was to be completely immobilized.

If the pug-faced woman would come a half step closer, Dakota could be done with whatever this conversation was. But she needed to gather intelligence from this woman. She was probably some kind of leader, so as tempting as it was, Dakota tamped down the urge to hurt her and then walk out of here. Right now she needed answers more than she needed escape.

Dakota turned her head to the side and spat out the blood-mixed saliva that had collected in her mouth. Her head throbbed like crazy. It was distracting enough she wasn't sure what to do next. She recited more of the Declaration of Independence while the woman stared at her with resting pug face.

Okay, so she wasn't doing as well as she wanted to believe. But lying to oneself was like balance—some days it was there, other days you had to work harder to get a good tree pose going.

It was the smell. And Austin being in here earlier. The taste of blood in her mouth. Hearing the teen whimper when she was hit. He might have dumped Maggie's body, but he was no hard-nosed criminal. The kid was new, being inducted into how this whole thing worked so he could take over in a few years, maybe.

Pug-face woman finally said, "That's all you're curious about? What time it is?"

"Can't say I don't have questions."

Maggie. Austin. The shipments. The orchard.

Dakota didn't know what to ask first.

Pug-face woman said, "Too bad it's going to be me asking the questions and you giving me answers."

"Fire away," Dakota said.

The woman actually reacted. Just a tiny glint. Not quite humor but there was something. She mushed her lips together, and the glint was gone. "Why are you snooping your fed nose around my orchard?"

Well, that was telling. *Her* orchard. "I've met the owners. Nice people. I don't think they'd take too kindly to you claiming their property."

"*Our* territory is vast. The fact the federal government isn't aware of who owns what is kind of the point, don't you think?"

"Yeah, I know. Stick it to the man. Live free, but ready for war." At least, that was what most people thought of them. They figured that with these militia guys it was mostly bluster and not much else. Except the amount of guns they have stockpiled.

The woman snorted, like she thought Dakota was hilariously misguided. "We don't need no feds poking their noses around."

"Just following the stink."

"Of what?"

Dakota curled her lips up. "Why don't you tell me all the things you're up to, and I'll tell you which ones I've heard about?"

The woman actually chuckled.

"Worth a try," Dakota said. "How about we start with Maggie? You kill her?" She knew Austin and Terrence hadn't done it.

"That airhead."

"Wrong place at the wrong time? Overheard something?" Dakota paused for a second. "Someone got mad at her and went too far, maybe?"

She'd been strangled. A personal death that put two people face-to-face, close enough you could hear their last breath. See the look in their eyes. It wasn't something done by accident, or without reason. Whether that reason was by order, or because of overwhelming anger, was the question she wanted an answer to.

"Do you want me to confess?" the pug-face woman asked. "Are you going to arrest me?"

"Did she get this treatment?" Maggie hadn't looked like she'd been beaten, but that was just her face.

"What you're experiencing—what you're *going* to experience—is reserved for feds."

"So Maggie was different."

"That *piece of trash*. She was nothing!" Spittle flew. The woman's face turned red.

"And you got rid of her," Dakota said. "Then you had Austin dump her at the orchard like the trash she was." Her voice was measured. Cold to her own ears. She'd never liked that tone. The one she'd had to learn, that contained no emotion whatsoever. No life.

She sounded dead.

"So what if I did? It's not like you're going to tell anyone."

They were going to kill her. That wasn't the part Dakota was so worried about. It was the stuff that came before it that was concerning. Her face and head both hurt like nobody's business. She needed to spit again. Had he cracked a tooth? Ugh. She hated the dentist.

"… even *listening* to me!"

Dakota blinked. "What?"

The woman screamed in rage. Close enough Dakota saw her uvula.

She tipped her head to the side, ignoring the pain. "You seem like you're having a bad day." Even though it was the middle of the night. "Why don't you tell me about it? Maybe I can help. Then if you let me go, I'm sure things will smooth out. I won't mention this to anyone."

Her scratchy palm slapped Dakota across the face. The blow whipped her head to the side, her cheek stinging.

Dakota spat. Inciting rage in the pug-face woman could wind up being a good thing, or it could go very badly. "Is that what happened to Maggie? You lost it, and she wound up dead? Maybe things just went too far, and you didn't mean it."

"Tell me what led you here."

"You," Dakota said. "And whatever you're up to."

She wanted to trust that she would be rescued. But she couldn't rely on it. The door wasn't going to blow off its hinges. No armed gunmen would burst in all of a sudden.

Was her team here? Were they coming?

Was Josh dead?

She'd seen him get shot but had forced away those thoughts. Until now. She couldn't fight back the surge anymore.

She didn't like the fact she might actually *feel* something for a man she'd met only yesterday. Not that she would like, cry, or anything. But she would feel the loss.

He seemed nice enough. Like he was a good guy who loved his dog and didn't deserve to die just because he tried to help her.

She wasn't worth that.

Where was Sal? And Niall? Was Talia looking for her? Was Victoria pacing her study at home, waiting for the phone to ring?

"What exactly do you think I'm up to?"

Dakota said, "Something. Or you wouldn't be so concerned that I've found out about it." She spoke the thought aloud, unable to fully process it in her head. Not when it currently felt like it was about to split open.

The pug face woman swung around and flung the door open. "Find out what she knows!"

She stormed out, letting the cold air blow in. Dakota's skin prickled, and she shivered. Shouldn't have downed so many sparkling waters at dinner.

She hopped up out of the chair before anyone came in. Then plopped her butt down on the floor—gross—and shifted her arms to the front so she had use of her bound hands. Her head swam, but she ignored it. She wasn't going to be able to get out of here without brain power and use of her limbs.

Disable the guards. Run for it.

Not a great plan but hopefully her team was ready to assist.

Terrence came in just as she climbed to her feet. He stopped. Blinked.

Dakota struck fast and hard. She poured all of her frustration and discomfort into her attack.

• • •

Josh moved between two containers at the edge of the property, the kind of shipping containers that transported freight on the back of semi-trucks. He held his gun in a loose grip. Shoulders shifting. Feet moving. Stiff or tense didn't help anything when an attack could come out of nowhere.

He stopped at the end and surveyed the expanse of dirt between him and the shed. Ruts from tires. Piles of dirty snow. Someone had made a snowman. It was halfway melted now, with the wrinkled carrot lying where it had fallen.

Air puffed white from his mouth as he stood and watched. Terrence Crampton had passed a heavy-set woman and entered the shed. The woman had stalked off.

Cigarette man was still there, not paying attention to much beyond his habit and his phone. He lifted his head and glanced at the woman's back. Didn't think much of her but wasn't willing to share that opinion to her face.

Something from the shed drew his attention. The man shifted that way and looked over. His shoulders shook with humor over what was happening inside.

Too far to run over and put him down before he turned back.

The guards at the north entrance were a quarter mile to Josh's left. Whatever he did would put him out in the open where they'd see everything.

The shed door flung open. Dakota stumbled out. It was too dark to see her face, but he saw her go down.

Josh ran before his brain could catch up and tell him rushing over there wasn't a good plan.

Cigarette man dropped his phone and fumbled behind him. Gun?

Josh brought his up.

Dakota rushed at him, ducked her head to change levels at the last second, and tackled his stomach. The man landed on his back, her on top. She swung her hands together in front and hit him. Tied up?

Josh's boot dipped sideways into a rut. His leg caught and his other knee landed in the frozen dirt. *Ouch.* The force jarred his shoulder, making it impossible to ignore it any longer. The pain was blinding. And while pain meds were a beautiful thing, he'd been shot, and it hurt.

Josh had to push a breath out between gritted teeth and get his footing back under him so he didn't pass out.

Cigarette man shoved Dakota aside so she rolled, ending up flat on her back a few feet away. Struggling to get up. The guy pulled a gun from the back of his waistband and pointed it at her.

Josh went with instinct and cried out again, running. It was enough to distract cigarette man.

The guy looked at him.

Josh winced at the pull against his wound but held his gun up and put a bullet in his chest. And he didn't miss the guy's heart. The explosion echoed in the night. Terrence Crampton stumbled from the shed. Josh ignored the yelling in his earpiece, clambered to his feet and ran for Dakota. A dog barked. She was already up, and grabbed cigarette guy's gun.

Turned.

Pointed it at Terrence.

But he wasn't armed. Josh yelled, "Let's go!"

Automatic gunfire peppered the ground between them. Dakota and Josh both cut toward the south. "On me." He ordered, assuming she'd understand he knew the way out.

Josh keyed his radio as he ran. "I need cover—"

Before he even finished, answering gunfire sounded across the compound. The cavalry had come.

Josh raced with Dakota to the hole he'd cut in the fence, bullets dogging every step.

Chapter 10

Dakota raced after him. He would never know how much trust it took to concentrate only on him, push out everything else and just follow. Submit to his leading.

She was never going to tell him how much that took.

Josh cut right around the back of the container.

She could hear the jingle of metal tags. "Dogs." She didn't want them to race up behind her and grab her pant leg. Bite her.

A sob burst from her throat, but her eyes remained dry.

Josh stopped at a fence and waved her through the hole. She scrabbled on hands and knees through the gap, grimacing at how useless her bound hands were. A gun fired.

She spun around, expecting to be shot. She'd dropped the gun right before they ran, and hadn't been able to stop and grab it.

Two big dogs stopped in their tracks right behind them. Both barked, paws lifting off the ground.

Josh fired again, weapon pointed at the dirt. The dogs yelped and backed up. With a swift head nod, he motioned for Dakota to go through first. She glanced back. Guys with automatic weapons raced between the containers, headed right for them while the dogs paced. Waiting for orders.

Josh tugged her elbow, and they ducked through, skirting the fence line. "This way."

"K." It was all she could get out.

They had to put distance between them and those guys with automatic weapons. There was no way they would win that fight.

And the more distance between her and those dogs, the better.

Every step felt like it took forever. As though time had slowed, and every breath was drawn out. A lifetime between each one.

"Copy that," Josh said, his voice breathy. He grabbed her hand and tugged her forward.

She wasn't going to last much longer running at this pace before her body shut down and she collapsed.

Dakota glanced back but couldn't see anyone.

An engine revved. Not the throaty sound of a car. This was different. A four-wheeled vehicle headed right for them, lights on. So bright she had to shield her eyes.

Josh said, "I know," into his radio.

Whatever that was about, there wasn't time to ask him. The all-terrain vehicle cut left, off the path they were on, and headed between two trees at a slower pace. Dakota saw the word POLARIS on the side.

Josh darted after it, still tugging her along with him. He let go of her hand and jumped on the back, grasped a bar at the top and tucked his feet up on a shelf at the back. He shifted and held out his hand. "Jump."

Dakota grabbed his hand. She planted her foot two more times, then launched herself up. The shin of her trailing leg hit the shelf, and she grabbed the bar. Josh nudged her forward with his free hand. "Climb through."

A bullet sang past her head. Josh ducked. Dakota's whole body flinched.

"Hold on," Niall yelled from the front seat.

There was no way she could climb through to the seat. Her fingers didn't want to lose their grip on the bar. The wind was killer. *So cold.* A whimper escaped her mouth.

Josh shifted closer to her, but there wasn't much he could do without losing his own grip. He turned to Niall and called out, "Slow down a fraction. About twenty feet."

Niall eased off the gas, both hands a death grip on the wheel.

Josh stuck two fingers from one hand in his mouth and whistled. Loud and sharp. Dakota winced as the sound reverberated through her head.

Seconds later, Neema ducked out from behind a bush and jumped. She cleared the passenger side and landed on the seat, skidding into Niall. Her teammate yelped. At any other time it might've been funny.

Niall drove through the woods. Neema panted, mouth open and tongue hanging out. Josh shifted and Dakota glanced at him.

He winced and leaned closer so their faces were almost touching. "You don't look so good."

"Probably about as great as I feel." She could hardly talk around the discomfort of her swollen face, numb from the cold air. "You were shot."

He nodded, eyes on her. Unreadable. "I'm okay now."

Niall eased on the brakes and she saw they were approaching an SUV. Niall stopped the ATV. "Go with Josh." The look on his face was one she didn't want to argue with. "I'll draw them away."

"Are they following us?" She glanced back.

"Go Dakota."

Josh jumped off the the back and lifted her. It took a second to disconnect her fingers from the bar, then he set her feet on the ground. "Come on."

She looked at Niall, even while Josh led her to the vehicle. Should she be doing something?

"Go," Josh said. "Get warm."

"What is—"

Josh flung the door open. "Get in." He glanced at the animal. "Neema, up."

Dakota flinched. The dog hopped into the car and moved to the backseat.

Niall drove off. Without thinking about it, her body turned to the ATV. She needed to help her team, didn't she?

Josh gave her a gentle push. Her legs gave out. He tucked them inside and shut the door in her face.

Neema laid her head on Dakota's shoulder. She recoiled and shifted in her seat so the dog had to move away.

Josh got in, saw her body language, and said, "Neema, platz." He turned the key and started the car. The dog settled into the backseat with a grunt. He backed around in a U-turn and set off down the dirt track, tapping his finger on the steering wheel.

"What?" He needed to say *something*. She could feel the shakes coming over her, so she cranked the heat and pointed the blowers at her face. "Tell me."

"Alvarez hasn't checked in yet."

Dakota grabbed the cord to his earpiece and stuck it in her own ear.

"…on. Come on."

"Talia, it's me."

Josh bent toward her so their faces almost touched. So the cord was long enough.

Her teammate blew out a breath that made the connection crackle. "Thank You, God. You're all right?"

"I'm fine." Like that was important right now? "Where's Salvarez?"

"Hunkered down would be my guess."

"But you don't know."

"You think he let them capture him?"

Dakota pressed her lips together. "He better be okay."

Josh said, "We're headed back to the motel. Keep us posted."

"Copy tha—"

Dakota interrupted Talia. "We are not. We're going to help him."

"That's Niall's job right now." Josh actually pulled the earpiece out of her hand. "Not yours."

"Go back."

"No."

She balled her fist, teeth clenched.

"Are you going to hit me? I figure you don't have the strength to do a whole lot of damage, but there's a chance." He shook his head. "Do I need to remind you we just *saved your butt?*"

Dakota sat back in her chair. Folded her arms. "Planning to talk until my head explodes?" Sarcasm dripped from her words.

He made a sound, air pushed out of his nose. Like he wanted to tell her to shut up. He should. What was the point in being nice when things needed to be said?

"Close your eyes and take a break." His voice sounded pained. "When I know something, I'll tell you."

Dakota didn't close her eyes. "I better know the *second* you find out."

Josh reached over and squeezed her hand. "He'll be okay."

"He better be."

. . .

First she got mad. Then it became clear she needed a little compassion from him because she was hurting and worried about her friend. Now she was silent. Evidently if something happened to Sal because Josh hadn't turned the car around and gone to help the guy, then it was going to be his fault.

She wanted to go and rescue her friend. A friend who'd been there to rescue her. She was in absolutely no position to be doing anything right now. Unless that was taking pain killers and lying down.

Josh really shouldn't be either, considering the bandaged gash just below his neck.

He glanced at her once, then pulled out onto the road. Her face was a mess. If the rest of her was half as bad, then she might have internal bleeding to go along with that concussion.

He drove into town and headed to the doctor's office instead of to the motel. She would probably prefer to not be in the room she'd been kidnapped from.

Josh ignored the radio and handed Dakota his phone. "Do me a favor and call Talia?"

She didn't look at him, or give anything away, but she did dial the number. When she handed it back, it was already ringing.

Talia answered. "Weber?"

"Yeah."

Before he could say more, Talia interrupted. "Is Dakota okay?"

Josh answered with, "Rouse the doctor out of bed."

Dakota shifted. "No—"

He ignored her right back. "She needs looking at, and I'm pretty sure I need stitches."

"Copy that."

"I'm headed there now. Have him meet us."

"Uh…" Talia paused. "Looks like it's a woman."

"Then have *her* meet us."

Josh hung up and pulled into the parking lot. The sign outside said, *Doctor J Stevens*. Probably better for Dakota that the doctor was a woman, as she'd likely be more comfortable being poked and prodded by a woman. Especially considering what might have happened between her being taken and running out of that shed.

He pulled into a spot right by the door and tossed the phone in the cup holder. He shifted toward Dakota, and fussed with the heater some more so it blew warm on her. "Still cold?"

He shifted again, trying to get comfortable. Neema set her front paws on the center console and sniffed at his face. She knew how he felt about face licking, so she didn't try that. Just kept her nose close to his. He scratched under her chin. "You okay, Dakota?"

She spoke to the window, her body still. Fingers intertwined together on her lap. "Sorry about your truck."

"You didn't ask them to toss a grenade under it. I'm just glad we're both in one piece." Except neither of them were all right, if they were honest.

She sucked in a breath that shifted her chest and couldn't quite hide the wince.

"Tell me what they did." He didn't want to ask, but maybe she needed to say it out loud.

"Tied me up. Punched me. Tried to talk me to death."

"That's it?"

She shrugged one shoulder. A delicate move. One he didn't think she realized told him more about what had happened than any of her previous words.

They'd shaken her, despite her strength and capability. The pain she was in, the quiet and dark of the car. Maybe even the fact it was him here and not her team. All of it allowed her mask to slip just a little.

She was far from okay.

The clock on the dash read 00:47 when the doctor pulled into the parking lot. She met them at the door and took a look at both of them. She motioned to Josh. "Gunshot first."

She showed Dakota to a room, and had her get into a gown while she stitched up Josh next door. When she'd finished up, she headed to check out Dakota.

Josh paced the hallway while the phone rang against his ear. Dakota would want an update. When Talia answered, he said, "Anything?"

"Niall thinks they have Salvarez pinned down so that he can't respond or he'll give himself away. But Niall can't get any closer without confronting them. How's our girl?"

"In with the doctor," Josh said.

"Soon as I get word about Sal, I'll let you know. So you can tell her."

Because they were friends and teammates, or more? Josh didn't know if he wanted an answer to that. "Are they…"

"*No.*" She dragged out the word. "What a nightmare that would be. No way. He would probably shoot her inside of a week, after she first drove him crazy, of course. Dakota needs someone who can settle her. Someone who can bring peace to her life, not more of that Type-A, butt-to-the-flame, win-at-all-costs thing they both have going on."

It sounded like she needed an elementary school teacher, or at least someone with a job completely different to hers. Josh wasn't sure he liked that.

"She also needs someone capable of protecting her and keeping up with her. Not someone she's going to railroad, or walk all over. Not that she would do it intentionally, but if they just bend under her strength, then what's the point?"

"Mmm." Josh didn't really know what else to say. Equally strong, but not the same? Soft but a fighter? Maybe Talia just knew all the facets of Dakota's personality, so she had this level of insight. Maybe she saw the contrasting things and knew what would match up to her.

Would he?

Did he want to find out? It wasn't like he was any good at relationships. So far he hadn't had one that actually worked. And if he admitted it to himself, that actually hurt. He knew it wasn't totally his fault. Relationships took two people working to make them last, and maybe he hadn't met anyone willing to do their part. But he was almost thirty. Everyone he'd grown up with was married. Some of them even had kids already.

He had Neema, and his job. And Eden.

A dog and an old lady neighbor.

The doctor pulled the door open. Josh said, "Gotta go," and hung up on Talia.

Dr. Stevens closed the door behind her. "One second." She tapped the screen of her iPad for a few seconds, then locked it. Looked up. "Okay."

Josh lifted his eyebrows, leaving the question unspoken.

"Lacerations and bruising, mainly concentrated on her face. Her hip has a nice-sized bruise as well. She's getting dressed now."

"You're releasing her?"

"She doesn't want to be admitted, so there's nothing I can do more than what I've already done. The concussion from earlier still stands. She needs monitoring, and she needs to sleep. The woman is exhausted. She's not going to feel better for a few days."

By which time he'd be back to work. Long gone with nothing but a gunshot wound to remember this lovely time in his life.

Yes, Victoria had made his boss sign that paper, but it wasn't like it extended beyond Monday, right? He needed to get back to his desk. Keep working on those open cases he had.

"Thank you."

Dr. Stevens nodded. She walked away down the hall, and he waited a minute. Then tapped on the door.

"You can come in." Her voice was muffled.

Josh cracked the door and peered in. She was dressed in her jeans and a T-shirt, the other layers beside her on the bed. Her feet were bare. Hair down. Ponytail holder on her wrist.

Aside from the bruising, she looked considerably younger. It made him want to hug her so she felt better.

"Can you help me with my shoes?"

Josh knelt in front of her and assisted. Her socks were thick. He tied her boot laces, and even zipped her coat for her.

She stood. "Thank you."

The words were a whisper between them. "You're welcome."

Her lip was split. Josh leaned close to the other corner of her mouth. Just a tiny kiss. A small amount of comfort for her, when she clearly didn't feel good at all.

When their lips were a hairsbreadth apart, his phone rang.

Chapter 11

Dakota settled into the chair, not thinking too much about the fact this was Josh's room and not hers. Her head pounded. She would've been grateful for that fact, as it meant she was still alive, had it not hurt so bad it eclipsed everything else.

"You can lie down if you want." He even shooed Neema off the bed.

Dakota said, "No." It came out too strong.

He shot her a look. "I didn't mean anything. You just look like you need to lie down."

That soft look was back in his eyes. The same one that had been there before he was going to kiss her. She knew he'd been about to. No one moved their face so close to someone else's without that being on their mind.

Then his phone had rung. Niall found Sal, and they were headed back here.

After that it had been all about getting in the car and arguing about who was worse off, and who should drive. Heading back to the motel. She wanted to take a shower, but that would mean getting her things from her room, and right now, it was the last place she wanted to go. Asking one of the guys to get her stuff also wasn't going to happen.

"You do look like you need to rest."

Dakota was about to answer him. Someone knocked on the door. She moved to get up, but Josh waved her back in the chair. "Stay there."

He had a gun in one hand, and peered out the peep hole for a second before he grabbed the handle and let them in.

Niall, followed by Sal.

Relief was enormous. So overwhelming she actually smiled, even though it hurt a lot. Sal looked about as grateful to see her as she was to see him. He strode over and crouched in front of her. "Pierce?" His voice was hoarse.

Dakota bit her lip against the rush of tears. Why was this affecting her so much? Too tired. Too much headache. She didn't know why, but she could hardly speak past the emotion clogging her throat. "I'm okay."

Josh made a noise that sounded an awful lot like he disagreed with her.

She ignored him. "You?"

"They pinned me down, and I didn't want to be in the middle of a gunfight. I hunkered down and stayed there until they passed by me. Then I ran for it with Niall."

Dakota didn't think that meant they'd come out unscathed, necessarily. But she was going to wait until she could think straight before asking more questions.

Sal would absolutely refrain from telling her the truth, or the *whole* truth at least, if he thought she didn't need it. Or couldn't handle it. For the first time, she thought he might actually be right.

And if he wasn't, she didn't have the energy to argue.

"What are we going to do now?" She didn't want to be the focus. And if she was going to stay awake, then they needed to make a game plan.

Sal sat on the edge of the bed. Niall's usually glass-half-full face looked decidedly darker than normal. She didn't like that at all. He was the happy, hopeful one among them.

Niall said, "Victoria is on her way."

"*What?*"

Sal waved at her. "Deal with it. You think she's going to sit at home when one of her people got hurt?"

"Guess not."

Niall cracked a smile. "When she gets here, we'll figure out a plan."

"Is she getting a warrant for the compound?" Dakota figured the plan would be to raid the place where she was taken, round them all up and start filing charges.

Sal nodded.

"You think they'll be there when we go back?" Josh asked.

"We?"

He nodded. "Victoria got permission from my boss. I'm attached to the team. At least for another eighteen hours. I should be back in the office Monday morning."

Dakota didn't know what to say. She glanced at the clock, counting down the minutes until Josh left. It was the middle of the night right now—early Sunday morning. Josh was part of the team? Victoria had pulled strings so that he was attached to the Northwest Counter Terrorism Taskforce.

Sal said, "Don't count on going home anytime soon. This is far from over."

Josh opened his mouth to say more, but another knock on the door sounded. He pulled the door open without looking this time. Talia strode in, followed by Victoria. The difference between them couldn't be more apparent than it was just now.

They introduced themselves to Josh, then Talia sauntered over, her gorgeous thick curves showcased as she peeled off her thigh-length fluffy coat to reveal a pair of skinny jeans and a fitted blouse. Her gold toned makeup was still perfect against her dark skin even though it was the early hours of the morning, and her short bob of tight curls looked just right.

"You okay?" She cocked her hip and set her hand there for extra emphasis.

Dakota shut her eyes and nodded.

Talia touched the sides of Dakota's head, her fingers warm and pressed a kiss on her forehead.

She opened her eyes to Talia licking her thumb, then going in to wipe her forehead. Dakota said, "Did you leave a lipstick mark on me?"

"The purple is bruise-colored as well." Talia paused. "I'm not sure if it's fabulous or very very sad. I think I'm done with the eggplant."

Dakota smiled as Talia sauntered to sit next to Sal. He sighed and scooted over.

Victoria had crouched by the door. Her pencil skirt pulled tight across her knees as she held out her hands. Neema sniffed and licked the boss's hands then moved closer and aimed for Victoria's face.

The boss ruffled her hands through the hair on Neema's sides while the dog slurped kisses all over her cheeks. "What a beautiful girl you are."

Dakota glanced at the men. Transfixed. Victoria had that way about her. Long, straight blond hair. Classy. Late forties, but she had something about her that was…timeless. Like European vacations, and those perfume commercials.

Next to her, Dakota would always be the girl who grew up with dirt under her fingernails and one pair of shoes. A girl who got haircuts at home. And had never been on a vacation in her life.

Josh called Neema away and then held out a hand to help Victoria stand. Looking a little more smitten than Dakota would've liked to have seen on the face of a man who had nearly kissed her not even an hour earlier.

"Dakota?"

She blinked and focused on her boss. A woman whose lips had curled up. Like there was anything funny about this?

She started to get up. There were entirely too many people in this small motel room, and she needed to move.

Victoria said, "Sit down."

Dakota sat back down.

Victoria surveyed her, mostly her face. Though she knew better than to comment on any of it. Then she glanced around. "The warrant is on its way."

"Good," Sal said. "Then we can haul them all in." He looked about ready to kill someone, not arrest them.

Dakota told them everything that had happened in that shed.

Sal said, "So the woman is in charge?"

"I think so. From what I can tell she's the brains and the guys are all muscle." Maybe they could pin down Austin Crampton again. Get him to talk this time.

"Unless they're gone," Niall said. "Maybe they split."

"They have." Talia pulled an iPad out of her giant gold purse. "Heat signatures moved away in different directions right after you guys took off."

Dakota wanted to run her hands down her face, but that would hurt.

"We can still serve the warrant," Victoria said. "See if they left anything behind. But we need to find them. Maybe even get *someone* on the inside of their group to dig up what they're hiding." She shot Dakota a pointed look.

"Austin." Tomorrow she was going to find him.

Victoria shook her head, "That wasn't who I was thinking of."

Dakota stared at her boss. Seriously? She was going to bring *him* into this?

"No. I said 'no' after the grenade and I'm still saying no. I mean it."

The situation didn't warrant that. It wasn't a plan to solve this. It was no better than tossing in a nuclear warhead that would destroy everything…and everyone.

"But—"

"No."

Victoria had no idea what she was even asking.

. . .

Josh didn't ask what that was about. "Is it worth having Dakota look over mug shots to see if she can identify the woman?"

Talia spoke before anyone else. "I have something that might help." She swiped at the screen of her iPad, her gold glitter nail flickering in the overhead light. "Austin Crampton, younger brother of Terrence Crampton."

Dakota nodded.

Talia said, "They have an aunt. Their mother's sister, Clare Norton." She turned the iPad.

Josh leaned to the side to see what Dakota saw. Then he looked at her, so he could read the reaction on her face.

A muscle in her jaw shifted. She gave a short nod.

"Clare Norton?" Victoria said her name as a question. Evidently that meant something to the rest of them, a question she needed an answer to.

Talia nodded as she read her tablet screen. "Served ten years in the state of Oregon on drug charges. Got out three years ago. Austin and Terrence have no family, except her."

"Maybe that's why they're sticking close," Josh said. "Humoring her."

Was Clare the one who'd killed Maggie? And why? He knew there wasn't always a good answer, or even a satisfying one. Still, he wanted to be able to go back to Eden with an explanation that would give her peace.

"Looking to her for direction," Sal said. "Maybe she has connections."

"They're definitely up to something." Dakota pinned Victoria with a stare. "But nothing that warrants your move. This orchard thing could be big, but more likely they're just squirrely because we've been asking around about them."

"So killing Maggie was a screw up?" Josh thought for a second, then said, "Maybe Austin, that other guy, and Terry were there to cover for their Aunt. Get rid of the evidence. Terry didn't seem too upset that she was dead." Though he had cared where she was. Josh just didn't know what his motivation might've been.

Dakota said, "Their focus is still whatever they have coming up."

"Do you think we stumbled onto something?"

She shrugged in answer to Victoria's question, then said, "Maybe."

"Then we need more information, so that we can know for sure."

"Your nuclear option is not our answer. That's like throwing napalm on a BBQ."

Victoria's lips twitched. "Visual. I like it." She paused. "I can control the situation."

Dakota shook her head.

Sal said, "You two wanna let the rest of the class in on whatever you're talking about?" He sat straight. His body reed thin, but in no way conveying weakness.

Josh glanced at Niall. The younger man had a thoughtful look on his face. Talia bit her eggplant lip. "No," Dakota said. "We don't."

"Then there's nothing more to say." Victoria picked up her purse. "I'm leaving to go get a room for the night. Josh?"

She headed for the door, like that was all she needed to say to get him to come with her. Josh gave Neema the command to stay, then shut the door behind them, and followed her to a black SUV. She stood by the rear door, waiting. Josh opened it.

"The gray suitcase."

He was supposed to carry her bag for her? Of course he'd offer to. He was a nice guy, and this wasn't *exactly* entitlement on her part. Depended on who she was. Some people demanded that level of respect. And maybe she was one of them, he didn't know.

Josh set it down, pulled up the handle, and they were off. Headed for the main office.

"So, Special Agent Weber."

He nodded.

"Word was passed up the chain at the DEA that I should watch out for you. Be careful, as it were. Want to tell me why that might be?"

"Can't say I know the answer to that." Although, he could guess who said what. "But since I won't be sitting at a desk, drowning in paperwork while working with your team, I can't imagine what my supervisory agent thinks I'm going to be doing. Probably that I'll be getting shot at while running from gunmen."

The skin at the corner of her eyes shifted.

"He's likely certain I'm going to learn all kinds of bad habits from you guys. Renegades, he probably calls you. Like what you do is black ops."

"He's punching the clock until retirement?"

"He's got eight months left." To say the guy was playing it safe was a serious understatement.

"And you got stuck with him?"

"I'm learning. I am. It's just…" Josh didn't know how to word it without sounding ungrateful.

"You want to know what else there is."

He nodded.

"Good."

"How's that?"

She said, "The DEA might be a solid fit for you, and it sounds as if this training agent you've been assigned just isn't your kind of agent. It's helpful to learn how to blend in. That skill alone, swallowing the dissatisfaction, will come in handy. But you have to be who you are, which means eventually you have to find the spot where you fit."

Did she know where that was? Josh didn't want to wait to get there.

As much as he'd have liked it to be with Victoria and her team, it wasn't like this was a permanent assignment. He was on loan. Not for any good reason, just because he'd been here looking for Maggie and wound up being part of it. They didn't exactly need his help to figure out what Clare Norton and her family were up to.

Victoria pulled open the door to the main office herself. Before she stepped inside, she turned back. "I'm going to send you a file. I want you to head over to Inland federal prison tomorrow afternoon for visiting hours. He's being transferred in first thing, so he'll be there."

"Who is he?"

"Someone who may be able to get to the bottom of this for us."

"Does this have anything to do with what you and Dakota weren't talking about?"

The last thing he wanted was to be placed between the two of them, pitted one against the other.

Victoria said, "It's the same as your being here, is the easiest I can explain. The way that sometimes it takes someone else's action to shift things. Then we end up where we were supposed to be in the beginning."

That sounded like playing God with someone's life. Whoever this woman was, she evidently had no problem rearranging things to suit her.

"It's for the best."

Josh wanted to go ask Dakota if she would agree with the sentiment. Victoria left him outside in the cold, wondering if this wasn't the real reason she'd had him kept here.

To do things she didn't want her real team doing.

Chapter 12

Dakota sat up, breathing hard. Tangled in motel bed sheets, her forehead damp with sweat. She kicked the covers off and headed for the bathroom. Talia had suggested they leave the light on in there as well as the door cracked, and now Dakota was glad for it.

She splashed water on her face to push the images from her mind. Sensations and sounds. The sharp intake of breath. A whimper.

She gripped the sides of the sink and hung her head. Probably the fact Victoria had brought it up had something to do with the resurgence of that nightmare. Or the pug-face woman. Both. Past and present blurring together.

Either way, it didn't matter. Her brain was just processing the fact she'd been kidnapped. That was all. Vulnerability was something she'd never dealt well with.

Dakota wandered back to the motel room. Talia's light snores came from the second bed. Her dark curls were pointed in every direction now. She wore a pink eye mask and earplugs. Her iPad was on the covers, close to the open fingers of her hand. Like she'd been half asleep, locked it, and then not had the energy to set it on the bedside table.

The screen lit when she lifted it.

Across it flashed a message that said, "Don't even think about it."

She wrinkled her nose and set the iPad on the table. Dakota only had like, three apps on her phone, and one was for her local pizza franchise. She never went on the internet, though she did use email on her work computer. She'd never even used any kind of tablet. About the most technological thing she had was her wireless headphones—and the GPS watch. That was only because Talia forced her to wear one.

She sat on her bed, back to the headboard. 04:32.

Her head didn't hurt, so that was good. Not much point trying to go back to sleep, but neither did she want to head out for a run. Injuries and no backup weren't a good mix for being alone in an unfamiliar environment.

Victoria might think that throwing someone in undercover was a good idea, but there was no way her idea would work. Nor would she get information out of her "source." At least, not anything helpful.

Dakota couldn't argue that having someone on the inside to feed information back would be helpful. Their team had all been seen. It had to be someone Clare and everyone with her didn't know. Talia wouldn't work—she couldn't pull off "country chick" if she tried—and Dakota *loved* that about her. She knew who she was, and she was proud of her individuality.

Half the time Dakota didn't even like the woman she was. But that was for another time. Or another life, where she was the kind of person who self-examined. She had too many things to do.

Too many bad guys to catch.

She'd been doing that for years. Moving at one hundred fifty percent and then sleeping on her days off. Through college and the police academy, at Homeland Security training. Since Victoria had spotted her, and she was picked up for the task force.

The alternative was having way too much time on her hands to think about her life. Past, present, future. Things would be what they were. After a childhood never knowing what was going to happen next, she was content with the familiarity of her routine of closing cases and then going home. A simple life.

She had her friends and her job. What else did she need?

Her thoughts jumped again, and she saw Josh's face. That split second when he'd seen her for the first time after she'd been kidnapped. Right after she'd taken a healthy amount of frustration out on Terrence Crampton.

That look on his face. She'd never seen anything like it and couldn't even imagine what it meant. Relief that she was all right. With a side of, "What happened to your face?" She looked worse this morning, according to the mirror in the bathroom, but she didn't have more ice to put on her bruises.

Dakota shut her eyes and drifted. She needed coffee. And the files for Austin, Terry and their aunt. They had to figure out what the group was up to. If not someone on the inside, what other options were there?

They'd asked about them around town and wound up with Josh's truck getting exploded by a grenade.

Josh.

Since she'd met him in the dark at the orchard there had been...something about him. She'd never been all that interested in a man before. Too busy. No time for guys who made it clear they were interested. Because what were they interested in, anyway? What kind of person did they think she was? How could they even tell she'd be worth getting to know after just a few minutes?

Dakota had never understood that. Attraction was fleeting. Everyone wrinkled and aged eventually. Some people headed in that direction with class and a sense of style she'd never had in the first place, but Dakota couldn't help thinking that wasn't going to be her.

She'd hardly be surprised if she ended up some grouchy cat lady. Or a sixty-five-year-old hit woman. What, were they going to send her to jail? Whatever. She'd had a good run.

Or she'd be dead. Struck by some illness, or taken out at work. Did it matter which?

There wasn't much point trying to pretend that a "forever" relationship would work. Life almost never actually went that way.

Dakota pushed away the lull of sleep and pulled on some clothes. Maybe the night desk clerk had coffee. At least going outside would clear her head of random thoughts about romance and a good looking guy. Okay, *seriously* good looking. Not that two days of beard shadow was cute. It looked more scratchy than anything else. Anyway, he had a dog. Dakota didn't like dogs.

She sat to pull on her boots, her brain flashing back to carrying a brown and white dog through the house in her arms so she could grab the leash and take her outside.

Daddy didn't like it when Eliette woke him up.

Dakota strode out the door and flung it shut. The slam cut through the quiet of before dawn. She winced. Probably shouldn't wake everyone up.

A dog barked anyway.

Dakota sighed. Busted by Neema.

She wandered along the sidewalk in front of the doors. It had been shoveled and salted. The cold cut through her fleece jacket. She zipped the collar over her mouth.

"Dakota?"

She spun around and almost slid over on the sidewalk. She flung her arms out to get her balance back. "Whoa."

"You okay?" He stood with his head out the door, a frown on his face. T-shirt. Sweats with white stripes down the sides. Thick wool socks.

Neema leaned against his knee in a sit. The way she'd rested her weight against Dakota's leg last night when he'd gone to talk with Victoria. As though, in his absence, the dog had decided she should stand guard.

"Dakota?"

"Yeah...what?"

"Are you okay?"

"Just looking for coffee." She motioned over her shoulder to the main office. He nodded. Silence stretched between them. "Okay, so I'm gonna go."

He nodded again, made a face and said, "Want some company?"

"Uh...sure."

"I'll get my shoes."

"I'll meet you over there." She turned away before he could say anything else.

He caught up to her in the office. Jacket on. Wool cap pulled down over his ears. There was no coffee though so Dakota drove them to a truck stop, and they ordered breakfast. It was after five now anyway. Not much point in trying to get more sleep.

She settled back into the booth, coffee mug in one hand. Sipping.

Josh studied her. "You eat in places like this often?"

She looked around. "Truck stops?"

When he nodded, she shrugged. He said, "You seem completely at home everywhere I've seen you so far. The orchard, the motel. Even running out of that compound."

"What does that mean?"

"It's like you know exactly who you are. The good, the bad, and the ugly. And you're completely fine with it. No pretenses."

She shrugged again. Talia knew who she was. All Dakota knew was that she'd made the most of who she was—and of where she found herself. Was that a good or bad thing? She couldn't tell from just his face. She shifted in her seat.

"Dakota."

She set her cup down. "What?"

"Not many people know who they are to that level. It's kind of amazing actually."

Who she was had been inked into her skin—and she'd had that laser removed. Still, she'd been marked by her history on an elemental level. As much as she tried to forget any of it, or all of it…she couldn't, could she? She would never be able to escape it.

He spoke again, still studying her. "I wonder if you would have that same level of complete at-homeness in a city."

"Maybe not." She shrugged one shoulder. "I don't like to be around a lot of people."

"Me either. Not even for the Super Bowl will I succumb to the crowd." He shot her a self-deprecating smile. "I'll occasionally go as far as a sports bar, but that's rare. I prefer my recliner at home."

She smiled wryly. "And how old is this recliner?"

"About fifty years." He laughed. "It was my dad's."

Humor drained from her face. She felt her cheeks go cold, like someone had touched an ice pack to her skin. She took a sip of coffee, which made her split lip hurt. She probably looked like she'd been dragged through town by a horse. No wonder the waitress had done a double take.

"He died three years ago."

"I'm sorry." Isn't that what you said?

Josh nodded, that intense gaze of his still taking her in. She *felt* his gaze, warm on all the places she was cold. Some kind of mythical creature or a dream guide that could see into her soul. She didn't believe in any of that. But if she did? Well, she might think he had some part of one of those beings in him.

Intensity might be uncomfortable, but so far he'd noticed things about her that no one else had. Not even the people she was closest to. It wasn't entirely unwelcome, the idea she could be "seen" at that level. Still, she couldn't decide if she liked it or not.

One of the ladies at the church she went to sometimes had told her that God saw everything she did and said, heard everything she thought—even the intent behind her thoughts. Mostly Dakota didn't want to acknowledge it. God was God, and she was down here. Working.

Considering how it felt with Josh, maybe she should think about God more. Dakota liked her privacy, but was that a reality?

Maybe she needed to face the truth.

Josh asked her how she got started with Victoria's task force, so she told him. As for why she joined Homeland Security in the first place, Dakota gave him the pat answer she offered everyone. The one about serving her country. Justice, and all that.

When he started to ask another question, she said, "How about you? DEA?"

He fingered the handle of his mug. "Saw too many people go down that way. Even in the service, guys I rode with got hooked. Long days, killer hours. We had to stay awake." He sighed. "Stuff was passed around. A buddy of mine OD'd." His eyes didn't meet hers, but she could see he was lost in memory. In the sting of losing someone close.

Dakota didn't know what that felt like. She'd never lost someone she actually cared about. Couldn't imagine what it would feel like if one of her teammates was killed. "So you're fighting the good fight now?"

"Trying to," he said. "The agent I was assigned to is content logging hours pushing papers until retirement."

"And you were hoping for more action?"

"How did you know?"

She shook her head, the pull of a teasing smile on her lips. "You just have this…sense about you. Like you know who you are. What you want."

He smiled back. "Touché."

She laughed, then finished off her food. When the waitress brought the check, Josh said, "Can I get four sausage links and two pancakes to go?" He pulled a couple of twenties from his wallet for the bill.

"Sure." The waitress brought it in a box, and they headed outside.

The sidewalk had been salted, but the parking lot was slick still. Dakota turned on the car engine and rubbed her hands together.

Neema stuck her head between the seats, her nose twitching with rapid breaths.

"I know," Josh said. His voice was soft, his affection for the animal clear.

"Was she your dog in the marines?"

He nodded, tearing the pancakes into pieces. He handed Neema a piece of sausage. "Got hit by a ricochet, tore up her hip. She's good, but she can't handle long days anymore. Took months and a whole lot of paperwork, but I got approval for her."

He was quiet for a second, then said, "Thought about kidnapping her a couple times. The family they gave her to was nice and all, but she wasn't their dog. When they saw her with me, they were good enough not to make a stink about it."

Dakota nodded, not sure what she was supposed to say. They were a matched pair. But if Neema should have been adopted out after being retired, then there would've been nothing he could do.

Neema had been the property of the US Marines and assigned where they decided. Some partners would certainly have given up long before Josh. But it was clear both of them were far happier together than they ever would have been apart.

Neema shifted her muzzle toward Dakota's face. The tongue swipe came out of nowhere.

"She likes you."

Dakota made a face. "Or maybe I just smell like pancakes."

He chuckled. "That's possible, I guess. Not a dog person?"

"Is it that obvious?"

"Maybe you just haven't been around dogs all that much."

She shrugged.

"Or you had a bad experience."

Neema settled on the backseat, and Dakota pulled out onto the highway.

"Have you?"

"What?"

"Been around dogs that much?"

Dakota didn't know how to answer that. There had been dogs in the yard when she was a child. Not the kind you pet, though. Then there was Elliette. Her dog.

Hers.

"Dakota."

She glanced at him but couldn't read the look on his face, not while she was driving. "So where are you headed to today?"

He was quiet for a few seconds, clearly knowing she didn't want to talk about dogs. Then he said, "Victoria has an errand."

"Right." He'd mentioned that, and she was more than curious what it was.

"I'm borrowing her rental. She has me headed to Inland Federal Prison to see a guy named Harlem Roberts." Everything inside her turned to ice. "I don't know how he fits, but Victoria thinks he can give us something that'll help, I guess. So that's where I'm going."

Dakota hit the brake. She stopped so fast Josh had to brace one hand on the dash. "Get out."

"Right now?" He turned to her, incredulous.

"Get out."

"We're in the middle of nowhere."

Dakota leaned close and screamed in his face. "GET OUT."

Chapter 13

Josh saw Victoria's rental car turn the corner. When it neared him, she swung the vehicle in an arc and pulled up beside him. He opened the passenger door and got in.

Victoria hardly waited for him to shut the door before she hit the gas.

He shot her a look and buckled up. "So you're mad at me too?"

She glanced over. Shook her head once, a sharp movement. "Why would you say that?"

He pushed out a breath. Maybe because she was driving like this was the Indy 500 and she was already two laps behind?

Frustration boiled in him. Dakota hadn't even given him the chance to get Neema out of the back seat. She just sped off, leaving him by the roadside.

"Maybe you could just call Dakota and tell her to bring my dog to my motel room." No point in him sticking around now. He'd been here to help the team. But she clearly didn't need, or want, any help. Once she brought his animal back he could figure out transportation and get home.

Did she forget he'd been shot for her?

He should've brought the meds the doctor had given him to the restaurant so he could take a dose. Now he was full from eating too much and in enough pain it couldn't be ignored. Which made him grumpy.

"On it."

The voice from the backseat made him twist around. He groaned aloud as a sharp pain surged through his shoulder. He faced forward again.

"That looked painful." It was Talia. But her voice sounded far away under the rushing water in his ears. "I sent Dakota a text."

At least he had a few hours before she wanted him at that federal prison. Given how Dakota had reacted, he wasn't entirely sure he should be going. The can of worms was fully open now. He could either continue to tick her off, or he could act like a defiant child and tell Victoria, "No."

Right now he was in entirely too much pain to decide. He didn't want to whine about it but had all of these people forgotten he'd been shot yesterday? He thought he'd pushed through pretty well. Maybe now it was finally hitting him.

Josh breathed through the pain. He wanted to touch a hand to his chest, but it was almost excruciating. In the diner he'd been okay. Talking to Dakota, whose eye wasn't totally swollen this morning but still puffy. She'd seemed better. Maybe just happy to be free of that shed and those people. Restless to get on with doing something to get back at them. He'd been satisfied for food to make him feel better. That was short lived. Now he couldn't ignore it.

"You need a hospital?" That was Victoria.

"No. Just a pit stop at my room."

"Okay."

Josh hit the button to lower the window, enough he could suck in a few breaths of crisp air. Push down the nausea.

Victoria sent the SUV careening around a corner. From the backseat, Talia chuckled. Josh groaned.

"Oh," Victoria said. "Sorry." But she didn't slow down.

Josh needed to distract himself. "Who is this Harlem guy, and why is Dakota so fired up about him?" He heard an intake of breath from the back seat, but Talia said nothing.

Victoria drove, eyes on the road. "They have…history."

That was supposed to explain the situation to him? "Why do you think he'll help in this case?" It wasn't like anything related to Dakota, or her *history*, was at play here. Or any person. It was about that orchard, and Clare and her crew.

"She called it the 'nuclear option' for a reason, right?" He knew there was a tone in his voice. Frustration and pain were bleeding through.

Maybe he should be a little more respectful with a superior, but it seemed like Victoria was going her own way. Like she was willing to dredge up something personal Dakota didn't want to revisit, all to get a win on this case.

The question was, would it be worth it? Was she willing to burn a bridge just to get the result she was looking for?

Victoria said, "I'm exploring options at this time."

A diplomatic answer, and one that meant exactly nothing. "I think you seized an opportunity to pull in someone not part of your team. To get me to do something you'd never assign to them—because Dakota would see it as a betrayal no matter who did it."

Using him as a scapegoat was a gutsy move. Not something he'd ever entertain, but Victoria evidently was prepared to do it.

He glanced over. She bit her lip. Maybe with doubts. "I'm not under any illusion he doesn't know who we all are," she said. "If I were him, I'd know."

"So you want me to go because this guy, whoever he is, doesn't know who I am?"

She nodded. "He's a potential source of information."

"On what?"

"Militias, specifically. Along with transporting stuff across the state, and even into Canada—though that was never proven."

Maybe it wasn't as bad as he'd thought. Especially if it could help. But there still had to be a reason why Dakota reacted the way she did. Who was this guy to her? Josh needed to get his hands on the case file for Harlem Roberts. Or his rap sheet.

"Why do I think there's a whole lot you're not telling me?"

She glanced over for a second before returning her attention to the road. "Because there's a whole lot I'm not telling you. The bottom line is, I'm hoping you showing up to talk to him will trigger something. We need information. That means we need someone who will spill when knocked off guard."

"Not Austin?" Dakota seemed to think the teen could still be a good source of information. Assuming he hadn't split with the rest of them and gone underground—though, Josh was only guessing that was what happened after Dakota escaped from them.

"Another angle to explore. That's why we're headed straight to the compound. Dakota and Sal will go to the orchard, talk to the residents again. Today is about seeing where the chips fall."

So long as Josh could get some Ibuprofen soon, he had no problem with that. "I'll need to hit town at some point. Get a new car." Otherwise he'd be stranded here. He hadn't even had a call back from his insurance guy yet.

Josh shut his eyes and took a few breaths. Everything was moving so fast, and the last two days had been insane. Normally at this time on a Sunday he would be getting Eden into his truck to take her to church. How was she going to get there this morning?

He hadn't even told her that he'd found Maggie.

His eyes burned. Josh kept them squeezed shut. As soon as he got home, he was going to have to tell her that Maggie was dead. That she'd been murdered.

Someone tapped his shoulder. Josh opened his eyes to see Talia's dark-skinned hand stretched out toward him. In the center of her palm was a collection of little red pills. He took them, and she handed him a bottle of water.

"Thanks."

"Hardly going to fix all your problems." She patted his shoulder. "But it's a start. So you're welcome."

He wanted to smile. Seriously, he did. But what was there to smile about? His life was in shambles. What had started as a trip out here to find a young wayward woman had turned into a full-fledged investigation with him in the middle. Getting shot. Running through the woods, rescuing Dakota. Trying to figure out what these people were doing.

Did he even care what Clare Norton and those Crampton guys were up to? It wasn't like it had anything to do with him, except for the fact he'd quite like to get back at them for shooting him. But right now he had no truck and his dog was with someone who, by her own admission, didn't exactly like dogs.

Was she taking care of Neema?

• • •

The driveway at the orchard was long and looked different than it had the night they'd found Maggie's body.

Sausage-flavored breath blew against her cheek. Dakota huffed out a laugh. Fine. Neema was the one who'd found Maggie.

"You like this dog."

Dakota shot Sal a sharp look from her spot in the passenger seat. Now that she didn't have to pretend she was okay—mostly because Sal would see through it anyway—she was having him drive. Plus, he wasn't worse off than her since he hadn't been shot.

The way Josh had been.

She wanted to feel guilty about the way she'd just left him there on the side of the road. Maybe part of her was. A small part. But he didn't have to know that.

She also didn't expect him to know, and she wasn't planning on telling him. Even if he asked.

It was none of his business.

"I don't like dogs," Sal said, not to her exactly. "I just like *my* dog."

"What?"

"My dad always said that. Didn't like dogs, just liked *his* dog."

It struck a chord in her. Not unlike Josh saying *his* name. Harlem Roberts. Ugh. That was the last thing she needed—more nightmares.

Harlem. Dogs. Her past. All of it was like some nightmarish gift she'd been given. One she now carried around with her everywhere she went.

"So what's the deal with dogs?"

"I had a sheepdog puppy when I was little." Dakota stared out the window. "My father shot her."

"Dakot—"

"Don't." She shook her head. "It was a long time ago."

This whole weekend was supposed to have been about recon. Then she met Josh in the orchard and everything went wrong. Now she had a concussion, she'd been beaten. Her father's name was being thrown around.

Harlem Roberts.

Inland Federal Prison.

The whole thought was like salt in one of her wounds. A painful scratch that wouldn't heal. A—

"If you think any harder your head is going to explode."

Dakota said, "Maybe it already has."

"Yeah, I heard about Josh. Guess he found out what happens when you stick your hand too close to the flames." He lifted his eyebrows and threw the car in park.

Dakota didn't want to go there. In fact, she seriously did not want to talk about it. Or be *here* at all, for that matter. She thought she might be in dire need of a vacation.

She pulled out her phone.

"We need to go talk to these people," Sal said. "Stow that thing, and let's go."

She shook her head. "I need to find out how many vacation days I still have left for the year."

"How about…all of them."

"Oh yeah. Right." She lowered her phone and looked at him. They might not spend all that much time together in the grand scheme, but she thought they might actually be the closest thing each other had to a real friend.

"Running away to Rapid City isn't going to help."

"You think I'm going to head to South Dakota for a vacation?" She wanted to laugh. "I was thinking more like Maui. I hear it's a balmy eighty degrees about this time of year."

"Sure. If you like sunshine." He made a face that had her finally laughing.

"I really do." She sighed. "But not too hot."

He smiled, and they climbed out of the car. Neema pressed her nose against the back window.

Sal took point. Dakota hung back, eyeing the hound sniffing at weeds on the driveway.

When the front door was opened, Sal introduced them both. Even though she'd been there Friday night.

Mr. Johnson mashed his lips together. He held the door like he might want to slam it in their faces. "Pretty sure we've already said everything we're going to say about that dead girl. And we're about to head to church."

Sal said, "We just have a few follow-up questions. We won't take up too much of your time, and then you can be off to church."

Johnson frowned. The wife moved to his side, her steps completely silent even though she wore brown flats and the floor was bare tile. It had to take serious practice to move that quietly.

Mr. Johnson said, "Whatever. Just make it quick."

He stepped aside, half bumping into the wife. She took a side step and laid a hand on his arm. He didn't react to it. It was like he didn't even see her there. "Living room." He turned and led the way.

The wife followed him in. Then Sal. Dakota shut the front door and made her way through the dim hall—all the blinds closed. The living room was the same. It smelled like the air never moved, and the fireplace was cold even with the chill in the air. Mrs. Johnson's thin sweater probably wouldn't keep her warm, but they had a roof over their heads. Food in the fridge and the pantry. Or she assumed so, given Mr. Johnson's build.

That was more than some people had.

Dakota had learned through the police department and into her career as a federal agent that some people wanted to live their lives. They didn't want change. They wanted things to be the way they were, and you weren't to interfere in that. Helping just got your hand slapped.

Mr. Johnson spun to face them. "So ask."

No one sat. Or was invited to sit.

The wife said, "We didn't know the dead girl. We've already told you that." She directed her statement to Dakota. "What else is there to know?"

Presenting a united front. Or appearing that way. But there was something Austin Crampton had possessed that was missing here.

Since she had the wife's attention, Dakota bent her wrist to point at her face. "The people who did this to me live in a compound north of town. They're the ones the dead woman was tied up with. They're the reason she's dead." She paused a second to send a prayer of thanks to God that she wasn't dead too. The first time she'd acknowledged what could have happened.

But she couldn't afford for that to trip her up right now.

We hold these truths to be self-evident...

Mrs. Johnson's eyes flared. She sucked in a breath and ended up coughing.

"What do we care?" the husband said. "Probably stuck your nose in as well."

"As opposed to you," Sal returned. "Someone who keeps his nose out of their business and turns a blind eye to what's going on at your orchard. Still means you're an accessory to whatever they're up to."

Dakota turned to the wife. "What is it? What are they shipping through here that makes them willing to kill a young woman in order to keep a secret?"

"Doesn't matter," the wife said around another cough.

Mr. Johnson folded his arms. "It is what it is."

Dakota figured that meant they thought they had no choice but to put up with it. They didn't want to face the consequences of dissension. "You'd rather be under the thumb of people who would kill just to protect themselves?"

No one said anything, so Dakota offered up a morsel. "Clare Norton called this orchard 'hers.' Not yours. She thinks her people are the ones who own this place." She paused. "And that they own you."

The husband shrugged one beefy shoulder. "Like I said. It is what it is."

Chapter 14

Sal pulled the vehicle all the way into the compound. Dakota bit the inside of her cheek, not allowing any other reaction to slip through.

In the daylight it looked like any other compound housing a local militia. People living off the land. Under the radar. Off the grid. When they got bored of meat they'd raised and vegetables they'd grown, they would call and order a pizza. Just like everyone else.

She flung the car door open and Victoria approached. "Okay?"

Dakota nodded. Neema jumped out. The dog brushed past the back of her right knee, nearly knocking her over in her haste to get to Josh.

He grinned as she ran at him, then patted his chest. Neema placed her front paws on his shirt. "Hey there, beautiful." He rubbed up and down her flanks until she hopped off, her tail swishing side to side.

His eyes met Dakota's. "What?"

Still mad at him.

She shrugged one shoulder and said, "Nothing." Then walked with Victoria toward the main house. "Is it just me, or did he seem like he wanted me to say something?"

"Maybe you could have tried apologizing."

"For what?"

One of Victoria's perfect eyebrows rose. "How about stranding him on the side of the road and abducting his dog? Getting him shot."

"I didn't shoot him. That wasn't my fault."

"You're right," Victoria said. "*That* wasn't your fault."

Dakota frowned. "What are we doing here, anyway?"

"They cleared out. When Niall got here, he found the gate open and called me. Talia, Josh, and I showed up half an hour ago. Closets were partially cleaned out. Storage sheds cleared of weapons. They packed, but they did it in a hurry."

"Did they leave anything we can use?"

"So far we've found some correspondence. Nothing that gives us anything we didn't know already from running their IDs."

"But it's physical evidence," Dakota said. When Victoria nodded, she went on. "Anything else?"

"Niall is searching the last building. Josh was helping, but he came out when he heard you were here."

Dakota glanced back to see Josh wandering the edges of buildings. Neema squatted and peed on a patch of grass. He clicked his fingers, and they set off.

"He was mad."

Dakota didn't say anything.

"He got shot for you."

She spun to face her boss. "And that gives you the right to dredge up my past, hang it out for all to see?"

"No one else knows except me." Victoria folded her slender arms. "In fact, I'm not even convinced that *I* have the whole story."

"You think I lied to you?" She wasn't the one who did that. Victoria had dragged Josh in, planned on using him to speak with her father. "Nothing he can give you is going to aid at all in this case. It won't help."

"Not even a window into their state of mind?" Victoria paused. "Clare and her people are still up to something and on the run. We're sniffing at their heels. Where will they go?"

"We'll find them."

Victoria eyed her. After a minute or so, she sighed. "I think they received a transport that came over the Canadian border a few weeks ago."

Dakota bit the inside of her mouth again, then winced because it was sore. "Another way *he* might be able to help."

Dakota shook her head. "That was years ago. You think my father's contacts are even still alive, let alone still active? It's a long shot."

"Long shots are what I do," Victoria said. "Why do you think *you're* here?"

Before Dakota could react to that, Victoria tipped her head back and let out that delicate giggle of hers.

Dakota rolled her eyes, just to make a point. Yes, she'd been a long shot. Victoria had written counseling into the contract for her employment, and Dakota couldn't deny it had helped. She'd long since let her father's neglect and abuse go. It might have been better if he'd picked one. As it was, the constant back-and-forth, never knowing how he was going to act, had been the worst part.

"Guys!" Niall's voice rang out across the compound. She had to hand it to him—he had excellent timing.

Dakota jogged over to where he stood in the doorway of one of the Quonset huts. "What is it?"

His face had darkened, his eyes serious. Enough she knew that though it might not be as bad as that Colorado Springs thing, it was still bad. He shook his head. "You're gonna want to have the dog stay outside on this one."

Josh gave Neema two commands. Dakota didn't know what they meant, but the dog laid down on the grass. She watched as he lifted his hand, palm out and said, "Bleib." And then moved to the doorway. Neema didn't get up, but all her attention was on Josh.

Dakota realized she was staring at both of them and turned away. Yes, it was clear they were close. Or, maybe "bonded" was a better word. She'd had that with Elliette, at least for a few months. Until...

"What is it, Niall?"

No one missed her tone, not even Josh. Dakota ignored all the glances and raised eyebrows and lifted her chin. "Well?"

"Inside." Niall led the way.

Just inside the door hung a plastic curtain. He pushed it aside and she followed him through with Josh on her heels.

Josh said, "Now I see why you didn't want Neema in here." Niall glanced back and Josh said, "Appreciate it."

Liquid had pooled on the floor, most of it a brown color. Tables stood in two rows. They walked down the middle. On top, crates had been stacked on both sides. Open, empty. Beyond that, half of the right hand row of tables was an elaborate set up of beakers and tubes. She knew basically nothing about chemistry, having long forgotten what she'd learned in high school.

She said, "Maybe they were making moonshine."

Niall said, "It was medical."

How he knew that, she had no idea. "Whatever was in here, we're thinking they took it with them?"

No one disagreed, but until they caught up with the woman and her nephews, the Crampton boys, they weren't going to know what it was. Or what Clare planned on doing with it.

Sal turned in a circle. "This isn't saying, 'slaughterhouse' to me. Nor is it saying, 'murder happened here.'"

Niall asked, "So what does it say?"

Dakota wandered farther. All the way to the end of the tables, where a metal barrel had been placed. Maybe muscled in somehow. Too heavy to put on the table.

On the side of the barrel was a sticker.

"Biohazard."

"Do we need to rush outside?" Josh asked. "I don't want to get a disease from these hillbillies."

Dakota wasn't sure that's what they were, exactly. She shook her head. They'd have taken different precautions if whatever had been in here was hazardous. No one was that stupid.

She picked up a screwdriver on the floor beside the barrel. Using it on a groove where it'd been opened before, she pried off the lid like a paint tin.

"It's empty." She glanced up from her crouch and looked at the team— and Josh. "Whatever was in here, it's gone now."

"They took it with them," Victoria said.

Niall evidently agreed. "That's what I think, too."

"So what was it?"

Sal folded his arms. "Nothing good."

"This changes everything." Victoria slid a phone from her overcoat pocket. "The item being transported was a biohazard. Maybe they needed medical personnel—or equipment."

"Like a special truck?" Dakota asked.

She nodded. "I'll get Talia on it, and we'll see what she comes up with."

"You think Mr. and Mrs. Johnson know?" Dakota didn't have the first clue what militia guys wanted with a biohazard barrel. But there was no way it could be anything good.

"You keep going back to them," Sal said. "Why?"

Dakota took a second. "I don't know. I guess I just can't believe they don't know what it is. More likely they're just too scared to tell us."

He nodded. "I got that from them, too."

"And maybe they're the only ones left in town who can tell us."

Victoria said, "You wanna go talk to them again, I'll get you a warrant to search their property. This—" She pointed around the room. "—should be enough for probable cause, given they're possible accomplices."

Dakota said, "Great. Let's go then."

• • •

"You wanna go back to the orchard? Take Agent Weber with you."

Josh blinked. Dakota didn't look at him. Not that he expected her to. She'd been strategically ignoring him since she showed up here. Except for staring at him when he'd greeted Neema. To say he didn't understand her was a serious understatement.

She hadn't apologized even though she'd essentially kidnapped his dog. He generally tried to go with the flow and not get frustrated with people, but that resolve was getting tested frequently. Especially in the past two days.

Wasn't she going to ask him how his gunshot wound was doing?

It was like the woman cared about nothing. Not even herself.

And yet, he saw so much feeling left unspoken behind her eyes. There was something about dogs she wasn't telling him. And the whole Harlem Roberts business. Who was that man to her? No way she didn't have at least some kind of feeling about that guy. Not the way she'd screamed at him.

And yet, he'd guess if he was to ask her about it, that she'd deny having any feeling at all. Josh was pretty sure she'd just lie to him. Maybe she was even lying to herself. Pretending she felt nothing.

Maybe it was safer that way.

He'd seen guys do that in the Marines. They would stuff down their feelings. Their reactions to the horrific things they saw. Did it help? Josh had found someone to talk to—an older guy at the gun range. A Vietnam vet. Maybe it had helped, he didn't exactly know. But it was better than walking around a powder keg, primed to explode at any moment.

Dakota backed off from her hushed conversation with Victoria. Jaw set. Hands curled into fists.

Josh folded his arms and waited, watching her flushed cheeks. Color looked good on her. Even with the bruising and the fact one of her eyes was still pretty swollen. He knew better than to allow sympathy to birth the urge to protect her. Dakota Pierce wasn't a woman who would accept protection—if she knew that's what you were doing. Still, he couldn't deny those feelings were there.

He wanted to help her, even now. Even though she'd stranded him by the roadside. That was the part that frustrated him the most. The fact that even despite how she'd treated him, he honestly still wanted to be there for her. Make her weekend easier. Aid the team in solving this case.

When she glanced at him, he lifted one eyebrow. Ready for whatever she was going to say or do next.

"What are you looking at?"

His lips twitched. So, yeah. She knew he found this amusing. And she didn't agree with the sentiment, that much was plain to see.

Someone snorted.

She swung back around to Victoria. Nothing to encourage whoever had that particular reaction. She ignored it all and said, "I'll take Sal."

"You'll take Agent Weber. The rest of us are going to be busy all day going through the stuff in this compound," Victoria said. "I've called the Spokane FBI office. They're sending a team of agents to help with evidence collection. I can't spare anyone, Dakota."

The implication was clear. If she wanted to check out the orchard again, she was on her own. Josh was the only one who was expendable. That was fine; he was a rookie and an unknown. He didn't particularly want to root through the personal belongings of a group of anarchists anyway. That wasn't going to make for a fun day. He would much rather keep moving, go chat with witnesses, and so would Neema.

Josh lifted his chin, as much of a shrug as he could manage with stitches on his shoulder. "We'll bring back food with us."

Sal pointed over at him, not lifting his attention from the table in front of him and the equipment he was looking over. "And coffee."

Josh said, "Copy that."

Dakota glanced between them.

"Ready?"

Her eyes narrowed. "Fine."

Victoria turned to the door, but Josh saw the hint of a smile before she moved out of his field of vision. Her phone rang as she stepped outside.

Dakota moved to where Josh stood. She opened her mouth, said nothing, and closed it. He said, "Your car or mine?"

"Your truck exploded."

He winced. "Oh yeah." Shook his head. "Guess I need to go shopping as well. Maybe we can do that while we're driving through town."

"You want to buy a car today?"

He wanted to shrug, but knew that wouldn't be a good idea. The thought of it was enough to send pain shooting through his shoulder. He pressed a hand to the wound and took a breath. "Why not? It'll be a good distraction. For both of us."

"We do look like a couple of invalids, don't we?" She gave him a small smile.

"Sure do." He was about to make a suggestion about them both needing a nap, but realized how that would sound when it came out of his mouth. *Thank You, God.* He didn't need her thinking that he was thinking that.

Except now he was totally thinking that.

Josh cleared his throat. "Ready?"

She held the door for him. Neema trotted over to greet them, despite the fact he'd told her to *stay.* She went straight for Dakota and licked her hand.

Dakota rubbed under Neema's chin. "Hi, dog." Then kept walking.

Like nothing had happened.

Yeah. He did *not* believe she wasn't a dog person. People who said that, Josh mostly figured they just hadn't met the right dog. Dakota had a past that made her wary of dogs, but she liked them. Neema was winning her over.

Josh grinned and petted her, rubbing all the way down her flanks. "You're such a good dog. Yes, you are. Ready to go?"

Neema leaned back, front paws out straight in front of her, and groaned through the stretch.

"Let's go."

She trotted with him to the car and hopped in the back. Dakota handed Josh her keys and spent the whole drive on her email. Probably a good plan.

When they pulled up at the orchard he said, "How do you want to play this?"

"I've asked them what they know already." She frowned, her gaze on the front windows. Then the drive. "Maybe you should come from a different angle. Appeal to their civic duty or something."

Josh wanted to laugh. Before he could say anything, she had cracked the door handle and was halfway out.

He pulled the handle on his side.

Over the roof of the car she said, "Don't let Neema out."

"What—"

"Don't let her out." She motioned to the driveway, and he saw it.

"That their dog?"

They both shut their doors and wandered over to the stiff form while Neema barked from inside the car. The dog's tongue was out, covered in white foam. Neither of them got too close.

"Chest isn't moving," Josh said.

They headed for the front door. Both had one hand on the butt of their weapons. Josh closed his other fist and pounded on the front door.

It swung open on its own accord.

A woman lay in the hallway. Angled like she'd slumped to the ground. White stuff had collected on her lips and around her mouth, her face completely pale. Dead.

"That's Mrs. Johnson."

Josh hardly knew what to say first. He choked out the word, "Biohazard," like it was a question.

"If it is," Dakota said. "Then we've been exposed."

Chapter 15

Exposed. Dakota held the phone out, the call on speakerphone, while her stomach roiled. She'd lived through nights spent in the woods only dressed in her nightgown. Being beaten. Broken bones. Days of no food.

This was what would kill her?

"I can only see Mrs. Johnson." She glanced again inside the open front door. "I have no idea where the husband is."

She felt fine. If she had actually been contaminated by whatever had killed Mrs. Johnson she would be feeling the effects by now. Right?

They needed to look in the windows, see if they could see the husband. There was no way she was going to step inside without some kind of protective clothing. She didn't even have gloves right now. And while she didn't think it was airborne—more like they'd been poisoned somehow— she wasn't going to take the risk by touching anything. Or anyone.

Victoria's voice was clear and strong. No trace of the nervousness moving through Dakota. "How is it that I put up with you when you wind up doubling my workload, *every time*?"

Dakota almost smiled. Her boss's humor gave her the focus she needed to push aside her emotions and focus. "We need the CDC, right?"

"I'll put in a call. The medical examiner is on the way; should be there in a few minutes."

"And the sheriff?"

"On his way back to town, but he won't be here before this evening."

Josh blew out a breath. She'd been mostly ignoring him so far, save for the initial conversation they'd had when they realized the homeowner—and the dog—were dead.

At the end of the drive, the medical examiner's van pulled in at a crawl and headed toward them.

"The doc is here."

"Okay," Victoria said. "Keep me posted."

The line went dead.

"Not one to waste time with sympathy, is she?" Josh shot her a wry smile.

"Why would we need sympathy?"

"Maybe because we could've been exposed." He frowned. "We could be hours from death, and she's working through the logistics of getting the CDC here."

"The CDC is the help we need," Dakota argued. "They've got that whole compound to go through, every scrap of anything left behind. All the places they could've hidden something."

"Okay." He held up both hands. "You don't need to bite my head off, just because I don't get it."

"What don't you get? We need help if we're going to figure this out before whatever happens next. Not her sympathy. Whether that means we end up in body bags is either a given at this point, or something we can continue to prevent."

"So you do your job not slowed down by silly emotions."

"Now you're getting it."

Josh shot her the weirdest of looks. One she didn't even know how to decipher. Thankfully, right then, the medical examiner slammed the van door. Dr. Stevens got a duffel out the back and ambled over with raised eyebrows. "I beat the sheriff's department?"

Dakota met her halfway. "This is a federal investigation. We're keeping them in the loop and all. At least for now."

"Okay then." She set the duffel down. "How are you both feeling?"

"We might've been exposed, but I can't be sure," Dakota said.

"Wait." Dr. Stevens waved a hand. "*Exposed?*"

Dakota nodded. "To whatever killed Mrs. Johnson."

"And the dog." Josh pointed to where the animal lay.

Doctor Stevens blew out a breath, her gaze on the animal. She pulled a phone from her jacket pocket and tapped, then swiped the screen. "I'll let the vet know. If we have to run tests he may get answers faster than I'm able to. Especially if we're dealing with a contaminant."

Dakota led her to the house and showed her the body from the safety of the front porch. "Could be a simple poisoning, the dog maybe getting ahold of whatever it was she ingested."

Doctor Stevens' brow furrowed as she studied the body in the hallway. Then she bent and pulled a flashlight from the duffel, which she shone at the dead woman. "What makes you think it's some kind of pathogen?"

"She coughed."

It was the first thing out of Dakota's mouth and the second she said it, she realized how ridiculous it sounded.

Josh to the rescue. "Plus the fact we found a lab at the compound."

"Yes." She pointed at Josh in agreement. "That too."

Doctor Stevens glanced at her. She reached up and touched the back of her hand to Dakota's forehead. "Your face still hurts?"

She said, "Yep."

"I'd wager you have a slight fever, also. Did you take the meds I gave you?"

Dakota glanced at her watch. "I might be due for the next dose." Where had she even put them?

"You should be resting right now, not out here working. But I'm not going to argue with you when I have other things to do." Doctor Stevens shot Josh a look. "Another stoic federal agent determined not to let on that they're in serious pain?"

"No, ma'am." Josh touched a hand to his chest. "Hurts like judgment day over here."

Doctor Stevens chuckled.

Dakota spun around. "Why didn't you say something? Go sit down."

"I will when you do."

Doctor Stevens said, "Both of you should go take a nap. I'll call you when I'm done here."

Dakota didn't like that idea when it meant leaving someone at an unsecured scene with no law enforcement experience.

Acknowledging their silence, the doctor said, "Okay, I didn't figure you'd actually do it." She chuckled and stepped inside the house. "Worth a try."

Dakota said, "Be careful in there."

Another vehicle pulled in. Dakota stepped past Josh and down the front walk, purposely not looking at the dead dog on the drive over by the garage.

The vet was gray-haired with rough hands. Josh went with him to the spot where the dog lay. She watched them talk. Saw the reaction on the veterinarian's face at the sight of a dead dog. The vet felt the loss of an animal like a physical blow.

Dakota glanced back over her shoulder at the front door and could make out Doctor Stevens inside. Professional. Like Victoria, she kept her emotions divorced from her work.

The constant grind helped Dakota tamp down the hot ball of frustration and anger in her stomach. It whirled, slithered like a snake curling into a circle, and threatened to send her breakfast back up. Part of her wanted to know why she even cared about a dog and a dead woman she didn't know. The other part of her couldn't get past being tied to that chair.

It was done. She'd survived it just the way she'd survived everything else. And just like every time and with everything else, she was left with anger. Rage, actually, over the fact she'd been helpless. Frustration that she couldn't fight hard enough to have freed herself before the pain started.

"You don't look so good."

Dakota shrugged. "It is what it is."

He moved to touch her forehead like the doctor had done. Dakota shifted her head and stepped back. He frowned. "Sorry."

She shook her head. "Don't make it worse."

Josh leaned close and spoke low, so only she heard him. "Perhaps if you're barely hanging on, you should let go. You might be surprised to find that the people around you are here and ready to catch you."

. . .

She looked at him like he'd grown two heads. Josh sighed. It had been worth a try, at least.

He wasn't an expert at relying on the people around him. He would much rather be fine on his own. The reality was that most of the time he *wasn't* fine, and it wasn't realistic to try to be either. Eden had encouraged him to share what was on his mind. To find someone to speak to who knew the kinds of things he'd seen and done.

Dakota seemed determined to ignore her feelings. To push aside any attempt he made to sympathize with her, because she didn't think it worked.

Like she thought feelings were a weakness, instead of one of the best parts of living.

Another vehicle pulled onto the property, this time a sheriff's deputy. The vet had agreed to look over Neema as well, just to make sure she hadn't come into contact with anything nasty. An older guy, and nice it seemed, who clearly cared about the animals under his care.

Neema stared at him through the window of the car while Josh wandered to meet with the deputy sheriff.

The man retucked his shirt and shook his head as he ambled over. "Feds?"

Dakota called out, "I'm Special Agent Pierce. This is Special Agent Weber."

Never mind that they were with two different agencies, and she worked with a counter terrorism task force. Right now he did as well, but was that the point?

The deputy didn't seem all that impressed. "You're gonna have to explain to me how this isn't harassment. Cause last I heard, Mr. Johnson didn't want y'all at his house."

Josh said, "If you can find him, I'm happy to apologize."

Dakota came to stand beside him. "I won't. And not only because he's probably dead."

The deputy blustered. "He...what?"

"We'll let you see for yourself," Dakota said. "Mrs. Johnson is dead."

"So is the dog," Josh said.

"And Mr. Johnson needs to be located." She waved at the house with a sweep of her hand. "Whether or not he's still breathing, we have no idea. But we'll leave finding him up to you. After all, we wouldn't want to be *harassing* him."

Josh bit down on his molars to keep from smiling. The deputy sheriff muttered a string of expletives under his breath and made his way over to the house. "I don't think you made him happy."

Dakota shot him a look, a gleam of humor in her eyes. "Not part of my job."

She really did look like she needed a hug. And a nap.

He sighed instead. He had no idea if Dakota was even attracted to him. But really, how could she be immune? The sparks between them were obvious enough to him.

From the look on her face when he'd nearly kissed her in the hospital, he'd say she knew. But maybe she was in denial about this, the way she was in denial about certain dogs. Maybe that was why she'd stopped him from touching her forehead this last time. Definitely in denial—at least, he hoped.

The deputy strode out, pink-cheeked. "The doc says it looks like poison. Some kind of chemical killed her."

"Any sign of the husband?"

"Kitchen."

Josh said, "Dead?"

The deputy nodded, looking a little sick. "Same as the wife."

"So someone *else* did this to them?" Josh glanced between the deputy and Dakota, not necessarily looking for an answer.

Dakota said, "I got the vibe the husband might've been the kind to snap and hurt his wife. Maybe even kill her. But it'd be a spur of the moment, grab what's handy. Beat her, or strangle her."

The deputy swallowed.

"Both of them dying like this, plus the dog, though?" Dakota paused to let her question hang in the air. "They were targeted."

Josh said, "Getting rid of loose ends?"

"Pretty drastic way to do that. Why not just shoot them?"

If they'd done that, they wouldn't have had to kill the dog. Josh chewed on it, then said, "So they're testing a substance, seeing how effective it is. Using it or getting rid of it. Or both."

"Two birds?"

He shrugged.

"It's a good idea," she said. "I'm interested to know what Doctor Stevens comes up with as far as the substance. See if we can trace its source."

He turned his body to face her. "And it's what they were working with at the compound?"

She nodded, doing the same so they were face-to-face. "Some kind of drug, or chemical weapon maybe."

"Excuse me—the compound?" the deputy cut in, his tone incredulous.

"Yeah," Dakota said. "Clare Norton and her posse." She pointed at her face, with its patchy purple spots. "The ones who did this to me." Then she pointed at Josh. "And shot this DEA agent. Any idea where they are?"

The deputy blustered. "They're God-fearing folks. Live off the land types. Not like bikers or vagabonds, who get their kicks out of breaking the law and hurting good people."

"Right." Dakota dragged the word out. "God-fearing or not, we need to know where they are." She stepped closer to the deputy. "And if I find out you have a way to locate them, or even a *clue* where they are hiding, and you didn't share that information with us…" She blew out a breath. "I'll have you charged with impeding a federal investigation."

"Now you…" He flapped his mouth open and shut. "Listen here…"

Dakota put one hand up, then drew out her vibrating phone with the other. "One sec." She stepped away and answered it, the look on her face inordinately pleased at the timing of the call.

Josh studied the deputy. "Any inkling whether Clare and her people have been up to something lately?"

Give or take throwing a grenade at his truck, kidnapping Dakota, shooting him and maybe also killing Mr. and Mrs. Johnson, of course.

The deputy blew out a breath and scratched at his stubble-free chin. "They're not exactly your run of the mill residents."

"No bake sales, or church potlucks?"

He didn't react to that. "I see them at church. And maybe they're a little rough around the edges, but poison?" He shook his head again.

"Right now we have agents at the compound combing through everything they left behind after Dakota escaped. Do you have any idea where they might've gone?"

It was clear enough to Josh they intended to keep what they were doing a secret. But how many others were going to get hurt before this ended? For the first time since he walked up behind Dakota at the orchard on Friday night, Josh didn't care about going back to his desk. This weekend had been exhausting and painful—not to mention the biggest test of his life so far—and it wasn't even over.

"I don't know where they'd go."

Dakota strode back over, done with her phone call. "I think we might be on track to finding out."

"Talia?"

"Gotta roll. Time to track down one of Austin's friends." She motioned to the house and asked the deputy, "You got this, right?"

"Uh…"

"Great." She walked away, and Josh figured that was his cue to follow. At the car, she said, "You think I hurt his feelings?"

"I think you blindsided him." He glanced at the vet, who had already loaded the dead dog into his truck. Then said to Dakota, "Do you have a problem with local law enforcement?"

"Generally, no." An expression washed over her face, and she shot the deputy a look. It was almost like she was mad at herself. She sighed. "Let's go find that teen."

Chapter 16

Dakota shifted in the seat and realized that not only was she back in the car, but she also had fallen asleep. The car was parked in the lot outside the gym, and she was in the passenger seat. Alone.

She moved some more, wincing when her bruises and aching muscles made themselves known. She hardly remembered what feeling "fine" felt like right now, she was so uncomfortable.

Josh stood by a grassy area to the left, his attention half on the front door of the gym and half on his dog. Neema sniffed around the base of a scrawny tree, then squatted.

Dakota shoved the door open and clambered out. *Ouch*. She tried to walk like her whole body didn't hurt, all the way to where he stood.

Josh saw her coming. "Hey." His voice was soft.

She was still pushing away the remnants of sleep when she said, "Hey back at you."

His lips twitched. "You feel better, then?"

Or she was just off her guard enough she was acting weird. "How long was I asleep?" She looked at her watch. It wasn't even noon yet. On a Sunday.

"Thirty minutes or so."

"Why does it seem like that breakfast we had yesterday morning was weeks ago?" She tried to stretch, but it just hurt more than it made her feel better, so she gave up and huffed out a breath.

"I know what you mean." A smile teased the corners of his lips.

"Did you get anything on Austin's friend?"

"He's still in there working out. I called the front desk, pretended to be his parole officer and got the guy to confirm he's checked in." Josh pointed at a rusty pickup truck. "That's his car."

Dakota nodded. Same kind of pick-up truck as Austin. The letters on the back had been picked off, leaving, "YO."

Neema wandered over, so she pet the dog on her head just to be polite. When she looked up, Josh was studying her. "What?"

He opened his mouth, then shifted. "There he is."

They closed in on the teen. The guy strode to his truck in basketball shorts, tennis shoes, and an oversized sweater.

Josh called out, "Gavin."

He didn't turn.

Dakota closed in enough to tap his shoulder. He spun around, elbow first. She shifted out of the way. He saw her and flinched, then pulled the headphone from his right ear. The white cord trailed to a bulging sweater pocket. "What?"

She pulled her badge out and flipped it open, giving him a nice view of the gun under her arm. Josh did the same. Gavin's eyes widened, taking them both in as well as the slender but imposing dog.

"Turn the music off, Gavin." She waited until he complied, then said, "I'll cut to the chase, no beating around the bush. Where's Austin?" She paused half a second then said, "Now you do me that same respect and answer."

She watched the battle take place on his face. Who were they? Why were they asking about Austin? How much trouble would he be in if he didn't answer? Why did she look like she'd had the crap kicked out of her?

She said, "Speak."

His mouth opened. Jaw worked side to side. "Fine." He shook his head. Disappointed in his friend? "His dad has a hunting cabin up in the mountains."

"His dad is dead."

"If Austin is hiding, that's where he'd go."

Josh said, "And if Austin is with his brother, his aunt, and all of the rest of them, where would they go as a group?"

"Not the cabin. It's tiny."

Dakota said, "Any other properties you know of?"

"I don't know where they'd go. I've never even been to that compound." Gavin sniffed. "Austin's changed. They've got him doing stuff for them. He's different, you know? Maybe it's better he split town. Makes it easier to get on with my thing, if I don't gotta explain why I can't hang. You know?"

"Uh."

Dakota ignored Josh's reaction and nodded. "You don't have to worry about letting down your friend, because he's not here. And you telling us where he is could save his life."

Gavin studied her.

"Give me the location of that cabin, and you can get on with your day."

Soon as he did they watched him drive off, then headed back to the car. Dakota sighed, tried to roll some of the tension out of her shoulders. She didn't want to empathize with the guy, but her emotions were on a knife-edge right now. Since she'd seen Mrs. Johnson dead on the floor of her hallway, she'd been having a hard time keeping them contained.

No good was going to come of it if she let go of the hold on her emotions. Last time proved that.

She just couldn't help commiserating with a teen living in a small town with little prospects for the future. Friends falling victim to things they weren't equipped to handle—whether that were family pressures, drugs or alcohol.

This whole case hit entirely too close to home. As much as she wanted to believe she'd lived life past that point, coming here felt a whole lot like walking back in time. Different town. Different Dakota. She wasn't that scared kid anymore.

Still.

She called Talia and explained about the cabin.

Her friend sighed. "Let me get to my computer. I'll pull up an image and get you some pictures of the area so you know what you're walking into."

"Thanks. You're a doll."

"Remind me of that when I tell you what I want for Christmas."

Dakota laughed. "I've created a monster." Wait a second. There had to be a reason Talia thought Dakota owed her big. "Are you at the compound? Wearing your purple boots?"

Josh frowned at her from the passenger seat.

Talia said, "We have a winner."

Dakota groaned, a smile on her lips. "Sorry."

"Really?" She sounded suspicious. "Are you okay?"

"Are you?"

Talia chuckled. "We'll be talking about that later. After I've washed this backwoods dirt from my life, and I'm at home in my fabulous condo sipping a Nespresso latte."

"Maybe I'll fall into a coma before then. Or drop dead." It should have been funny, but her brain decided to remind her of that dead dog on the driveway. And the dead woman with white foam on her lips.

"I'm not laughing," Talia said.

"Neither am I." Dakota leaned her head back and closed her eyes. "Sorry you have to do the dirty work."

"You got me back on my computer, so I'm hardly going to say no. But seriously. Someone should have taught these rednecks to take care of their PC. It's like they were living in the Stone Age with this thing."

"Will you be able to get anything from it?"

"Looks like they were off the grid for the most part. No internet connection here," Talia said. "They might've used it for record keeping, but it's so old it's taking forever to get into the files. Someone had a healthy appreciation for Minesweeper though."

Dakota laughed. "I don't know why they would. That game is boring."

Talia chuckled. "I'm sending you images for the cabin, but it's just Google Earth. There isn't time to hack a satellite, and I try to only do that when they owe me a favor, so—heads up—there could be an army there and I wouldn't be able to see them."

"Thanks."

"Better start saving for Christmas, chickie."

The call ended with Dakota laughing.

• • •

Humor changed everything about Dakota's face. Josh didn't pull out of the parking lot. He just wanted to look at her. She'd brightened. Her eyes wide and gleaming. Her cheeks with more color than he'd seen since he met her.

"Are you gonna go, or will we sit here all day admiring the scenery?"

A semi passed them on the highway, spraying gray muck on the front of the SUV. Josh pulled out behind it and ran his windshield wipers. "Are you going to try and nap again?"

"Probably not." She shifted to face him more. "Did you want to sleep? I could drive."

He shook his head. "It's distracting me from how much my shoulder hurts."

She looked at the images on her phone. "There's a hole in the roof. Though this image could be from months ago, so it might have been fixed."

"Months?"

"Like when you look up your house on Google Earth and the car in the driveway is someone you haven't dated in weeks."

He felt his eyebrows rise. "That happen to you a lot?"

"I mean…" She shifted again.

"I'm just teasing." Mostly. "Unless you want to share. I wouldn't say no to learning more about you."

She shrugged one shoulder as he drove the winding highway. "Not much to know."

"Pretty quick on that reply. If you keep repeating it often enough, then even you will start to believe it." He pressed his lips together. "You could just tell me you don't want to talk about it."

"I'm not currently dating anyone." She said it like he'd forced a terrible confession from her.

"Neither am I. And I haven't for a while now. Between DEA training and my first post, there hasn't been much time. Before that I was deployed." It had been him and Neema.

Maybe that was why he'd fought so hard to get her back after he'd been accepted as a federal agent. She was all he had that truly belonged to him. A big part of what made him the man he was.

"The job takes up a lot of time," Dakota said. "Most guys don't understand that. Or they do similar jobs, which makes scheduling a date next to impossible."

"Favorite date of all time."

She chuckled again, a flash of that lightness he'd seen on her face when she'd been talking to Talia. "Gosh. The county fair…maybe, what? Twelve years ago?"

She had to have been in high school then. "He hit all the targets and won you a big prize?"

"As I recall," she said, "I'm the one who hit the targets and won the giant panda. So cute. I think I still have it in my closet. He got pissy and took off, met up with some friends. Only he'd given me a bunch of dollar bills. So I paid for all the other attractions with his money and then rode the Ferris wheel with Mr. Fluffy."

Josh nearly choked on his laughter. "I'm glad you made the most of him ditching you for his friends."

"Oh, I did."

"And the rest of your dates?"

She made a noise that sounded like a snort. "Not all that much different when I think about it." She was quiet for a second, then said, "Huh."

"That sounds like an epiphany about your dating life.

"Maybe."

"I had one of those."

"Yeah?"

He was heading them out of humorous-life-story territory, and firmly into things that were honest. Real. But maybe that was a good thing. "I've dated a few women. I'm twenty-eight, so that was bound to have happened."

When he glanced over, he saw her nod. He didn't want her to think he'd been alone, but it wasn't like he'd had a flourishing romantic life either.

"But it never lasted that long. It seemed like I was giving everything I could, but it wasn't enough. You know?" Maybe she didn't know. "Like I couldn't do enough, or be enough, to make them stick around. It wasn't like they were waiting for me to ask them to marry me, more like they just…got bored."

It hurt to admit it, though he figured it was also a good thing. Josh understood the value of sharing things that made him vulnerable, even painful. It was part of what he'd learned. No one could be stoic and unfeeling forever. Eventually you had to let someone into your life and hope they would stick around.

No one had so far. Except Neema, and maybe Eden. Would he get there one day with a woman? Find someone who stayed long enough to build a family—and make it a forever thing?

He didn't want to hope that was going to be what happened with him and Dakota. Life didn't work out that way. Or at least, it hadn't so far. Hope only gave him a side of heartache to go along with being alone. Neither was fun. Both together were seriously painful.

She was facing him. He could see her study him out the corner of his eye. "You ever think…maybe it's you?"

Josh swallowed against the lump in his throat. "I did what I could. But sometimes I wonder if it wasn't enough."

"That's not it." She shook her head. "I just wonder if…maybe it's me. Maybe I'm what's wrong. Like there's something broken in me."

"There's nothing broken in you, Dakota." He reached over and squeezed her hand. He desperately wanted her to hear him. To take his words on board. "You might be different than any other woman I've ever met in my life, but that doesn't mean there's something wrong with you."

And maybe that difference was going to be the thing that made this—whatever relationship they could have—unlike any other relationship he'd had so far.

Maybe she didn't want that with him. But that thought wasn't enough to stop hope from birthing in him. Warm, glorious hope that saw no problems. Just promise.

He sighed. The pain would come later.

It always did.

"Okay." Her voice was soft.

They drove in silence for a while, and then she needed to direct him from her phone. He followed the turns and they ascended the mountainside up a thin dirt track that was mostly sharp corners and switchbacks. Anyone not familiar with the area probably got lost pretty frequently.

"Thank God for GPS."

Dakota nodded. "Right? This place is a maze."

Houses and cabins were scattered up the hillside. Their destination was the farthest end of the dirt "road." When he pulled up outside, he grimaced. "Mud."

The car was covered with it.

"No smoke from the chimney." Dakota motioned to it with her finger. "Could be laying low, or no one is here."

Josh climbed out and angled left, seeing something around the side. His boots quickly got caked in mud. "His truck is here. Looks like he pulled it around back." He glanced at the ground in front of the cabin. "Must've rained since."

Dakota shivered.

"Not a fan of rain?"

"Not when I'm anywhere except on my couch with a book and a mug of hot water."

"Hot water?"

"Don't knock it till you try it."

He smiled, one hand still braced on his holstered gun just in case. "I'll take your word for it."

She glanced up at the overcast sky. "I don't like getting caught out in the rain."

Josh climbed up the porch steps and knocked on the front door. When no one opened it, Dakota said, "See if it's locked."

He turned the handle and pushed it open without entering. He'd already been shot once this weekend.

Dakota gasped. "Austin." She rushed across the cabin's bare wood floor.

The inside was threadbare, not much more than a bed, one chair, and a tiny circular table with two chairs. Austin lay on the floor like he'd been trying to drag himself to the bed.

Pale. Sweat-stained shirt.

Another victim of whatever killed the Johnson's? "Is he…"

She pressed two fingers to his throat and blew out a breath.

"He's alive, but only barely."

Chapter 17

Dakota leaned forward in the hospital chair. Austin's hair was matted to his forehead with sweat. His eyes were glassy, but they were open and he was coherent.

The teen shook his head. Those glassy eyes were wide with fear. Of dying, or what would happen if he talked? Whichever one it was, she had to figure out a way to use it. To leverage his fear in order to get him to talk.

Might not make her an especially nice person, but it made her a good agent.

"You're gonna make it," she said. "You're gonna live, but the quality of that life is up to you. If you wanna spend it doing twenty-five years in federal prison, that's up to you. Or you want to go to college. Get a job, maybe meet a girl and have a family? That's up to you as well. The rest of your life is entirely up to you, Austin."

She heard Josh shift behind her, but didn't break the connection she had with Austin.

"It's about the choices you make right now." She paused. "The rest of your life starts *right now*."

His gaze shifted to Josh, then the TV. A local channel was playing a rerun and she'd muted the volume as soon as she came in, just before one-thirty. The day was marching on.

Tomorrow Josh would be gone—back to his desk. The alternative wasn't something she had time to entertain right now.

Dakota was pretty sure they hadn't been exposed to anything. They would have been showing symptoms by now. But what was it? What did Clare and her posse have?

And what did they intend to do with it?

"You went to that cabin to hide out. To get away from them."

Austin said nothing.

Josh said, "Didn't know it was too late, and you'd already been exposed."

Austin scrunched up his nose.

She said, "Where did they go?"

"Does it matter when you can't stop them?" Austin's voice was quiet. Broken. A single tear rolled from the corner of his eye.

"They got their hands on something. A drug, a virus. You could be dead right now, but you're not." She did think things happened for a reason. That he was still alive for a purpose. "It's my job to stop them, and you get to help me."

It wasn't an invitation. She wasn't going to waste her own time, appealing to whatever sense of nobility or duty he might have. That would take too long.

She said, "Means you tell me where they are, what it is, what they're going to do with it and who sold it to them. And you're going to tell me *right now*."

He had to know this was time sensitive. But a teen who had been screwed up in more ways than one probably wasn't going to think logically about any of this.

"I left. They didn't tell me where they were going."

"In the lab it looks like they were conducting a science experiment."

He nodded stiffly. "It has to be doctored. They have like…a concentrate. It's in a tiny vial, with instructions on how to mix it to make more."

"What are they going to do with it? Is it a virus?"

"They're gonna make a statement." Fear washed over his face. "That's all I know."

"So you'll trade your ignorance for a life in jail? Because I can have charges brought up on you. Accessory to kidnapping, assault, the attempted murder of my friend here." She motioned to Josh with her finger, but didn't turn around. "Because you're telling me you're so honorable you never eavesdropped. Maybe you heard something you weren't supposed to have."

Austin sniffed. Pressed his lips together.

"Where did it come from?"

"Terry picked it up."

"Why was Maggie killed?"

"She was going to leave. I heard them arguing. She said they were going too far."

"You dumped the body." She let that statement hang in the air for a second, then said, "Who told you to do that?"

He swallowed.

"Who?"

"Aunt Clare."

"Did your aunt kill Maggie?"

Austin nodded.

She sat back and breathed against the persistent ache in almost every part of her body. Her head was the worst. "You want to be dragged down with them? They're your family. I get that. More than you'll ever know, I understand the pressure you're under to be part of who they are. How they get in your head and twist everything you think about yourself and the world. But maybe that's not you."

"They're good people."

"Are they? Or do you just not think you're any better than them."

He sniffed and scrunched up his nose.

"I get that you want to belong. You feel like you're supposed to be part of it, because it's what you were born to do—to be part of that legacy, right? But you know what? That thing they're building—"

He said nothing.

"—they're going to hurt a lot of people. Good people who didn't ask to be dragged into your family's war. People trying to live their lives right and honest. And *your* family is going to destroy what they're building. That's what they are set to do. Destroy."

"Maybe those people deserve it."

Dakota shook her head. "They don't. They never do. Just like you don't deserve jail time just because you were born into their family. That's why you've got to choose. Like *I* had to choose when I walked away to live the life *I* wanted. Not the one I was told I should have."

Talking about it made a lump stick in her throat. She had to swallow it back down while she ran through those opening lines of the Declaration of Independence, just to get the past to dissipate. This case was dragging so much garbage back up in her head. Stuff she'd buried and laid to rest. Stuff she had no interest in dragging out to deal with again.

The door to the hospital room opened. Dakota saw a flash of uniform—the state police officer stationed outside—before the doctor stepped in. "Your chat is over. You've had long enough."

Dakota stood, and the gray haired MD moved past her. At the door, she turned back to Austin. "Think about what I said, okay? The choice is yours."

Josh followed her out. She glanced at her phone but didn't have anything new from Talia, who had swung by and picked up Austin's phone. Hopefully their tech would get something from it, and it wouldn't be a wasted trip.

In the hallway, Josh said, "It's not really a choice, is it?"

Dakota shrugged. "Jail or betrayal."

"You really think it's betrayal."

"I think he'll see it as that." She blew out a breath and ran her hands through her hair, wishing for a hairband so she could secure it in a ponytail. Get it out of her face.

"What did you have to walk away from?"

The question was quiet, but jarred her out of her head as though he'd shouted it at her. Dakota lowered her hands.

"There's something, isn't there?"

"We all have past experiences we wish we'd never lived through, right?" She shrugged, trying to pretend it wasn't a big deal. "Mine is no different."

"What did you survive?"

Everything inside her wrenched. Contorted. Like a blow to the stomach. She wanted to bend over and succumb to it, but forced herself to stay upright. "Who says I survived it?"

• • •

Josh had never in his life been more tempted to run his own background check on someone. The desire to learn about Dakota's past, that thing she'd lived through but hadn't necessarily survived, ate at him the whole way down to the morgue.

They exited the elevator and he shivered. "Whoa. Cold."

"Brr." She glanced at him before she wrapped her jacket tighter around her. Not exactly happy, but at least the trace of sadness was gone. He didn't want her to be swallowed up by things she refused to tell him.

The urge to hug her was still there. Plus the nap. The almost-kiss from Friday night. He sighed as they strode down to where the music was coming from. Some kind of soft rock, but it sounded like the kind you'd hear on a street corner in New Orleans.

"Why are you being weird?"

He glanced at her. "Long day?"

"Long weekend." She smiled ruefully. "I swear you're not meeting me at my best."

"You think I care about that?" He tugged on her elbow before she stepped inside the room where Doctor Stevens was performing an examination on Mr. and Mrs. Johnson. "I'm just glad we're both okay."

"Define, 'okay.'"

"Point taken." She'd been beaten, and he'd been shot. "Maybe we'll just have to meet up after this is over, get to know each other when things return to normal."

She eyed him. "Not sure my life is ever actually normal, to be honest."

"True."

"And if this case turns into another case? If we end up working together for a while?"

Josh frowned. He had repeatedly felt like they were testing him. Was this whole thing, him being here, some kind of interview? Was this how Victoria scouted out new team members?

"We're a team member down since we had a guy get injured and retire before Christmas." She made a face, like she didn't approve of anyone quitting. For any reason. "Now he's licking his wounds in Alaska."

"So you're having me tag along with you just to check me out for Victoria?"

"And to keep you from getting into the kind of trouble we can't get you out of." She shrugged. "With the added bonus that I get a break from Sal and all that 'cupcake' stuff."

Josh smiled.

"Are you two gonna stand out there all day," the doctor called out from the examination room, "or will you actually come in at some point?"

He turned the corner and stepped in. "Hey."

Doctor Stevens glanced between them. "Did you two figure it out yet?"

He said, "Figure what out?" Dakota glanced at him, but he shrugged.

"This thing happening between you." Doctor Stevens motioned between them with her finger. Gloved, and smeared with dark blood.

Dakota said, "Nothing's happening between us."

Josh nodded. "Right."

He couldn't let anything happen. Not if they really were interviewing him for the open position on their team. Even just dangling that possibility in front of him gave Josh an additional level of pressure he hadn't needed. But he was glad Dakota told him—or at least she'd inferred it was on the table.

If he could get a job with the Northwest Counter Terrorism Task Force, that ruled out the possibility of something happening between the two of them. Fraternization wasn't against the rules, but it also wasn't encouraged. Agents with relationships got distracted. Emotions affected choices. In the heat of a tense situation, people diverted from training and regulations because someone they cared about was at risk.

It definitely made things sticky.

The doc said, "If you say so." And turned back to her body, shaking her head. "Shame."

"Mrs. Johnson?" Dakota wandered over to look at whatever Stevens was looking at.

Josh didn't particularly want to stare into a dead woman's chest cavity. "What did you find about the substance that killed her?"

"I was right about the vet helping," Stevens said. "He was able to run the test much faster, and we've already confirmed what he discovered. It's a form of the chemical weapon, VX gas."

Dakota gasped. "What?"

The doctor nodded. "This is different, and likely they ingested it. But from the test results we have, someone took VX gas and did something with it. Tweaked it."

"You know all that, already?" Dakota asked.

Stevens's eyes darkened. "I worked with the Red Cross in Bosnia and Sarajevo. Saw some awful things used on people. This is very similar, though it's far more sophisticated now compared with what has been used previously."

"But not a gas?" Josh asked.

"No." She shook her head. "Not anymore. Someone who knows what they're doing worked with it. The end result is similar, but it's not airborne. Deaths are targeted with this, because you have to inject the person directly. Or get them to ingest it in some other way."

Josh said, "And the dog?"

"Must have come into contact with it." Doctor Stevens motioned to Mrs. Johnson, then beyond her to the table where Mr. Johnson lay. "Because these two were injected."

"What about Austin?" Dakota said.

"Who?"

"The teen upstairs who got infected. He's being treated."

"He's alive?"

Dakota nodded. Doctor Stevens said, "I'll speak with his doctor. See if there are any injection marks."

"I figured he got exposed when they were working with it. That can happen, right?"

The doc shrugged. "Possible. With VX, clothes are contaminated for a time. The two of you are watching for symptoms?"

Josh nodded.

"I'll find out how Austin got sick." Dakota shook her head and blew out a breath. "I just assumed he was exposed to the same thing, since he looked pale and clammy."

Josh said, "It's the most likely scenario." Thinking about the set up at the lab they'd found in the compound. An amber-colored liquid, purchased by Clare Norton to do serious damage. But who did she buy it from?

The doctor said, "I can help whoever is treating this Austin person, and they can potentially shed some light on it for me." Stevens pulled off her gloves. "But at least we know it's not an airborne contagion."

Josh nodded. If it had been, he and Dakota would likely be dead by now.

"And if Clare has a way to make it into one?" Dakota glanced at both of them in turn.

Josh said, "You think she has mass casualties in mind?"

"Buying something like this is overkill if you're just looking to murder a couple of people. She might've killed these two to tie up a loose end, but in the process also exposed what substance they have and plan to use. And we know they've got something planned. It's just a question of figuring out what it is."

"So they tipped their hand." Josh shrugged one shoulder. "So what?"

"Just seems dumb is all."

He was inclined to agree with that. People were people, some were smarter than others, and criminals weren't that different. Still, he'd expect a little forward planning. He said, "Could be a measure of how smart they aren't."

"I'm not betting on that."

"Or an indicator of something else." What, he didn't know.

Dakota shook the doctor's hand, and Josh did the same. "Austin needs to tell us what he knows." She shifted and pulled out her phone. The screen lit with an incoming call. "Or maybe his phone already has."

She answered the call. "Yeah, Talia." After a few seconds of quiet, her gaze flicked up to his. "We'll be right there."

Chapter 18

Dakota led the way inside her and Talia's motel room, where the whole team had gathered. Josh shut the door behind them. Dakota had zero energy. It was way past the point where she could pretend otherwise.

She walked to her bed, sat down and flopped back with a moan.

Sal's horchata-smooth voice said, "Rough day at work, dear?"

"To be honest, it's been a rough couple of decades." She smiled but didn't open her eyes. Not that there was much to smile about. She might not have been willing to share with Josh, but that didn't mean she'd quit thinking about it. Sal and the others knew some. Not all of it.

Only Victoria knew everything. And yet, the director had her father transferred to the local federal prison, *and* she'd been about to send Josh to speak to him.

"Whatcha got for us, Tal?"

"For real?" her friend said. "Don't call me that. Ever."

Dakota cracked one eye open. Across the room Talia stood with her hand on her hip, looking down her nose. Josh covered his laughter with a cough.

"Sorry."

"It's official," Talia said. "You've lost your marbles." Her eyes glinted behind her tiny designer glasses. How they were even functional, Dakota didn't know.

She rolled over, grabbed a pillow and pulled it down the bed to stuff under her head. "You learned something from Austin's phone?"

"Don't I always?"

Niall opened the bathroom door and stepped out. "What'd I miss?"

"Nothing," Dakota said. "She didn't start yet."

"Do you want me to drain your retirement accounts and change the password to access your bank account online?"

Dakota grinned. "Again?"

"Last time was just a taste." Talia linked her fingers, then stretched her arms in front of her and cracked her knuckles. "You have no idea what I can do."

"I don't wanna know."

The motel room door lock clicked, and Victoria entered.

Sal muttered, "Attention on deck."

Dakota glanced at him, already halfway to sitting, before she realized what she was doing. Josh had snapped straight and looked at Sal as well.

Victoria shot him a look. "Funny." She took off her coat and laid it on the back of a chair. "Talia?"

The NSA agent spun to the TV, which she'd linked by a cable to her computer. "From Austin's phone, we were able to get all of their numbers. Email addresses. We even got into Terrence Crampton's bank account, since the brothers' accounts are linked."

Several images flashed across the screen, too fast for Dakota to read anything but a blur of numbers. Josh had been standing by the TV. He wandered over and plopped down on the bed with a good amount of space between them but not too much it was weird. One of several things she'd found worth appreciating about him.

Talia continued, "From there we got a warrant to get into Clare Norton's email. It was pretty sparse. As in she's barely ever used it even though she signed up, like, ten years ago. From the contents of her junk mail, I'd say either Terrence or Austin—or both—use it to access all kinds of um…entertainment. On the internet." She glanced around. "And I don't mean Netflix."

Sal said, "We get it."

Dakota made a face, because that was gross no matter who was watching it. She'd seen the ugly side of the sex industry and could rarely watch movies anymore because there was so much nudity in them. It wasn't about taking the moral high ground. It was about not wanting to be reminded of things she would never be able to unsee.

"Anyway," Talia said, "There was an email a few months back that piqued my interest. A link. The address is for an online file server on the dark web. You log in with the credentials provided, and you can access whatever is there."

Dakota said, "Like read whatever message they left you?"

Talia nodded. "Easier to control than a message board just anyone can see, because they're alerted whenever someone logs in. And they don't have to speak in code. Whoever set it up knows who accesses it, when, and from where."

"Can you get into it?" Josh asked.

Niall tipped his head to the side. "And is it worth revealing your IP address just on the off chance it's related, and not something that has nothing to do with all this."

Talia clasped her hands to her chest. "Did you just say, 'IP address'?" She wiped an imaginary tear from the corner of her eye. "My baby. He's all grown up."

Dakota snorted. Everyone looked at her. She cleared her throat. "How *do* you know if it's related? Could be they bought the contagion online, and this server thing has nothing to do with it."

Talia said, "I would put money on the fact it's whoever they bought the VX from." She turned back to the TV and clicked on her wireless mouse. "The email address the link came from is too good. It's a ghost. Doesn't even exist as a domain now."

"And that makes sense to you?" When Talia nodded Dakota said, "What about the login?"

"All I can say is that Clare Norton didn't receive the credentials by email. The phones are all unregistered, and we can't access anyone's but Austin's. How she got the username and password for the server, I can't say with certainty at this present moment."

Which meant that later was an option. Talia was severely hampered being this far from their office in Portland and away from her good toys. The mobile version of her system that she'd—in her words—pared down and packed into the laptop she traveled with was, "woefully understated." Whatever that meant. Seemed to Dakota she always managed just fine.

Victoria said, "As soon as you access, or even attempt to access the file server, you'll be detected?"

Talia nodded. "Past a certain point, yes. I could maybe mask my penetration from the office a little better, but even that would buy me…maybe a few minutes. However I do it, the person who set it up will get an alert that someone is trying to get in."

Victoria lifted her hand and ran her index finger across her top lip. Supposedly it was her, "thinking" face, but since she never ate until the afternoon, mostly Dakota figured she was deciding what to eat later.

Finally, Victoria said, "Okay, go ahead."

Talia's eyes widened. "Hack the server?"

Victoria nodded. "Use Dakota's computer."

Dakota said, "Hey—"

"Actually, that's a great idea. It essentially has no personality. It's perfect." She turned to Talia. "What—"

"The added anonymity will give me more time." Talia paced the small space between TV and bed, tapping a pen on the palm of her hand. "I can create a persona that he'll discover first. Until he realizes it's a smoke screen. After that…" Her words drifted off into silence as she thought some more.

Victoria picked up where she'd left off. "Figure out a way to track him the moment he starts to track you. Turn the tables. Find out who it is and what that server is."

Talia nodded slowly. "Okay." Still nodding—her version of a thinking face. "Give me an hour to get set up."

"Good." Victoria turned to Sal. "What have you got?"

Conversation continued around her while Dakota put the pieces together in her own head. An online, dark web server. A chemical form of VX gas that had already been used to kill. Militia—anarchists. Not the usual kind of people to deploy a chemical weapon.

The target? She had no idea. Could be anything.

The one thing she knew for sure was that this was far from over.

Beside her, Josh pulled out his phone. He typed on the screen and then bent it so she could read. His notes app.

Could Harlem Roberts help us?

. . .

She covered her reaction well, but something was clear enough to him. Once again, Josh had pushed her too far. Enough to where she hit that place where she shut down. Kicked him out of the car. Screamed in his face. Walked away.

Kidnapped his dog.

Thankfully he'd left Neema in his room, sleeping off her morning outing in the car. Adventure was a dog's life and his appreciated the best of them, so long as they featured sausage. And pancakes. She'd been snoring by the time he left the room.

Now he had only one adventurous woman to contend with. And she was pulling away.

Josh waved his hand, dismissing the idea, and stowed his phone. She didn't need to worry about a mere suggestion. It wasn't important if it was going to birth this kind of reaction in her. She could just forget he mentioned it in the first place.

Only, there had to be a reason Victoria had gone so far as to have the guy transferred to a local federal prison and arrange for Josh to go see him. Visiting time had passed, but surely he could use his badge—and Victoria's pull—to get in.

Sal, Niall and Victoria were talking about what they'd found in the trash at the compound. A package had been delivered by courier. It could've been the VX, or not. A small vial of the amber liquid concentrate could have been easily transported. It was likely far easier to move the smaller it was, and maybe they had just sent it in the mail. Could even be carried on a person, in a small cylinder, like a travel mug. One vial could get to its intended destination basically anywhere—even through some airport screenings. A little doctoring and that small concentrate could turn into a huge batch of killing agent.

Was it going to be converted into a gas and dispersed in a populated area? Or added to the city's water treatment tanks?

Either way meant multiple casualties.

Josh leaned over to Dakota and spoke quietly. "Sorry, but Victoria planned enough to move him local. I just wanted to know if it's an option." He shrugged.

"Don't bring him up again."

Did it have something to do with what she'd survived? Clearly her past wasn't on the table as far as topics of discussion. Dakota wasn't interested in lowering her walls and letting him get to know her. Maybe he should take that as a sign. Even with the most traumatic of circumstances, trust was pretty crucial between two people. To be vulnerable with each other. The fact she wasn't willing to do that should tell him what he needed to know.

She wanted to keep things professional between them.

Well, that was fine by him. They had enough to do today without either of them overcomplicating it with messy emotions and distractions.

She pulled out her own phone, occupying herself while conversation continued to swirl around him.

"I'm in," Talia said. She hadn't been sitting at Dakota's laptop for ten minutes.

"That was fast." Josh felt his eyebrows rise.

She winked at him. "What can I say? I'm good."

He opened his mouth to fire a quip back, but saw Dakota glance at him. Josh figured that wasn't a good idea.

Victoria said, "Let us know when you get something." Then she turned back to Sal. "What about targets?"

"Within a hundred miles? The usual soft targets like churches, shopping malls. Schools." Everyone shuddered at the idea of a school being a target yet again. "Farther out you've got stadiums and concerts."

Niall picked up the thread. "Then you've got federal buildings. State facilities."

Like the federal prison Harlem Roberts had been taken to?

Josh shook his head at his own idea. That was way too out there. Especially if Clare and her posse didn't even know Roberts. Josh had no clue how the man fit, other than with Dakota.

She shifted beside him and handed over her phone. He took it on a reflex, then said, "Wha—"

"That."

He looked at the screen.

Local man arrested for murder.

Josh's stomach flipped over, then settled far lower than it should've been. The victim was Imelda Packer, fifteen years younger and Roberts' girlfriend. Shot in the chest and head. The only witness a seven-year-old girl.

Roberts' daughter, Katie.

Josh looked up.

"I changed my name."

Dakota Pierce was Katie Roberts. A little girl who had witnessed her father shoot his girlfriend.

Josh took a breath, not even knowing what to say. She was a survivor…of one of the worst kinds of violence a person could do to another person. At seven years old she'd seen that, and it had shaped everything about her—as much as she'd tried to shove it down. Deny it. Forget about it.

He *knew* with everything that was in him that Dakota had changed her name and separated herself from who she had been, and what she'd seen, as the next step of her survival.

He realized the room had gone silent. Josh looked at each of them.

It was Victoria who said, "You told him?"

Dakota lifted her chin. "You didn't really give me a choice. I don't want to talk about him, or *to* him. Not even if it's one of you."

"I thought—"

"I know," Dakota cut in. "And I want to say thank you, because you care about me. You want me to face it and move on, but that's not going to happen. I know you mean well." She shook her head. "I'm not even at the place where I can appreciate the fact you had good intentions."

Victoria pressed her lips together. Like she wanted to apologize, or cry.

Okay, maybe not tears.

The depth of respect between them, forged through years of working together, was plain for Josh to see. They did care. Even if they went about things entirely differently and had completely different personalities. They'd made a friendship work. But professionally, they were a family.

All the people in this room were.

The family Dakota had never had for herself.

And Josh had never wanted more than to be part of it.

Conversation wound down. Sal and Niall headed back to the compound. Victoria headed to her room to continue working. He checked on Neema, made a few calls from the classifieds online—asking around about a truck. Nothing much came of it, except he had a guy who was going to text him photos of an F150.

He knocked on their door again, but it was ajar.

Inside, Talia paced in front of Dakota's computer. "Anything yet?"

She shook her head. "All quiet, except the layers of security that keep coming up. And when I get through one, there's nothing behind it. Literally nothing. Not even a trace of something that used to be there."

Behind her on the bed, Dakota was curled up. Fast asleep.

"So weird."

Shoes clipped the concrete walk outside. He spun around just as Victoria trotted in, out of breath. "The prison."

"What is it?" Should he wake up Dakota? Was this going to make her mad again?

Victoria squeezed her phone tight enough her knuckles went white.

Talia came over, pulling off her wireless headset. "What is it?"

"There was an incident at the federal prison thirty minutes ago. People foaming at the mouth, seizing and then collapsing."

Josh said, "The VX?"

She nodded. "Can't be sure, but it's too similar to be a coincidence." She took a breath. "Guards. Prisoners. It's chaos, and communication is spotty. But there's been a breakout. Some of the inmates escaped, and a contingent of guards took off."

Josh knew why she'd come in like this. He opened his mouth to ask but not before a voice behind said, "Harlem?"

He spun to see Dakota sit up. Hair mussed, and with a crease down the side of her face.

Victoria said, "The whole place is a mess. Total chaos."

"Tell me."

"They have no idea where your father is."

Chapter 19

Dakota couldn't stand. There was no strength in her legs. "Are you kidding me?"

He was loose? Fear slithered through her like frost creeping across a window.

"That was my reaction." Victoria ran slender fingers down her hair. A nervous gesture. Not sure how Dakota was going to react.

Dakota shifted on the bed and tried to shove away the fatigue in her muscles. She could practically see her boss's thoughts race. Focusing on that enabled her to still enough to suck in a full breath.

Josh's attention was on her, unlike Talia who was fully focused on her computer. Dakota didn't want to look at him, though. She didn't need to process this one aloud. It was her deal, and no one else's. What Harlem had done wasn't anyone's problem.

It was hers, and she didn't share. Besides, she'd dealt with it. This was just an understandable hiccup in the process of getting on with the rest of her life.

There was just one other hiccup she had to deal with first.

She pinned Victoria with a look. "Did you do this?"

Her boss seemed surprised more than guilty, but she had been planning on sending Josh to talk to Harlem. Wasn't it logical for Dakota to wonder if Victoria had planned this?

What if Josh had "happened" to be there, right when a prison break took place? Dakota would never put something like that past her boss. Victoria did *whatever* it took to get a result on a case. And everyone knew it.

Josh said, "Seriously?"

Dakota made a face like, *What?* She turned back to her boss. "Victoria, did you plan for Harlem to be loose in order to gain his assistance on the case?"

Her boss pressed her lips together and blew a breath out her nose. "Special Agent Pierce—"

"Answer the question, Victoria."

"This is going in your file."

"If I do it right," Dakota said, "It'll go in yours too. And I wonder which of us can't afford to get written up about something else."

Victoria sighed. "I did not plan for a modified version of VX to be released at the federal prison. I have nothing to do with these militia people."

"And Harlem?"

"I didn't take steps to get him released, or to somehow break him out," Victoria said. "And anyway, we don't even know if he escaped. Right now he's just missing."

"He escaped."

"Perhaps we should go and find that out for certain before we continue jumping to conclusions."

Dakota reached for her boots. "Fine."

"Marshal Alvarez is headed to the prison already. He'll be spearheading the hunt for whoever is missing."

She stood and grabbed her jacket.

"Hold up." Talia held up one finger but didn't look away from her computer screen. "Seriously?"

Victoria had one hand on the door handle already. "What is it?"

"Nothing." Talia blew out a breath and sat back in the chair. She shifted to face them. "Okay, so this is weird. I got in there, right? But there was nothing. So I look around. More layers, more logins. Every time I think I've broken into the server, on the other side there's nothing."

Dakota didn't know what that meant. "So they're hiding the information."

"It's more like a Russian nesting doll…with nothing in the middle. Like I'm being strung along."

Josh was the one who said, "Are they onto you?"

"Possibly." Talia thumbed her lip with a gold-tipped nail. "I'll have to look around. See if I can find a trace of whoever is giving me the runaround."

"Like a distraction?" Dakota asked before she'd even really thought it through. "Which is interesting, considering it all broke loose at the prison around the same time."

Victoria nodded. "Very interesting timing."

"So they're connected?" Josh asked. "Because I can't really see a militia being all up on technology."

"Maybe they have a guy…or know a guy."

Talia said, "Or it's the person they got the VX from. Someone smart enough to modify a chemical weapon."

Josh nodded. "The server *was* connected to where they got the drug from." He looked at each of them. "So it stands to reason that whoever's behind what they're doing is the one giving Talia the runaround."

"No one is controlling them." Dakota shook her head. "At the most, it's a partnership but even that is going to be loose. They don't get into bed with anyone. Its family, or you're not a part of them."

"So they bought it and whoever they got it from is covering their tracks," Josh said. His eyes were a little too knowing. It wasn't a secret now. She'd shown him the article. He knew that Harlem had killed his girlfriend, the woman who would have been her step-mother in a few weeks.

The flash of light erupted across the screen of her mind. A single gunshot, the sound so loud it was like a firework she could still hear even after all these years. Dakota's body flinched. She couldn't control the reaction. For a second she shut her eyes, but that only made the images more prominent.

She hadn't even liked Imelda. The woman had never said anything nice and when Dakota's dad wasn't around, she had slapped her frequently. Not that he'd have cared if he had been there to see it. Harlem's parenting style wasn't all that different.

The foster family she'd been sent to had been the opposite—they'd never touched her at all. Dakota had spent most of her time alone, while the family went out to dinner or to the movies. She'd been shuffled through families and homes and by the favor of God hadn't gotten caught up in anything she couldn't control. She knew the horror stories, but the worst she'd suffered was the gaping loneliness.

Something she still felt, but had learned how to manage.

He said, "They're making it so Talia can't access their stuff?" His voice a whole lot more gentle, as though he didn't want to disturb her from her thoughts. He was looking at her like he had in the doctor's office—his face close. Soft.

"Yet." Talia shifted in her chair. Her fingers flew over the keyboard.

"Let's go." Victoria led the way outside.

Dakota zipped up her jacket as she moved through the door.

Josh said, "Got your key?"

She nodded and called out, "Bye Talia!"

In reply she got a distracted, "Yep."

Josh pulled the door shut. "You okay?"

She opened her mouth to dismiss him, but what was the point? "No. I'm not okay, not really."

Josh made a sound, deep in his throat. Like a pained moan. He grasped her elbows and pulled her into his chest. "C'mere."

Dakota frowned. He wrapped his arms around her and held her close. She lifted hers and wound them around his waist. She supposed she probably did look like she could use a hug. Who couldn't? Hugs were nice. But maybe that was just Josh.

Victoria honked the horn.

Dakota pulled away and turned to stare down her boss. Behind her, Josh made a choking sound that came across a whole lot like laughter. She turned back to him, "I'm learning your noises."

"My what?"

"You don't need words sometimes. You make noises, and you're very expressive." She studied him. "I'm figuring you out."

"Then I'll have to endeavor to be a whole lot more mysterious."

She snickered. "Please don't. I'm not sure I can handle it."

He grinned, and she realized he'd successfully pulled her out of her head. She'd been in a funk. He had brought her out of it. And he knew it, judging by the gleam in his eyes.

Then reality crashed back in, just as relentless as ever.

Dakota headed for the car. "Get your dog and let's go."

• • •

Victoria had been right that the prison was in chaos. Sal stood at the center of a circle of people, all with those silver star badges of the US Marshals hung from chains around their necks.

Dakota opened the rear door of Victoria's SUV. She pulled off her jacket and strapped on a vest that said POLICE, with the letters HSI underneath. Homeland Security Investigations. She handed him one. "Put this on."

He looked at the front—just POLICE written across it. "Thanks."

Victoria strode over to Sal and his group, her trench coat billowing around her hips.

Dakota nodded towards Victoria. "Watch what happens."

Josh frowned at her, then glanced at the men and women with Sal. Most of the men had their mouths hanging open. The women stared, too. Not Dakota. Her brow had furrowed, her lips pursed. Jealous at her colleague's reactions?

"She has that effect on people."

"Huh. I guess. If she's your type." Josh turned to Dakota.

That was it? He wasn't going to give her some kind of reassurance?

Maybe he thought his lack of reaction said enough.

He sat on the edge of the SUV to relace his boot. Neema hopped over the seat to lick his ear. "Hey." He pushed her away, and she came back to try again. Josh chuckled.

Dakota strapped on her weapon. She used a hairband to secure back her hair, then slipped her ponytail into a ball cap. Josh strapped up Neema so everyone would know she was working.

"Bulletproof?"

He nodded. "Didn't help last time, but we don't take chances. Plus it's a mental thing, you know? If she's wearing it, then she knows we're working. Watch her. You'll see the change."

"Business face?"

He smiled. "Something like that." And then got up. "Hier."

Neema hopped out and trotted to sit beside his leg. He gave the top of her head a scratch and checked his weapon while Dakota shut the back doors of the SUV.

He pulled his DEA badge out and used the Velcro to strap it to his chest. "Let's go find out what's happening."

As they approached, Victoria began to shake her head. The other Marshals had broken off to look at a laptop someone had set up on the hood of a car. On the screen was a map.

Sal saw them coming and said, "It's been confirmed. The VX was in an aerosol can and released during visitation." He must have anticipated their reactions, because he quickly said, "How they got it in there is anyone's guess.

I didn't believe it when they told me that we had to wait out here until the poison dissipated."

Dakota paled. "And Harlem?"

"Looks like in all the confusion, they purposely beelined to grab him," Sal said. "I watched the footage myself. They took him specifically. Handed him a gas mask before the gas reached him. They got a transport bus that hadn't left yet and fled the prison while the others were dealing with what they believed was the outbreak of a deadly virus."

Josh said, "How many dead?"

"Eight inmates and three guards. More in the infirmary—or what's left of it. They started a fire also. The whole place is in chaos."

Victoria sighed. "I feel like I played into their hands. Brought him right to them."

"You can't know that." Sal didn't sound like he was placating her. "It isn't like you served him up."

That they knew of. Seemed like it was possible that that was *exactly* what'd happened. But they didn't know who Dakota was. Or, at least they hadn't known she was Harlem's daughter when they kidnapped her.

Maybe, figuratively speaking, Victoria had left the door open. "You didn't know they'd go in there and release the gas."

They hadn't even known Clare had a canister. The Johnsons had been contaminated a different way.

Dakota spoke up, "But it can't be denied that someone took advantage of the opportunity to grab him."

"Maybe the prison was part of the plan," Josh suggested. "After the orchard, maybe that was next on their hit list?"

Sal shifted his weight. Like he was ready to get out of there and get on the hunt. "And Roberts was a bonus?"

Josh shrugged. Dakota said, "What about Talia's hack? Was that related?"

"Seems like she's being purposely distracted." Josh took a minute to think it through all the way so the pieces coalesced in his mind. "And the same with us."

"One real, one virtual," Victoria said, her voice distant. "Leaving them time to get set up with whatever they're going to do with that contagion next."

So someone knew about Harlem Roberts and his connection to Dakota? And whoever it was had to have passed the information on to Clare.

"You think there's a larger plot yet?" Josh didn't like that idea, even while he understood it was likely the reality. Maybe he already knew the answer to his question. But he still needed to ask it.

"I do," Dakota said.

"Me too." Victoria's agreement didn't seem to make either of them feel better.

"Something else." Sal's comment drew all their attention. "Terrence and Clare were both on the footage. Gas masks over their faces, but they got in during the confusion. They're the ones who took Roberts, along with three inmates who we believe were linked to them before they were sent here."

"So they got their people out also using the gas as a distraction?" Dakota asked. "We had no idea where they were before they exposed themselves here. Now we have a way to track them. And they've got extra people, which means it's harder to stay under the radar because now they've got to control Roberts as well."

Did she have an idea what her father would want to do when he got out? Maybe that would help them figure out where he would go. Then again, if he was under Clare Norton's thumb—because of duress, or cooperation—they were running her plays. And who knew what she was up to?

"Austin."

He said the kid's name before he even realized it.

"You think he has an idea where they're going," Dakota said.

"I think he might." Josh shrugged. "Worth a follow up conversation?"

She nodded. At least it put her elsewhere and not on her father's trail. It seemed that Dakota might be a whole lot better able to deal with the source of her life's pain running loose if she wasn't anywhere near him. If she didn't have to potentially face him.

Josh considered everything. "So maybe they knew about Roberts, or someone told them to go and get him?"

"Maybe Talia can find out how after she's done with the server," Victoria suggested. "In the meantime, Alvarez you go with the marshals. Track the transport vehicle. Find those inmates."

Two attacks.

Josh tried to think it through while she continued to dole out assignments. But he couldn't find a connection between a dark web server and a grass-roots militia apart from the sale itself. The two were completely different. There had to be a link between them—someone calling the shots. Not that he thought Clare Norton would take orders from anyone.

She turned to him and Dakota. "Go talk to Austin again. And then sit on Talia. I don't want her exposed. We need to have her back."

"What's Niall doing?" Dakota asked.

"Finishing at the compound and handing the scene over to the sheriff's deputy who is supposed to work with state police," Victoria said. "They'll let us know if they find anything we didn't."

An extra layer of protection? Josh figured these might be the first federal agents he'd ever met who were willing to admit they were humans. Fallible. Victoria might want her people re-tasked to more important assignments, but she also wasn't assuming the search of the compound and all its buildings was complete.

A new surge of respect for all of them rolled through him. The chance to be a part of this team would be great for his resume. It would also put him in the position to do what he had wanted to do when he'd applied to the DEA and with people he could learn from.

He turned to Dakota. "Austin?"

She nodded. "Let's go."

Chapter 20

The front doors to the hospital slid open. "Do you think they planned to test the VX at the prison by breaking out their friends?"

Dakota hit the button for the elevator, wondering how long this would take. Talia was going to hang tight until they got to the motel but had no backup until they arrived.

Dakota wasn't certain their teammate was in danger. Still, worry coalesced in her stomach, making her nerves sit on edge.

"Not really a test," she said. "More like a plan." They stepped inside the car, and she jabbed the button for the floor where Austin's room was.

"Like they had it figured out all along, that they'd cause a panic at the prison and stage a break out?"

She shrugged. "Guess we'll see if Austin wants to tell us."

"The alternative is running their backgrounds, right? Getting the case files that exist on each of them and going through them all in order to find a link between Clare's people and whoever else they might still have a grudge with."

"Seems to me like they manage to tick off basically everyone they meet." She shot him a wry smile. "It's going to be hard to tell who they hate the most."

"True. And that'll take days, right?"

She nodded.

"All for some kind of vendetta."

She didn't miss the tone in his voice. "Maybe whoever they target isn't so innocent." They had no idea what Clare was going to do.

"We still need to stop it. Those guards didn't come in to work today expecting to die from exposure to VX. I understand it. Mentally I comprehend the fact they need to be stopped. Your father needs to be found. But whoever they're going after, they could be worse than Clare and her people for all we know."

"So we let the bad guys kill each other?"

"No, because there's *always* fallout." He stepped out of the elevator first, and they headed for Austin's room. "Innocent people will always be caught in the crossfire."

She nodded, glad he understood that. And that he didn't feel like he had to hide from her. He was thinking it through. Coming to a conclusion. And he was using her as a sounding board—something partners did.

"And your father."

She paused at the door to Austin's room. Exactly what did he think her father would add to the mix that changed things? It wasn't like he knew—

She opened her mouth to retort, but Josh beat her to it. "Don't bite my head off."

"Do I do that?"

His eyebrows rose.

"I need access to a heavy bag if you want me to not yell at you on a regular basis."

He snorted. "Your people skills are astounding."

She grinned.

"All I wanted to say was that his presence adds a level of risk."

"For other people, or Clare and her gang?"

"All of them?"

She shrugged. "Maybe. Hopefully yes, hopefully no. I don't know his state of mind. I don't know *him*. Not to say with any certainty what he might do. Or what he'd want to do. He could go along with her. She could force him to take the blame for what they're going to do. He could be in charge. And he could kill them all and take the VX."

She blew out a breath just thinking about it.

"Let's find out what Austin knows."

She nodded, because the alternative was too frustrating to think through adequately. They needed information. The officer at the door noted their names on his pad and confirmed no one had been inside except hospital staff. And Austin had had no contact with anyone else.

Josh wandered into the room, moved to the far door, and scoped out the bathroom. The teen studied him as he turned back to them. "I'm going to go get Talia while you two talk."

Dakota nodded, wondering when he'd decided that. He thought Austin was more likely to talk openly if she was the only one here? Or maybe he wanted to make sure Talia was protected, and let Neema out of the car in the process.

He glanced at Austin once. Shot the kid a look that said a lot. He expected the teen to be respectful and to not try anything with Dakota. He made it clear she was under his protection, even in his absence.

Then he stopped beside her. "I'll be back."

Dakota nodded. He didn't touch her, but she saw the desire to do so on his face. After he shut the door behind him, she sat in the chair she'd used before. The one pulled close to Austin's bed.

"I'm not saying anything."

"You look better." She skimmed her gaze over his face. "Feel okay?"

He mushed his lips together.

"There was an incident at Inland Federal Prison. Multiple people are dead. Your aunt and brother broke Samuel Filks and Belvedore Staves out. They're in the wind."

The skin around his mouth tightened.

"No one came back for you, right?" She let that hang, then said, "They cut you loose, or did you leave of your own accord?"

"I'm done."

"You should tell Gavin. He'd probably be happy to hear that."

His gaze slid to meet hers.

"You didn't want to be mixed up in this?" She could see in his eyes that she was right. "That might be the smartest thing I've heard all day."

Dakota sat back in the chair. "Now, it could take me days to comb through their lives, and their criminal backgrounds, to uncover the connection. Who is it they hate enough to enter a federal prison and break their friends out using VX? You could just tell me right now. Save me the hassle, and maybe some lives in the process."

She didn't figure he cared about innocent people. Not the way Josh did. But she needed something from Austin, or you bet she would make good on her promise to drum up every charge she could against him. And make them all stick, too. He would have a legal battle ahead, but a good lawyer could argue duress, and there would be minimal consequences.

He had to want to be free. He didn't have the look of someone whose hope had died.

She knew what that looked like. Because she'd seen it in the mirror.

"Rough Riders."

"The motorcycle club?"

He nodded and looked away from her.

"Do you know who Harlem Roberts is?"

Austin frowned. "I…maybe I've heard the name before. But I don't know who that is."

She stood. "He was before your time."

The teen sniffed, disinterested now. "Okay."

Dakota wasn't going to thank him. That would only highlight the fact he'd just betrayed Clare and his brother.

Instead, at the door she said, "Sort your life out, Austin. It's never too late."

She didn't wait for his reaction. Just strode out, leaving him with that to chew on. The kid needed to make something of his life. Go to college.

She'd joined the police academy. Some cops had degrees, but education hadn't been her thing. She was too hands-on to be satisfied stuck behind a table, surrounded by books. She'd made her own way. Like she did with everything in her life.

She glanced at the cop on duty outside Austin's room. "Coffee?"

He nodded. "Black."

"My kinda guy."

She headed for the elevator, her steps in time to the sound of his laughter echoing down the hallway. Who didn't love coffee? Well, logically she knew some people didn't. But that didn't mean she understood it.

The elevator doors opened. Dakota didn't have time to gasp before the man inside grabbed her.

• • •

Josh knocked on the door before he used the keycard to let himself in. "Yep!"

He opened the door mid-word. The sound of crunching circuit board made him stop. Talia lifted her foot and stomped the thing to bits.

He felt his eyebrows lift. "Problems?"

"Fixing them." She looked up. "It's not only part of Dakota's job description, but mine too."

Josh grinned unable to keep from being captivated by her sheer personality. "Ready to go?"

"One second." She put one strap of a giant gold shoulder bag on her arm, then lowered things into it. An iPad. Phone. Keys.

He gaped at the pieces scattered on the table. "Is that Dakota's laptop?"

"She won't care. She hates the thing anyway." She lifted a slim computer and slid that in as well. "I've done her a favor, and he can't track me now."

They walked to the car, where she eyed Neema. "Does she need a walk?"

"Do *you* need to walk?" Josh figured Talia would want some air after being at her computer for much of the day.

She looked down. "In these shoes?"

She lifted one—also gold—a slender, strappy shoe with a high heel.

"Okay, maybe not."

She chuckled.

"I'm not really a fashion kind of guy."

She placed one hand on her breastbone, fingers splayed out so he could see her manicure. "Really? I'd never have guessed."

Josh laughed. "Yeah, yeah." He walked around the car and opened the passenger door for her. When he had Neema settled on the backseat, he turned the car on. "I threw the ball for her some, before I knocked on your door. She's good with short spurts of exercise."

"Roger that."

Josh drove back to the hospital. The entrance was considerably busier than when he'd left. "What on earth?" He dropped Talia at the door and found a space across the lot. She was tapping her index fingernail on her phone when he sprinted over to find her in the lobby. "What's going on?"

"I was just filling in Victoria. Apparently Dakota killed a guy in the elevator."

They took the stairs up to the third floor. The hallway outside Austin's room was packed with state police officers, though the officer on guard at the teen's door had kept his position. In the center of the commotion was Dakota, blood at the corner of her mouth.

"You okay?"

She glanced over. Pissed. "He's in there." She motioned to the open elevator doors.

Josh figured that was his cue to not get in her space and ask how she was doing. Right now she was in work mode, like Neema when he strapped on her vest. Surrounded by local cops, Dakota didn't want to be asked about her feelings.

He moved to the elevator, getting out of the way of investigators, and looked in.

Terrence's friend, the one who'd been at the orchard that first night, lay on the floor of the elevator. His chest was covered in blood. Black covered the area around the hole. Doctor Stevens was crouched over him.

Josh said, "Close range." Inside the elevator, there was nothing else it could be.

Stevens glanced at him. She lifted a tiny unlabeled bottle between two fingers. "On his person, he had a vial of what I'm going to surmise is the VX."

To kill Austin.

"Phone?" Josh asked.

"They retrieved it already."

He walked back over to Dakota. Talia was beside her, back-to-back, typing on her laptop she'd opened on the nurse's desk. A cord from her USB port was plugged into a phone.

"Is that his cell?"

Dakota said, "Yes."

"Anything?"

"Read it for yourself," Talia said, waving at it. "There's no passcode. Just a single text. *Get A. bring him to breakers.*"

Talia pulled up a map. The state police officer with lieutenant stripes on his shoulder pointed at the screen. "Right there. Three mile hike from the parking lot. State land, popular with outdoors people. Breakers is a campground."

"Bring him?" Josh asked. "Not kill him and then meet us."

Dakota shrugged. "Maybe he wasn't good at following orders."

"Looks like we might be going for that walk after all." Josh glanced between the two women.

"Have fun." Talia shot him a grin. "Get me a souvenir."

"You don't want any of what Neema's going to leave behind." Josh waved a hand in front of his nose. "Stinky."

Talia laughed. Dakota said, "What are you guys talking about?"

He shook his head, then turned to the Lieutenant. "Can Special Agent Pierce leave, or do you need her here longer?"

"She's good." The older man nodded. "We have what we need."

"And if I want to stay?"

"Do you?"

"No, but—"

Josh nodded in the direction of the stairs. "Then let's go."

The task gave him a focus point, one he used to push aside the pain in his chest. Dakota shifted as she walked and held her left forearm with the right hand. She stretched out her shoulder.

"Dislocated?" Maybe the doctors had put it back before he got there, but seriously? That would make her some kind of bionic woman.

She shook her head. "He slammed me into the wall. It's just bruised."

"I think we both used up our quota of allowable injuries for this year. No more fights until next year."

She grinned. "I'll add that to my list of goals."

Josh had a few things he'd like to add to his, like more hugs and maybe even a real kiss this time. But he didn't think she wanted to hear about that right now. He was going for baby steps. Introducing her to the concept of togetherness in a way that made it seem natural.

He'd never wanted to achieve a resolution more than he did the goal of getting something going with her.

Job or not, this was what would make him happy. Her too, if he did it right. The rest would fall however God allowed.

The ride to the park took forty minutes, the hike to Breakers another hour. Most of it was incline. A steep rise up the side of a mountain, along a winding trail probably used by animals more than people.

Both of them were breathing hard when they got to the campground—inaccessible by car—but Neema didn't seem fazed. The dog bounded to a tree, sniffed around. Squatted. *So much for that business face.* Then came back over to him, long enough to lick his fingers before she raced away again.

"It's beautiful."

"Off the beaten path," Dakota said.

He nodded. It took a certain kind of person to haul their belongings from the car to a place like this. Most would rather drive to the site and hook their trailer up to electricity.

He'd never understand why people needed air conditioning and Wi-Fi when they were supposed to be enjoying the outdoors.

"Think we missed them?"

Josh shrugged, turning his attention to Neema. Her body language had switched. "She caught something."

"Like a mouse?"

"No," Josh moved to follow his dog. "I don't think it's a mouse."

Neema barked once, then sat.

Beyond her was a body.

"Guess we should go and take that cadaver dog training course." He ran a hand over her chin, down past her collar to scratch her front while she leaned against his leg.

"Seems to me she could probably teach the course." Dakota stepped around the man, sprawled on the dirt. "That's two bodies in three days."

True. "Who is it?"

"I'm getting there." She moved to see the face that was angled away from him. She looked up, something in her eyes he couldn't decipher. "Is it bad that part of me doesn't want to know?"

He took a step toward her. "Let me—"

"I got it." She crouched. "Terrence."

"They killed him?"

Dakota sighed. "Pretty big knot on his forehead. Maybe he fell."

"You really think that?"

"No," she said. "I really don't."

Chapter 21

Tears threatened. And why? This guy had beaten her. Now he was dead. How was it that she even cared?

Dakota stood up. Her shaky legs took her away from the body. The scene. In this state she was bound to miss something and wind up compromising evidence.

She leaned her hand against a tree and hung her head. Sucked in breaths.

"Dakota?"

Those tears threatened to spill out. Why did he have to sound so gentle? Like he actually cared about her. That had never happened before.

She'd always kind of assumed that a deep level of concern was something that came after years of a relationship. Why else would she never have experienced it?

He took a step closer. She held up one finger then pulled out her phone and sent Talia a text letting the team know where they were and what they'd found. Then she stowed the phone away. "I'm okay."

He had the decency to not call her on her fib when they both knew she was far from all right. Neither men had been good. Not the friend—whatever his name was—she'd killed in the elevator. And not Terrence, either. But death was death, and it was always ugly. There was nothing noble about it.

"Hey." His hand slid under her hair, and his palm touched the skin of her neck.

Dakota sucked in a breath. "Cold." Enough to jog her out of her deep descent. She grinned. "Yikes."

Josh rubbed his hands together, then blew on them. "Sorry."

"Thanks." Even though it had felt like an ice cube down the back of her shirt. But the problems she had weren't going away. Terrence still lay there.

Tears threatened again. Josh tugged on the elbows of her jacket and pulled her in for another warm hug. Dakota sighed against his chest. Her breath broke in the middle a couple of times, but she managed to get the air out and back in without dissolving into a puddle of emotion.

His hand rubbed up and down her back. Probably warming his skin.

"Where are your gloves?"

He smiled down at her. "Lost them somewhere, I guess. Thanks for warming me up."

Dakota shook her head. "You're like a kid who got caught with one hand in the cookie jar."

"I make pretty good cookies. Eden gave me her recipe."

"Yeah?"

"Maybe next time I make them, you could come over and be my official taste tester?"

She felt the corners of her mouth curl up. "Depends. What do you put in your cookies?"

"Not a raisin fan?"

"Actually I love raisins. But they do not belong in anything except cereal."

"Good to know."

He leaned closer, and his lips touched hers. Thankfully warmer than his fingers were. Dakota tilted her head to the side and the kiss continued. Tentative, like a gentle exploration. And then his forehead was touching hers. She pressed her lips together, eyes closed. Still feeling the ghost of his touch against her mouth.

"Hmm."

She cocked an eyebrow. "You sound very satisfied with yourself."

"Maybe I should double check. Just to make sure—"

"Really guys?" Niall's voice rang out. Twenty feet away he stopped, cheeks red from exertion or the cold. Or both.

Dakota shifted back, like that kid with the hand in the cookie jar she'd just mentioned to Josh. *Oops.* His hand snagged her gloved one. She wound her fingers with his, just to warm them. Not because she liked the feeling of his hand around hers. That was hardly professional.

Niall dumped a bag on the far side of where Terrence had died. "Guess I'm on evidence collection duty. You want the camera?"

She shook her head. "You have the scene. Josh and I need to follow a lead."

His eyebrow crept up. "Is that what we're calling it now?"

"Niall!"

"Dude." Josh shook his head. "Not cool."

Dakota said, "What is it?" Something had happened, and it had nothing to do with her handing him this scene. She knew. She could see it in him. There was something wrong with Niall.

Her teammate sighed. He unzipped the bag and pulled out a camera. "Did you move anything?"

As if she didn't know not to do that? "I only touched him to check for a pulse."

"So you're off again? Leaving a trail of bodies behind you." Niall's jaw shifted. "Must be a Tuesday."

"It's Sunday." Josh wandered to where Neema had laid down on one of the few patches of grass not crusted with snow, resting in the afternoon sun.

"Need me to do the paperwork so you can save the world?"

"Yes," was Dakota's reply to his ridiculous question. "Actually, I do. Austin gave me the name of a group of bikers who could be Clare Norton's next target. Apparently there's history there. A grudge."

"And your father?"

It was getting harder to ignore his tone. "He ceased being my father when he shot a woman in front of me. You don't get to do that and still call yourself a parent."

Something crossed his face and she knew she'd hit a mark. "I wouldn't know."

Sore subject, apparently.

He crouched by the body and began taking pictures.

"Josh and I are going to head out."

"You need to stay for a bit. Help me."

That wasn't it. "You've done this yourself before. What's different today?"

He stood, and out the corner of her eye she saw Josh move. Covering her. A reflex as he read Niall's body language?

The subtle twitch of Niall's hand toward his gun gave her enough information. Dakota's heart sank. "Who got to you, and what did they say?" Clearly he'd bought it.

His face twisted.

"Your sister?"

"And my niece." His voice broke on the last word.

Josh stilled his approach. Beside him Neema leaned forward, her whole body alert.

"I can't let you guys leave. Not yet."

"And if we try?" she asked.

"They'll kill them."

Dakota said, "Are you going to shoot us?"

"Of course not, but—"

"Goodbye, Niall." She knew he wouldn't shoot her, or Josh. Dakota was willing to bet their lives that Niall wouldn't go against everything he believed and hurt a fellow agent. Not even to save his sister and niece. "I'll have Victoria take care of Patricia and Siobhan."

He shifted.

She lifted one finger, fully aware that Josh was about to give the command. Then there would be nothing to stop Neema from launching herself at Niall and taking him down to the ground.

As satisfying as that might be to watch.

"Don't." Dakota lowered her finger. "This is already bad enough. But if you want to do the right thing, then give Talia all the information on how they contacted you, so she can expose them."

"And if they kill my family before then?"

"You're the one putting their lives at risk." He was an agent. He knew the threat, even to extended family. Measures could be taken to protect loved ones. Surely he'd put those things in place already.

Not everything could be prevented. Still, he should have at least done what he could to minimize the risk.

Niall twisted to look at Josh. "Can I move, or is that dog going to take me down?"

"You can stay right there until we're gone." Josh clicked his fingers and the two of them circled toward Dakota. "Then I suggest you get on your phone, call Victoria and figure this out." His tone was one she'd never heard before.

Protective. Angry.

As he neared her, Josh put his hand out. She led the way. His palm touched the small of her back. The kind of cover she'd never experienced before.

Despite the circumstances, Dakota realized she'd like to have more of it. Uncertainty filled her. Was that what Josh wanted?

. . .

They still wore their vests, and when he pulled up outside the gated compound where Rough Riders lived, Josh decided it had been a good idea. These were bikers. Rough Riders was enough of a clue as to the kind of people they were.

He went around to the back of the SUV and opened the door. "Platz."

Neema, about to jump out, laid down instead. Chin up, ears perked.

"Stay."

He pulled his vest off, then removed his sweater. Rolled up both sleeves.

"What are you—" Dakota touched his bicep and the tattoo there. "Ah. You're going to appeal to their sense of duty?"

"I'd rather they shoot me because I'm a Marine and not because they saw two cops walk in their front gate."

"We are cops," she said. "And I thought you *were* a Marine, not that you *are* a Marine."

"Same thing."

"It is?"

"Once a Marine, always a Marine."

She smiled at him, like she thought that was cute and not supremely masculine. "You're going to freeze."

"I'll live. They need to see my tattoo, because if they're going to make a split second decision about who we are and why we're there, then I'm going to give them as much information as possible." He reached into his bag and pulled out two patches. He slapped the one that said *explosives detection* on the side of Neema's vest, but stowed the *narcotics* one back in his pack.

"Good idea."

He grinned. "How about you?"

"I'm a cop. There's no way to spin that." She gave him a wry smile. "Unless I wear a sign that says, 'grew up in a compound exactly like this.' Oh, and 'my dad's an escaped murderer.' That should go down well."

That was incredibly sad. But considering her tone, he said, "Might be too wordy."

Dakota laughed. "Shame."

He leaned in and kissed her, because he wanted to make her feel better. The smile she shot him when he moved back told him he'd achieved his goal.

"Neema, hier."

She hopped out of the SUV and came to his side. Josh said, "Ready?"

Dakota nodded and headed for the gate. A faded "No Trespassing" sign hung there. A camera had been mounted to a pole and was angled down, pointed at them. "You really think they'll just shoot us?"

He shrugged. "They've got to assume someone knows we're here. It isn't like we can simply disappear and no one will show up to ask questions."

She flipped the latch. Josh closed the gate behind them, and they headed down the lane. There was no way to tell what kind of bikers these were without meeting them. The deputy sheriff on duty hadn't returned their call asking for intel.

Josh said, "I'm praying they'll take the fact we're here to warn them about a possible threat as a good thing, and then we can get in and out peaceably. And without too much fuss."

"Amen to that." Dakota said, "I might not get to church as often as I'd like, but anytime I can pray I don't bleed any more than I already have in the course of an investigation, I do it."

"You seem better."

"Maybe you being here helps." She shot him a smile. "Or I'm so tired that I've gone crazy."

"Eden calls it, 'punch drunk tired.' Don't ask me what that means. Other than you're dizzy and falling down."

"I get it."

He wanted to kiss her again. Or hold her hand. Josh shoved away those urges—plenty of experience doing that this weekend—and surveyed what amounted to the front lawn. Minus any actual grass.

Tire tracks rutted the dirt that had frozen from the chill in the air. A big building stood to the left, one of those metal constructions that was shop underneath and rooms above. Some kind of meeting place. The house was huge, two stories and seemed to have been added onto several times over.

Two motorcycles were parked under a pop-up awning beside the house. A fire had been built about fifteen feet to the right at some point. Now it was a pile of charred wood and ashes.

"Where is everyone?"

Josh had been thinking the same thing. Before he could reply, a single man wandered out of the house. Baggy jeans secured with a belt, a chain hanging against his leg. T-shirt. Leather vest. His gray hair was pulled back, secured behind his head. Amid the sleeves of tattoos, Josh could make out the letters USMC in red on his arm.

Josh thought he saw movement at a window in the house. Everyone present had hunkered down. They'd seen Josh and Dakota, and they'd answered in kind. Sending out a Marine as their emissary.

"Can I help you folks?" Like they'd wandered up to his grocery stand on a Sunday afternoon.

Josh shifted, his body slightly in front of Dakota's. Not enough to cover her but enough to make a statement. She was here under his protection. It might be sexist, but bikers had a code. Women weren't subservient but they definitely didn't hold the same authority a man could exercise.

"You know Clare Norton?"

His head jerked back. Not what he'd been expecting.

"Heard word she might be on her way here. And not for a friendly visit like this." He gave the guy a pointed look.

He bit off a swear word. "That woman."

"What about Harlem Roberts? You know him?"

The man's gaze flicked to Dakota. Surprised she'd spoken. "This an interrogation?"

Josh said, "Do you know him?"

"Did." He didn't elaborate though. Just said, "Got a brother in lockup with him now."

"You're gonna want to check on your friend," Josh said. "There was an incident at Inland this morning. Several people, inmates and guards, were killed by a deadly substance that Norton managed to get her hands on."

He frowned. "Like a virus?"

"Not airborne as far as we've seen, but it's a gas in its usual state. It'll kill you. And she's using it. She started a fire at the prison. In the confusion, she broke two of her friends out and took Roberts with her as well."

Clare had also killed Terrence at the spot where Austin was supposed to have been taken. Or *had him* killed. But why? Perhaps there'd been a fight. Terrence fell and hit his head. Or he was hit *over* the head. Or he'd tripped.

Only time—and the medical examiner's assessment—was going to give them an idea of what had happened. Part of him was frustrated the group had been gone before Josh and Dakota got there. Then again, neither of them were one hundred percent. It was probably the grace of God they'd missed the group.

The man yelled, "Bunny." Over his shoulder.

A younger man, six-four at least, bounded out of the house. His leather jacket looked brand new. The old Marine whispered in his ear. Josh saw the moment the kid understood the gravity of what was happening.

He raced back inside.

"If you see a posse roll in that includes Harlem, Clare, or either of two men in a jumpsuit, I expect you'll want to call the US Marshals. Let them know where to find her."

"Um…sure." The man nodded.

Josh didn't buy it. "Good. We'd appreciate your input, and the chance to make sure everyone here is safe and remains so."

That got him a sincere nod. "Noted."

Josh handed over his card. Clicked his fingers for Neema to come.

The sound of gunfire erupted across the compound.

Chapter 22

Dakota's whole body flinched. Her knee hit the dirt, weapon already drawn. But she couldn't stay out in the open. She raced for the metal building, keeping her head as low as she could.

Praying she didn't get shot.

Praying Josh and Neema didn't either.

Men sprinted from both the house and the other building. A rush of heavy boots and jingling keys. More chains attached to belts. Angry shouts rang out, as frequent as the gunshots.

Rifles. Not automatic. More than one person. The source was concentrated to the west, behind the cover of trees.

She moved to go after the men. A shot hit the side of the building and embedded itself in the metal. She backed up, rounding the corner of the building. A man stood there, his gun aimed at the trees where his friends had gone. *Brothers.* That's what the old Marine had called them.

These people were a family.

She pressed her back against the wall beside the guy. Rough looking but that was to be expected. His eyebrows crawled together like fuzzy caterpillars. "Help you?"

She shook her head and tried to see Josh. "Is there a German Shepherd out there?"

Had either of them been hurt? Were they taking cover by the house?

"The dog ran with the other cop." He pointed east. "That way."

"I'm not going to arrest you, if that's what you're worried about."

"Who says I'm worried?" He disappeared around the corner, and she heard a slew of gunshots.

Dakota moved to the corner of the building and peered around. They didn't need to get in the middle of this war. She and Josh had been here to warn the Rough Riders. Now their job was to detain Clare and her friends.

It bothered Dakota that they'd been too late. The old Marine lay on the dirt, blood pooled out from underneath his chest. Dead.

The Rough Riders would be out for blood now. Clare was going to regret coming here and starting something.

If she lived through it.

Dakota moved to the back of the building. She could skirt the perimeter and come up on the gun fight from the flank, hopefully staying out of sight and the line of fire long enough to see what was happening.

The shots continued as she made her way around the back. Behind the buildings was essentially a parking lot. Motorcycles. Trucks. Even an RV had been parked back there.

A woman lay between the closest vehicle—a beat up car—and the back door of the building. Dakota sank to her knees beside the woman and pressed a hand to her stomach.

The woman's glassy eyes widened, and she gasped through the pain.

"Easy." Blood seeped between her fingers. "I'm Dakota."

She pulled out her phone with the other hand and touched her thumb to the home button. With voice commands, she called Victoria, then put the phone between her ear and shoulder to explain what was happening.

"I'm on my way with emergency services. Hang tight." Victoria hung up.

Dakota looked toward the trees. Where she should be going.

"I got towels!" Another woman, barely more than a girl really, ran out of the house wearing what appeared to be the uniform for female bikers—tiny denim skirt and halter top, with teased hair and heavy makeup. She saw Dakota and froze, nearly tripping over her feet.

"Give me those. Now."

The girl stumbled but came close enough to throw the towels at her. "Is Misty gonna be okay?"

"She will if you help her." Dakota snagged the girl's hand and pulled her the rest of the way over. She planted her hand on the towel, above where Misty had been shot. "What's your name?"

"Sunny."

"Press right here, Sunny. Harder than you want to," she told her. "And don't let up. Not until the paramedics get here. That is the *only* way she's going to make it."

Sunny let out a sob. Dakota didn't blame her. It was plain to see the woman on the ground was in a bad way. *God, will she make it?* He didn't answer back but sometimes she needed to ask the question anyway.

Dakota set her hand on Sunny's shoulder. "Got it?"

"Y-yes."

Dakota clambered to her feet and headed for the woods.

• • •

The second bullets started to fly, Josh ran for cover. Two guys rushed out of the building so fast he nearly ran into them.

Guns lifted.

He said, "Whoa." Praying in that split second that they didn't just drop him and go. He watched it register on their faces the second they realized who he was. POLICE. Josh moved around them, going for cover against the building. "Neema."

His dog was already at his side as he pressed his back against the wall and whipped his head back and forth. Finally he caught sight of Dakota's dark hair as she rounded the back of the building. Heading for a flanking position.

"Let's go."

It took a second to realize the guy was talking to him. What did he expect Josh to do? "Cover fire?"

The biker shook his head. In that second, Josh decided this guy was the man in charge. Older than him but younger than the Marine sent out to talk with them. He had a look about him. There might be a civil veneer, but it was pretty thin. "You're with us."

Bullets flew across the spot where he'd stood with Dakota just minutes ago. Maybe seconds.

Someone screamed. A window smashed, and gunfire answered. The sound of rifle fire. And if he wasn't mistaken, that make and model wasn't available to buy in this country.

They wanted him out of their space but where they could keep track of what he was doing.

Josh went with them, one guy in front and one behind. Skirting to the side. Coming around to the source of the gunfire.

"Foos."

Neema hadn't left his side. Giving the command for her to heel was a comfort to both of them. A shared plan. They were going to stick together in this, even though they had no idea what they were running into.

And maybe Josh was ascribing a whole lot more cognition to a dog who ate, slept, played and worked, but other than that, wasn't interested in much. But she was *his* dog. She was happier when she knew he was happy. Just like he was happier when he knew she was content.

"Two o'clock."

Josh saw one guy in a jumpsuit who stuck out between the trees. "How many?"

"One." The guy gave a hand signal. They slowed, then dropped to a crouch. "Dax, swoop around. Holler if there are more." Definitely in charge, his face maybe mid-forties but lined with experiences that could never be erased.

Dax whispered away through the trees.

"What do you say, Mr. Federal Agent? Wanna get your hands dirty?" The fire in his eyes preceded low growled words. "These people killed Sie. That means they pay."

"The jarhead?" Was Sie the older man now lying in the dirt?

The biker nodded.

Josh had seen the older Marine drop. If he was dead, and this man wanted to exact revenge, what could Josh do about it? Interfere and risk his own life? Maybe he should head back to the compound and find Dakota. Help her.

Regroup.

After that they could see what was left of Clare and her people. Clean up the mess.

Trying to decide what his mentor agent would do—write a report while drinking green tea—wasn't any kind of help.

"You need to let me take the escaped inmates back in." And Dakota's father. And Josh needed to arrest Clare. "They have VX, and they're going to use it. That needs to be contained."

The man almost smiled, but it settled into a kind of sneer. "When I'm done, you can have what's left."

Before he could object, the man raced away. Not good.

Josh moved into a crouch, still mostly undercover. He called out in the direction the man had gone. "This is the DEA. Lay down your weapons and surrender—"

Two shots hit the tree right by his head. Josh ducked so fast he lost balance and landed on one knee.

Someone yelled, a low roar that could only come from a man threatened. Gunshots. Three. Four. Josh lost count as his heartbeat thumped in his ears. Neema barked, way too close to his head.

Two dogs ran toward him. After them came a man he'd seen at Clare's compound. Then another man he didn't know. Josh yelled again. "Stand down!"

They lifted weapons. One fired at him, while the other fired to the side. Someone fired back. One man went down with a cry, blood spraying from his shoulder. Josh was going to run out of bullets.

The dogs pounced on Neema. Teeth snapped. Low snarls.

He pulled on one collar. The dog must have weighed more than a hundred pounds.

Neema yelped in pain.

Josh kicked at the dog closest to him. He fired over the other's head, barely missing it, then lifted up. Landed his weight on the dog and forced it into submission under him.

It let go of Neema's shoulder and snapped at Josh.

He put his arm up in defense and the dog latched on. Josh twisted off Neema, who was at the bottom of this pile of man and animals. He swung his leg around and kicked the dog until it let go of him.

Then he launched at it, praying the dog took notice.

It backed up. Josh didn't stop himself until the last second, making sure the dog wasn't going to retaliate.

He held his gun ready just in case. *Ouch.* His forearm stung, and he could see the red on his bare skin. Josh lost balance and landed on his butt.

The man who'd fired at him yelled, "Dumb dogs."

An assessment of their having backed down?

They broke off from snarling at Neema and went to the man. Called by their master using the most frequent name they heard. The man loped on, leaving Josh here with his dog.

He sank to the dirt beside her, blood dripping from his arm. The gunshot wound in his shoulder screamed but he ignored it. He watched each sharp rise of her chest. Blood seeped from her shoulder down onto the earth. He touched her muzzle, her eyes glassy with pain.

"Oh, baby."

Josh looked around, half expecting to get shot at any moment.

Where was Dakota?

• • •

She headed for the source of the sound—a gunfight between Clare and her people and the bikers she'd seen run. She slowed before she could even make them out. Was Harlem here? Duty warred against the fear he'd put in that scrawny girl with the ratted dark hair and too big eyes. Most of the time she still felt like that little girl. It was why she'd tried so hard to push out the memories, to forget.

A shot whizzed past her. Dakota crouched, shoulder against a tree. All her aches and pains decided that now was a good time to remind her she wasn't at a hundred percent capacity. Like she hadn't known that? Where was Josh, and Neema?

Maybe he'd been hit. Maybe she was out here, alone. The way she'd been when her father kicked her out every time he decided that's what she needed. Out of the house and outside the fence. She'd seen the looks on the faces of her father's friends. Associates. She didn't know what the relationship had been, just that other guys had hung around the house.

That one scrap of sympathy was something she'd never forgotten. Not because it had happened often, but because she had sucked up every smidgen of connection she could get her hands on.

Now she just tried to avoid it.

Not that it had worked. She had more of a family now than she'd ever known. And then there was Josh.

Where was he?

The gunfire had died down now. Dakota made her way over to the source, expecting carnage. She found one man dressed in a jumpsuit, clutching his leg and moaning. Across from him was a dead biker.

Two men stood over the injured escapee. Bikers from the compound.

"Easy fellas."

"Not hardly," the older one said. "He killed Sie. And now he's killed Smalls."

Dakota said, "There's a woman back there as well. Shot in the stomach but she's alive. Misty, I think the other one said."

The shorter of the two men spun so fast she took half a step back as he tore past her, back toward the compound.

Evidently Misty meant something to him.

"Guess it's just us," the other one said. His mustache shifted up and then down as he moved his lips in thought. "Means I could kill you. Blame him and then walk away." As if for emphasis, he kicked at the wounded man on the ground.

The inmate moaned, eyes wide and glassy.

She wasn't sure if he was serious or not, considering his face gave nothing away. "My team is on their way."

"Guess we're going to have to figure out what they'll find when they get here."

"Preferably not my dead body."

She held her gun in a loose grip, pointed at the moaning inmate. But not too far it would take her more than a split second to train it on the biker if she had to.

She lifted the other hand up, palm out. "If I get a vote, that is."

The biker flashed his teeth in what was probably a smile. "The committee is gonna take it into consider—"

He dropped to the ground. A hole blossomed blood on his forehead.

The inmate started laughing, still a half-moan as he bled out from his leg. Dakota spun around. She wanted to kick herself for not noticing anyone else approach. Her father strode over, a rifle in his arms. Clare Norton beside him. Her smile turned to a cackle as they neared. That was the only way to describe the noise she made above the rush in Dakota's ears.

"Gun down."

Everything in her stilled. Did he even know who she was? It had been years since they'd seen each other.

"You'll have to shoot me." She knew full well what he was capable of. "I'm not going to let go of my gun."

Clare sidled up next to him, her mushed nose red from the cold. "Or I could just jam this down your throat, and we can all watch you squirm."

She lifted the vial in her hand, a gleam in her eyes. She knew what she had. And she was prepared to cause maximum damage with it.

Her father didn't take his attention from her. "No, you won't."

His words had been directed at Clare. Which of them was in charge? Or was this simply a battle of wills, and one would die before they figured it out.

"Why?"

Dakota didn't even know what she wanted an explanation for. Something. Anything.

All of it.

It wasn't like he needed her. What did he care if she was dead?

Maybe he wanted to be the one to put her out of her misery himself. Had he been nursing dreams of revenge all these years? It wasn't like she'd said one word about what happened. They only knew she'd witnessed it because she hadn't moved from the time he fired the gun to when the sheriff had shown up.

Drawn there by someone's frantic phone call.

Just like then, Dakota was frozen to this spot right now.

There was no way she would let go of her grip on reality as well. Or her hold on the strength of what her training gave her.

His face was pitted, the bottom half peppered with the shadow of a gray beard. His stomach stretched the front of the jumpsuit. Never a small man, he'd always seemed so imposing in her mind. Now she was taller than him, and he seemed almost tired.

And angry.

"How'd you end up hooked up with her." Dakota motioned to Clare with the barrel of her weapon.

He kept a straight face. "Happy circumstances."

Clare said, "Money."

"And Terrence?"

"Waste of space." Clare rolled her eyes. "Good riddance."

Not exactly a confession. "Both of you put your weapons down and your hands up."

"I'm not going back to prison." Her dad didn't move the rifle at all. "You'll have to kill me."

She saw the intention in his eyes and cut him off before he lifted his gun. "Fine," she said. "Dad."

His eyes flared, and he held his aim on her. Dakota watched the anger surge in him.

Finger to the trigger.

He was going to shoot her, center mass.

Her father wanted to kill her.

In that split second between decision and the squeeze of his finger, Dakota fired.

• • •

Harlem's gun moved on impact. His bullet went wide, into the escapee who'd been shot in the leg. The man slumped to the side.

"No!" Josh raced toward her. He'd seen the tail end of the conversation after he carried Neema part way, then left her close, curled up at the base of the tree.

She needed help.

Dakota dived to the ground.

Harlem's body landed with a thud.

They *all* needed help.

Clare squealed and raced away.

Josh ran to where Dakota lay. *Don't be dead. God, please don't let her be dead.* His boot hit a twig and snapped it. Dakota sat halfway up, gasping. Pointed her weapon at him.

"Easy." He dropped to his knees beside her. "I saw you go down."

She blew out a breath. "That was close."

Her eyes darkened at the sight of her father. She stared, emotion washing over her face for the first time he'd seen. This evidently strong enough to break through that shell.

He spoke gently. "You killed him?"

She nodded, then looked away from Harlem as tears filled her eyes.

"I saw it," Josh said. "He gave you no choice."

She said nothing more

Josh motioned to the trees. "Clare got away."

"With the vial containing the VX." She paused a second and then said, "Go after her."

He shook his head. "Neema is bleeding, and so am I. We need to regroup." He sucked in a breath of his own, adrenaline still pumping through his system.

Dakota couldn't stand without help. Commotion drew both their attention. Sal and a team of marshals rushed through the trees. Vests and rifles. Sal wore aviator sunglasses that Josh thought looked ridiculous.

He slowed when he saw them and scanned the area. "You okay, Cupcake?"

Dakota called back. "Yeah, Puddin'. I'm fine."

One of the marshals snickered. Sal shot him a death glare over the top of his glasses.

"Clare Norton went that way—" Josh pointed southwest. "—if you're interested."

Sal tore off with his marshal friends.

"Guess that answers that." He heard a whine and spun around. "Neema?" They made their way to the spot where he'd placed her. She was breathing low now, and it was sporadic.

"She needs a vet." He looked over at Dakota and saw the wet in her eyes.

"Let's go then."

He had her call the vet and tell him they were on their way. Josh carried his dog, despite the screaming pain in his arm and shoulder. The vet could look at him after he saw to Neema. They reached the SUV, and he laid Neema in the back. There wasn't even time to reassure her.

He trotted to the driver's seat and climbed in.

Dakota was already buckling up when Josh shoved the car into drive. He was about to pull out onto the road when the cold barrel of a gun pressed against his neck.

"You go where I tell you to go." The voice belonged to a man. "Or both your brains are on the dash."

Chapter 23

Dakota twisted far enough to see the beige of the man's inmate scrubs. The one she hadn't left dead in the woods from Harlem's gunshot.

The tattoo on his neck shifted. "Want your head blown off?"

All she could think of was her father falling to the ground, dead from her shot. "Not especially." Dakota bit the words out.

"Drive." The inmate jerked his gun to the left.

Josh flipped a U-turn and got onto the highway. "Where are we going?"

"Just go. I'll tell you when to turn." He shifted to speak to her. "Pull out all the weapons you two got on you and hand them over." The inmate touched the gun to Dakota's shoulder. "Or you know what will happen."

She said, "I'm reaching for my weapon."

"Nice and slow." He pointed his gun at Josh while Dakota pulled her Sig out with two fingers nowhere near the trigger.

"Backup?"

"In my boot," she said.

"Hand it over."

She pulled out the tiny revolver and handed it over the exact same way. The guy tossed it to the floor of the backseat.

In the very back, Neema whined.

Dakota said, "That dog needs medical attention. She has a serious injury."

"You'll have a serious injury unless you shut up."

She pressed her lips together. Josh's hands were on the steering wheel, both sets of knuckles white with tension as he drove.

"Get his gun."

She reached over and pulled it from the holster on his belt.

The inmate said, "Backup?"

"Not today," Josh said.

"I'm supposed to believe that?" The guy shifted in his seat. Not overly stressed, or freaking out. Just tense. The *situation* was tense, and he knew it.

"It's the truth," Josh said.

"You'd better hope so." He rested the gun on Dakota's shoulder. Josh saw it. "Just drive. No one moves, and we won't have any problems." He shifted and she heard him root around in the back seat.

Dakota glanced at Josh. He kept his gaze forward, lines around his taut mouth. She wanted to say something. *Look at me.* She didn't like there not being a connection between them. But was it worth being shot, just for a glance?

Fear reared its head again. Curled up in her stomach, it shifted. Unfurled. Slithered like a snake until it filled her throat, trying to choke her.

The beige outfit was discarded, and he pulled on clothes. Stinky workout clothes, judging by the smell. Who did those belong to? She figured Sal. If they were Niall's then this guy was going to look ridiculous wearing high waters and a crop top.

"It doesn't matter how far you get," she said. "The man whose clothes those are is going to catch you. He's the best tracker I know."

"I'll be long gone by then."

But would she and Josh be alive? And Neema? She said, "Do you even have a plan?"

He needed money. Transportation. Were friends waiting for him? Anything he said now, Sal could use to track him down.

If Sal didn't catch up to them the second the SUV stopped.

Was he wondering where they'd gone? Talia would have their GPS. Both she and Josh had their phones with them in the car, and she was wearing her watch. Plenty of ways to track them if anyone decided they might need to be found.

They could be dead before the team thought to look.

"What do you care?" He shifted to bring the gun between the front seats again. "It's not like I'm gonna to tell you where I'm going."

"Then tell me what Clare is up to." She wanted to shift and look him in the eyes, but didn't risk it. "You'll have a better shot at getting away if we're all distracted looking for her."

"Crazy woman." He bit off another comment. "Don't want to be under the thumb of the government and then take a job doing some guy's dirty work he doesn't want to do? And for what?"

Dakota remembered the woman's comment. "Money, apparently."

"I don't care how good it is. You don't give away your freedom. That only makes you someone's slave."

"She broke you out." Dakota glanced over. Out the corner of her eye she saw Josh reach down between the door and his seat, slowly. Carefully.

"She owed me. Now we're square."

"So she's following someone's orders?"

He snorted. "You think I'll tell you who?"

"Could help. When the marshals catch up, you'll need leverage right? Get a deal." She paused for a second. "But if you kill us, there's *nothing* you could say that will make things easier for you. Not a single thing."

He shrugged. "So I keep one step ahead of the cops. Don't get caught."

"Forever?"

"All I gotta do is get out of the country. Get somewhere they don't make deals with America. Not that hard to find a country that doesn't like us, considering we're ticking people off left and right these days."

And this was different than any other time of history how, exactly? Dakota had paid enough attention in school to be able to graduate, and then she'd gotten out of there. Still, it wasn't like "world peace" had actually ever been a thing. From what she'd heard on the radio—that time she'd stumbled upon a pastor talking about end times—the idea and possibility of peace was literally a sign that "the End" was coming.

But how did knowing about that stuff help her right now?

The same way she'd purposely tried to forget the past, Dakota didn't usually worry about what was going to happen tomorrow. Or five years from now.

She could be dead by then.

Right now there was a gun pointed at her and Josh, and *that* was her priority. Not setting the goal to drink more water next month.

"How about we pull over," she suggested. "We'll get the dog and get out. You can take the vehicle."

"And get followed because this thing is equipped with GPS?"

"Then you get out." She bit off the words, frustration a poisonous strike of that snake. "Because we have things to do."

He chuckled. "Feisty. Maybe you should come with me."

Josh said, "That's not gonna happen."

"I'm the one with the gun."

Josh swung the wheel hard to the right. Dakota caught herself before her head hit the window. A concussion on top of a concussion wouldn't help anything.

The escaped inmate didn't do the same. She turned fast enough to see him fall almost all the way to the floor.

Dakota grabbed the hand holding the gun.

Josh slammed on the brakes. There was no time to say, "Thanks."

She swayed toward the dash. With her hold on the inmate's hand she pulled his arm hard in the wrong direction.

The gun went off. The front windshield shattered. In the confines of the vehicle, the noise was deafening. Her whole body flinched, and it was like her ears shut off…to a roaring noise like a waterfall.

He sat up.

She still had a hold on his hand. She tried to point the gun away from either her or Josh. The driver's door flung open and Josh dived out.

He was running away?

. . .

Josh raced around the car. Neema barked from the back, but there was no time to wonder if she had moved or was bleeding still. Or more.

He hauled open the back door of the SUV and grabbed the inmate. His ears rang through his head, like someone had stuck hot pokers in both. Gritting his teeth, he pulled against the pain in his arm and shoulder.

The man slid out onto the ground, his arms and legs flailing. Josh let go, then kicked the guy in the head. It wasn't nice, but he didn't want to shoot him. This fight needed to be over. Right now.

The man's head lolled to the side and he slumped. Out cold.

Enough of running for their lives. Enough of being shot and beaten. Kidnapped. Enough escaped prisoners, deadly substances, and having to face off with bikers who would kill anyone who threatened one of their people.

Dakota touched his face. Josh's whole body flinched, but she didn't let go or step back. He sucked in a breath and pushed it out slowly. He pulled her in, placed both hands on the sides of her face and touched his forehead to hers.

His breathing didn't slow. Adrenaline still too high, his blood pumped at a fast pace, lighting synapses and making his muscles twitch. He needed to run. To expel this energy somehow.

He started to move, but Dakota held onto his arms. He opened his eyes and shifted his face down.

"You saved us."

That, he heard. The sound was muffled, whispered against his lips. The ringing in his ears was still there, though not as loud. He wanted to smile. But exactly what was there to be happy about? She lifted her face closer, relief in her eyes.

He looked at the inmate again. Just to make sure he was out, and they weren't going to get blindsided.

Again.

He should have checked the backseat. He should have—

Dakota tugged his face around and pressed her lips to his. The buzz of thoughts in his head dissipated, replaced by silence. Her touch was like closing your eyes against the sun. The best kind of peace. Of rest. Like coming home.

She pulled back and bit her lip.

"What?" He heard his own voice more in his head than out loud. He needed to check on Neema.

She said, "Sorry." He started to shake his head, but she spoke again before he could. "I probably shouldn't have done that. I'm just so glad that we're all right—"

Josh kissed her back.

When he'd made his point, that she had nothing to apologize for, he pulled back. "I need to call the vet. Get him to come here and see to Neema." He dialed.

Dakota shifted to pull out her own phone. "I'll call Victoria." She glanced at the unconscious man. "We should find some cuffs."

Josh dug around in the SUV and found a pair, which he tossed to her while the phone rang.

"Thought you were headed here."

"Got sidetracked." He was more thankful than he could say that the vet was on the same page. "Any way you can come to me?"

"How is she?"

He looked over the dog. "Pretending she isn't hurt as badly as she really is."

The doc chuckled. "That's a Shepherd for you. Got a first aid kit?"

"Good idea." Josh gave him their location and hung up. He dug out gauze to hold onto the nasty wound on her side and climbed in the back of the SUV to be close to her. Dakota was on the phone still.

He saw her shift.

Josh lifted up so he could see the inmate. Hands cuffed behind his back. His right leg was bent up toward his hands. It appeared she'd tied the laces of one of his shoes to the cuffs.

Josh called out, "Did you tie him up?"

She moved the phone away from her mouth. "Better safe than sorry." She spoke for a few more seconds, then hung up.

One hand close to her weapon, she circled the man on the ground and came closer to the SUV so they at least didn't have to yell to hear each other.

"Victoria is sending Sal and the other marshals."

"Is that guy awake?"

She nodded, keeping her attention on the restrained escaped prisoner. "How is Neema?"

He smiled at her, even though she wasn't looking at him.

Then she glanced over for a second and caught him. She looked back at the inmate, shaking her head.

He said, "You like her."

"It's not nice to gloat."

Josh laughed loudly before he could hold it back. He glanced at his dog.

Dakota said, "The doc will be here soon, right? He'll fix her up."

Josh figured the vet would take her with him back to his office. Neema needed stitches and medicines. She didn't need them dragging her all over the countryside looking for Clare.

Sal and the vet turned up at almost the exact same time. Both climbed out of their vehicles, but the vet went to the back of his truck and pulled out a duffel.

"Let me see."

Josh petted Neema's nose, then slid out and went to Dakota and Sal.

"...take him in," Sal was saying.

One of the marshals untied the inmate's shoe from the handcuffs. Then he and another one lifted the man to his feet. The inmate glared daggers at Dakota and Josh as he was escorted away.

"One dead and the other is back in custody." Josh couldn't help the satisfaction. "Now we just have to find Clare." He folded his arms across his chest, mostly to keep from touching Dakota.

Now that they'd shared several kisses, he wanted more. He was past the point of trying to convince himself there was nothing going on between them. It was far more than nothing, and he wasn't going to disrespect whatever it was—or her—by pretending otherwise.

Maybe it wouldn't go anywhere past this. And what a shame that would be. They at least needed to acknowledge the fact it existed. Still, Dakota might not need to have that conversation now, or any time soon.

She had killed her father earlier today.

Sal glanced between them.

Dakota said, "What?" She also folded her arms.

Josh put his hands in his jeans pockets, just so they weren't standing the same way.

"You guys are weird." Sal didn't say more. Not before one of his marshal friends came over.

"We're headed out," the marshal said. "Are you going after Clare Norton?"

"Yes." Sal motioned to them. "I have a ride."

"Copy that." The man jogged off, and they pulled out. Headed off to return the inmate to the prison. Or wherever they were putting the escapees, considering the facility had dissolved into chaos.

Josh helped the vet carry Neema to his vehicle. He told her bye even though she was a dog. That wasn't the point, was it? And then the vet left as well.

"The SUV is a mess."

Sal said, "Was that inmate wearing my dirty gym clothes?"

"Yep," Dakota said. "Clare Norton?" Her smile quickly dissipated. "How do we find her?"

"She headed west, so we have people searching the woods between there and the next town. And we have roadblocks on the highway."

Josh said, "Roadblocks?"

"She released VX and set free three dangerous inmates. You think we won't use roadblocks?"

He shook his head, not sure what he was thinking. His arm really hurt. "And we have no idea where she's going now."

Dakota's phone rang. "It's Talia." She tapped the screen. "You're on speaker. Sal is here with me and so is Josh."

"I think I know where Clare went."

Chapter 24

Both guys shifted closer to the phone. Dakota gripped it, held out in the middle of their huddle. "What did you find?"

"I was listening to the police band. There's a guy. Has a farm east of the compound. He came home about thirty minutes ago to find his wife killed and her car gone."

Dakota's heart squeezed. That was the only way she could explain her reaction. Probably being so close to Josh before Sal showed up was the reason. Why else would she care that a man's wife had been murdered? It was her job to find and stop Clare. Not to get all emotional about another dead person.

She'd seen enough of that today. Maybe too much death. Some she'd killed herself. Like her father. So what did she care about one more?

But she was only kidding herself.

Josh's attention was on her when he said, "And Clare?"

Dakota didn't want either of their attention on her. Not when her eyes burned hot with tears.

Sal had been her friend for four years now. Then there was Josh, who had somehow gotten under her skin the past two days. Seriously, she could hardly believe they'd only just met on Friday night. Now it was nearly Sunday evening.

All kinds of insane stuff had happened, she could hardly process it all. Least of all the fact she'd killed her own father. Josh had stuck with her through it. Even when she ditched him, he'd forced her to explain why.

He made her care.

Because she cared about him.

Whether that would end up being a good thing remained to be seen.

Talia said, "Clare is at large. We have a BOLO out on her description and the car to all the local entities. Considering the level of police presence within fifty miles of Dakota, I'm thinking it won't take long to get a result."

"Wait, what—Me?"

Talia chuckled. "Honey, you're a walking disaster."

"I didn't make Clare break those people out of prison." Just like she wasn't responsible for *all* of the deaths that had occurred today. "And I didn't sell her that VX."

Sal said, "Let's get in the car. You guys can argue about whose fault this is while I drive."

"It's Clare Norton's fault." Dakota pulled the passenger door open.

Josh grinned at her, though she could see the pain on his face, and he climbed in the backseat. "It's also the responsibility of whoever sold her the VX."

"Certainly not mine." She knew she was grumbling.

Sal turned the engine on and the call connected to the Bluetooth. Dakota set her phone on her leg and said, "Which way is she heading, anyway?"

Talia said, "East on highway eleven."

"So, toward Spokane," Josh said from the backseat.

"Or anywhere between here and there." Dakota pressed her lips together. "Or nowhere in particular. Maybe she'll just drive until she runs out of gas. Then she'll kill someone else and take *their* car."

Not a happy thought, especially considering Talia's jab that this was Dakota's fault. They'd been following the intel. It wasn't like she'd been able to stop their plans, and Clare hadn't jumped on this just because Dakota showed up.

Maybe she'd escalated the timeline a bit. They had dragged her father into this—with Victoria's "help."

Could the speed up in their plans have been prevented? The fact she'd forced Clare to accelerate things might have meant more people died than was necessary, but it also meant Clare was reacting instead of working through a calculated to do list. She was more likely to make a mistake if she was changing things up on the spur of the moment.

Dakota's mouth tasted bitter at the idea that any of this had happened because of her. That anyone had been hurt because of a decision she'd made. Mrs. Johnson. A farm wife, hopefully happy at home, was now dead. Misty had been shot. Josh had been shot. Neema was hurt. Her own teammate had tried to stop her and Josh from moving forward with the case.

She said, "Have you heard from Niall?"

"Not since he sent me all the photos from the Terrence Crampton crime scene."

"He wrapped up there?" She saw Sal glance at her for a second before he focused on the road again.

"The medical examiner picked up the body. Niall marked himself as off duty about thirty minutes later."

"He probably headed to Portland." Dakota explained about the threat to Patricia and his niece Siobhan. Basically the cutest Irish name *ever*. As well as being one of the more pronounceable ones. Dakota enjoyed saying, "shuh-vawn." It was as cute as the girl was. She said a little prayer in her head for their safety.

Sal bit back a curse word.

Dakota grinned. "You kiss your mother with that mouth?"

"Every time I see her, cupcake."

"Gross." She shook her head. "Talia, can you check on them?"

"I'll notify local FBI of the threat. Have a detail put on them." She paused. "Why did he tell us they were being threatened?"

"I honestly don't know," Dakota said. "We're here to help, aren't we?"

Josh leaned forward and squeezed her shoulder. She was thankful for his reassurance, but didn't want Sal to know how close they'd gotten. She could tell him later. Talk to Josh later. Right now there were other things on their priority list.

He said, "Maybe one of Clare's people is still working, trying to cover her escape?"

"Or the same person who sold Clare the contagion in the first place is the one covering for her. Trying to slow us down," Dakota suggested.

"The one who runs that dark web server?"

She nodded, even though Talia couldn't see her. "The inmate we took down said she was doing his bidding, taking his money and working for him. For whatever reason, I don't even care why."

Unless knowing Clare's motivation could give them a clue as to what she was going to do with the rest of the VX.

Dakota continued, "But if he's waiting for her to complete a certain task, then it stands to reason he'd be helping her. At least somewhat."

"Maybe." Sal worked his jaw back and forth.

"It's the best suggestion we've come up with so far."

"But taking down the seller doesn't stop the threat. It just stops the money. And anything *else* he's planning."

"Or she." Dakota fired at him, just because he was right. "You're right that Clare should be our priority right now. But finding the seller could help us."

Talia said, "I'm looking into her financials, but I can't do everything at once."

"So tell Victoria. Punt some to the FBI."

"I'll have to explain what I'm doing. Then I'll have to make sure they're doing it right. Then, after they're done, I'll have to check what they came up with."

Dakota frowned. "That sounds exhausting."

"Now you feel my pain."

"Just not with the heels you wear," Dakota said. "That, I'll never know."

"Don't remind me. I've just about gotten over it."

The phone beeped, call ended. Dakota stowed it. "So we wait?"

Sal huffed. "Guess you'd better figure out how to do that. At least quietly enough Josh and I don't murder you for being annoying."

Murder you...In Dakota's mind she saw her father's body jerk. The surprise that registered on his face the second before he fell back.

Dead.

• • •

Josh shifted in his seat. If she'd been determined to keep the beginning of their relationship from Sal, she was about to be disappointed. He unsnapped his seatbelt and leaned between their seats, turned to face her.

Josh put his hand on her face. "Eyes."

Her gaze shifted up to meet his, her gaze full of tears.

"He doesn't know. But that isn't an excuse for him to be insensitive."

"Hey—"

Josh turned to Sal. "I don't need your help." He turned back to focus fully on her. "Just take a breath. This has been a long, stressful weekend. It's not over yet, but you are allowed to take a second for yourself."

It would take her longer than that to get through all that had happened. But he knew for sure she was capable. This weekend wasn't what would break her. Not a woman like Dakota, who had been forged in the hottest of fires. Forced to survive so many things, some she would never ever tell him.

He said, "You will find peace with this."

"How do you know that?" Her voice broke in the middle, but she got the words out.

He wanted to remind her that they both knew the Prince of Peace. But how could he do that without it sounding totally corny? "I'm going to pray."

"And so am I."

Hopefully they could do it together. After this he'd need some serious refocusing. Time to assess where he was at. Where he was headed. What he wanted moving forward. Some people might find that stuff hokey but it was what he'd been taught to do. Talk to God while you figure out what you want, and then watch for His direction as you figured out how to get it.

Otherwise he'd have floundered for years in life. He'd have wandered through every day with no direction and no purpose.

"Thank you."

He let go, reluctantly. At least he could admit to himself that it was reluctant. Now wasn't the time to go over all that in his head.

"You're welcome." He sat back and pulled out his phone because it was vibrating. Re-buckled his seatbelt.

"The vet is calling me." He answered the call. "Weber."

"Hey. Neema is resting now. She was pretty agitated after we left you, but by the time I got her up, stitched and bandaged, she was drowsy. I'm hoping you can be here when she wakes up tomorrow. I don't want her moving before then."

"I can try." But the reality was that he had no idea what would be happening tomorrow. "I'll keep you posted."

"Good enough. She's not going anywhere, and I'll have someone here to keep an eye on her tonight."

"Thank you. I appreciate you taking care of her."

"Wait till you see my bill," the doc said, partly laughing. "Then we'll see how appreciative you are."

Josh hung up, grinning.

"Say that again." Dakota hit a button on her phone. Josh shifted but couldn't see what was on the screen. He hadn't even realized she answered her own phone.

The call connected through the car's speakers.

"State police spotted the Nissan with Clare driving." It was Victoria.

Dakota said, "License plate?"

"They called it in, and it was confirmed. They were ordered to pull her over." Victoria sighed. "After that no one heard from them. So another pair of officers headed to the location. They found the state police car, one officer dead from a gunshot and the other wounded."

"She killed a cop?" Sal's voice was low. Deadly.

Even Josh was concerned about the tone. Not scared, though. The guy was a cop, which meant he operated within a set of rules even though marshals were a law unto themselves. That didn't mean Josh wasn't concerned as to the man's drive to catch up to Clare Norton and bring her to justice. And what that might entail.

The marshals had been policing America for more than two hundred years, making them the oldest federal agency. Still, even Sal had to obey the law. Procedure.

"She killed a cop." Victoria's voice resounded through the interior of the SUV. "The wounded officer said she took off, heading east."

Josh said, "To Spokane."

Dakota said, "What's happening there?"

"On a Sunday night, not much."

Josh said, "If she's intending to make some kind of statement, then she'll need a target where there are a lot of people. Maximum damage gets maximum news coverage." And wasn't that a horrible thought?

"Leave it with me. I'll get you a list of what I come up with."

"Copy that." Dakota pressed the button on the dash screen and ended the call.

Josh sighed. He stared out the window at the trees to try and get his brain to process everything. To push past the pain and focus. He'd wiped off his skin where the dog had latched onto his forearm. Not as bad as he'd thought. An older dog with not many teeth left. It was the bruise that hurt. Enough he was surprised he hadn't suffered a broken bone from that powerful bite.

"I guess we're going to Spokane, then." Dakota shifted in her seat.

He was only partly aware of her now. Fatigue and the pain in his shoulder and arm washed over him like a wave. He wanted to moan. Couldn't even remember where he'd put his pain meds. Or when he was due for another dose. Was Dakota feeling her injuries?

He shut his eyes.

Spokane. He tapped his phone against his thigh and thought about that city instead of his injuries. His office was there. The office he was supposed to be at tomorrow morning. Instead he'd be bringing down Clare. And *then* he would be driving back to the middle of northern Washington state to pick up his injured dog.

After that he was going to have to talk to Eden. Explain about Maggie. How her death had exposed and helped extinguish a serious threat. That was good. He should go with that in his attempt to give her some kind of peace in her grief. It might not help but maybe eventually.

And then what? He would have to go back to his desk at the DEA office in Spokane. Pretend none of this had happened. That it hadn't changed him or made him realize he could find what he needed on a different team.

He hadn't made the wrong choice, going for the DEA. He just wondered if God hadn't used that move to direct him to the next step.

Joining Victoria's team.

He wanted to ask the boss lady about a transfer. Dakota had said they were low one team member. Would she let him join? Should he tell her that he and Dakota had feelings for each other?

He had felt like they were testing him this weekend. Everything had erupted but that didn't mean the option was off the table.

What if he had to choose between the Northwest Counter Terrorism Taskforce and having a relationship with Dakota? Could he work alongside her, all the while denying his growing feelings for her?

"I got the email." Her voice was low. Like she thought he was sleeping, and she didn't want to disturb him.

Josh cracked his gritty eyelids open. "What does it say?" His voice was gravelly.

"There's a Senator hosting a town hall tomorrow. Big chain hotel, downtown Spokane. It's top of the list." She read off the senator's name.

"Big proponent of more government oversight, not less," Sal said. "A figurehead for 'the man,' trying to get everyone on federal programs. Beholden to government help just to get by."

Josh remembered that as well. Just not fast enough to have mentioned it before the marshal. "She thinks that's where Clare will release the last of the VX she bought?"

"Yes," Dakota said. "We think it's the most likely target. Make a big splash."

"And it lines up with her worldview. Anti-government." He figured they would know what he was talking about through the fog of his pain and fatigue.

"Yes, it does."

He heard the edge in her tone and figured she would know best. Her father had been exactly that type. She'd grown up as one of them. In any other time, Dakota could have been Austin—groomed to take over. Brainwashed for the cause.

Raised to fight as one of them.

A terrorist, threatening America.

Chapter 25

Dakota desperately wanted to sink into a chair. It wasn't even seven in the morning and she'd gotten about four hours of sleep. No police agency had caught sight of Clare, either late last night or this morning.

Josh stood beside her, the two of them providing legitimacy to the claim a possible terrorist was planning an attack on today's town hall meeting.

Across the suite at a tiny circle table, Senator Eric Walden ate a bite of his eggs. He'd tucked a napkin in the collar of his shirt, so he didn't get hollandaise on his tie. His dark hair had been styled with strategic use of hair dye, and his wedding ring wasn't on his finger.

Did he offer them a cup of coffee? No, he didn't. And at this point Dakota would have gnawed off her hand for some caffeine. Silly them, they'd considered a threat to the senator's life and the lives of innocent people to be a bigger priority than breakfast.

"And you think she'll bring this...gas or whatever it is with her?" He waved his fork in the air.

"Yes, sir," Dakota said. "This event is at the top of our list."

"Hmm. Aren't I lucky?" He shot a look at his aide.

The slender woman sitting across from him was on her iPad. She probably should have been eating. She looked like she needed some cheesy eggs in her life. She didn't smile. Just went back to her screen and whatever she was reading. Maybe the morning news report.

Josh took a step toward him. "With all due respect—"

"You know, Special Agent…what was it?"

"Weber."

The senator continued, "When people use the phrase, 'with all due respect' it usually doesn't mean anything good. Mostly it would indicate the fact you think I'm an idiot and you're about to say as much, but you wouldn't want me to get offended."

"I don't think you're an idiot."

Dakota wasn't sure if she agreed with the senator, or not. Josh was a nice guy and all. How a person treated animals said a lot about them. At least it was all she needed to know.

He had a good job. He hadn't whined when his truck was blown up. He hadn't minded when she took a handful of his fries last night. And his kiss?

Dakota felt her face flush.

Honestly, what else was she expecting? No man was perfect. Waiting for the perfect man was pointless because "he" didn't exist. But the man right in front of her? *This* man might just be perfect for *her.*

"I do think you aren't appreciating the potential danger here. Especially the lives of people who are looking to you as their duly elected official. For leadership and protection."

The senator's eyes narrowed as he considered Josh's words.

Josh continued, "Then there are those who didn't vote for you. I'm sure they're planning on attending this morning just to get in your face. Which group do you think will be more impressed that you've taken heroic steps to protect them? Those who already think it's your duty to do so, or the ones waiting for you to mess up so they can jump all over you?"

"Hmm."

"Yes." The aide didn't lift her attention from her screen. "Hmm."

What that was supposed to mean, Dakota wasn't sure. "So you're willing to cancel?"

The senator glanced at her as though he was surprised she was still there. Apparently he didn't consider her noteworthy enough to remember she was in the room.

His eyes also flared, along with his nostrils. As though he was just now remembering when she'd initially come in and he'd practically gasped. He'd asked her what on earth happened to her face.

"No," he said. "I won't be doing that."

"You'd rather a deadly contagion was released in a room full of people?"

"You yourself said there's a 'list.' Who's to say I'm even the actual target of this back-woods woman?"

Dakota was beginning to think about putting this guy on *her* list of targets. And she would start with punching him in his smug face. Josh might not approve, and Victoria certainly would not—bad for task force PR—but it would certainly make her feel better.

Her father had forced her hand, and she'd had to kill him.

Sadly, it hadn't improved her life any.

Thankfully Josh stepped in again. "Is it really worth the risk to you?"

"Perhaps it is," the senator offered back. "Perhaps the work I do is worth the risk, even the loss of life. What if my work is important enough that it justifies the potential loss of life?"

Dakota folded her arms. "If you think—"

"We understand, senator." Josh nodded. "It is important to see the bigger picture."

She had a new person she wanted to punch. His face wasn't smug. But if he wanted to kiss her again, he was going to have to disinfect those lips. She didn't want to kiss him when he'd just been kissing someone else…on the backside.

She shot him a death glare no one missed. But Dakota didn't care. Diplomacy wasn't her forte. "I'm calling my director. You want to have your little meeting? That's fine. You go ahead and try. Because when Victoria Bramlyn says no, it means *no.*"

The senator's face flushed red. "Victoria…" He blustered out her last name in a jumble. "That's what this is about? She's trying to sabotage my town hall meeting!"

Josh came back with his diplomatic tactics. "You have something with Director Bramlyn?"

"The woman hates me." He shot out of his chair, sloshing milky coffee on the white tablecloth. The aide frowned. The senator pulled the napkin from his collar and threw it on the table.

The aide shifted his coffee cup and got a drip on her finger, which she sipped between her pursed lips.

"Victoria Bramlyn? I should have known." A vein appeared on the senator's temple. "I should have *known* she would try to sabotage this. Get out. Both of you."

Josh shot Dakota a look. Probably because she'd used the same words on him.

"I didn't mean to kidnap your dog." Why that came out right then, she wasn't sure.

But it made Josh laugh.

Beyond the handsome display of humor the aide began to gasp.

"Uh…ma'am?" Dakota wandered between the two men.

The aide glanced up, the whites of her eyes completely red. She jerked a few times, and Dakota realized she was trying to breathe.

She coughed the last of the air in her lungs and white foam appeared on her lips.

Josh yelled, "Medic!" All reflex. The ingrained muscle memory of years serving his country in a place where they needed medical personnel on hand at all times. At least, that was what she figured.

The aide slumped to the side of her chair and kept going. Dakota reached out to catch her, then thought about the VX and recoiled. She didn't want to risk getting some on her.

The woman fell to the carpet. Dakota knelt by her side. Whatever her name was, she took her last choking breath and then the life was gone from her eyes.

Dakota looked over at the senator. "She's dead."

Two uniformed paramedics came in.

"There's been a murder!" The senator's voice was practically a wail. "My aide has been killed."

"It was in his coffee." Dakota held out a hand before the first one could touch the aide's face. Even with a gloved hand they needed to know. "Her clothes could be contaminated. So far it hasn't been transmitted, only directly administered. No one should touch that coffee cup."

She explained what she knew about the VX.

"The doctors at the hospital need to know everything about it that you do."

She nodded. "I can have it sent over…"

"And in the meantime?" the senator wailed again. "What do you expect me to do?"

Dakota stood and faced him. She ignored the wary look on Josh's face. He didn't have to worry about what she was going to say. Because there was no way for him to stop it.

"You're going to have to call a speech writer," she said. "Because it's time to make a statement."

• • •

The door to the senator's suite opened and Sal strode in. "She's still here."

Dakota spun to greet him. "Here?"

Sal nodded. "In the hotel."

The senator took a step back. One more, and he'd be sitting on the table where he'd been eating casually just a moment ago. Now his aide was dead, the room was crowded with first responders, and he was...

What? Certainly not affected by anything that was happening. At least as far as Josh could tell. It almost seemed like he was trying to figure something out. Maybe how he could spin this?

He reached for the aide's iPad.

"That's evidence. And it could be contaminated."

"Well it's not like I have my own."

He wasn't worried about dying? Josh said, "Yeah, they're pretty pricey." Which was dumb, but it was what came out of his mouth.

The senator shook his head. "No. I just only have a phone and a computer. If I'm going to go 'live' on social media to announce the tragic murder of my aide, then I'll need to use something with a faster processor."

Wow. This guy talked a good game. What was it Eden called it? The "gift of the gab." Anytime this man smacked his lips together, the words that came out made Josh want to shake his head in disbelief. Though the senator likely would've preferred Josh to jump to support, or into action. Not sit by in an incredulous stupor.

There were so many problems with what he'd said that Josh didn't know where to begin. "First of all, that's going to be collected as evidence. You want to use your phone, go get it. But don't go making announcements of any kind until it's been cleared by us. First thing we're going to do is make sure the next of kin is contacted."

Josh motioned to the dead woman, though she was surrounded by cops and the paramedics. "Does she have family?"

The senator made a face. Like a preschooler trying to solve multiplication. "Um...maybe?"

So he had no idea.

"We'll find out." Dakota folded her arms. "I don't want you breathing without permission until this is sorted out. There's a woman in this hotel who wants you dead and obviously has the means to get a deadly substance into your coffee. Who knows how she's going to try again when she discovers it failed? So if I were you, I wouldn't go making social media posts. All you're doing is inviting another murder attempt."

Josh waved Dakota and Sal over to the corner of the room. "Unless that's exactly what we want her to do. You know, draw her out? Set her up and then take her down..." He registered the looks on their faces. "And you guys already figured that out."

A look washed over Dakota's face, but she didn't share. He was intrigued enough he'd have to ask her about it later.

Sal said, "All our scouring the footage in the hotel paid off." That was good to hear, since Josh had been doing it at two in the morning. They'd taken shifts to get through all of it.

The marshal continued, "We saw her enter. Tracked her movements in the hallways. And we found the waiter she drugged, dead in a closet. She delivered the food to this room herself."

"And then never left the hotel?"

Sal nodded in answer.

Dakota shifted her weight, a thoughtful look on her face. "So she's hanging around to see if the job was completed? Or she left, and we just didn't catch it?"

Josh didn't know how they were supposed to be able to answer that question. "Do you have a photo of Clare?"

Sal pulled out his phone and swiped to a picture.

"Can I borrow that?" Josh went to the senator and held it out. "Have you ever seen this woman before?"

"Is that her?" He squinted at the screen, then moved across the room for some reading glasses which he slid onto his nose.

"Please answer the question."

He studied the phone. "I've never seen her in my life."

"So you have no idea why this woman might want you dead?"

He shrugged. And yet, Clare Norton had delivered his breakfast. She'd been inside this room.

If the VX had been sold to her from a third party, and she was working on orders as her friend had suggested, that made her no more than a hired gun. Maybe it wasn't personal. Could be Clare had nothing against the senator, and this was just a means to an end.

Josh moved back to Sal and Dakota. Both of their faces indicated they felt the same as he did. "He's got nothing." He kept the words quiet, not wanting the senator to hear. Josh didn't want to get suddenly audited by the IRS for no reason, or whatever put-out government officials did to get revenge.

Dakota pulled out her ponytail, flipped her hair forward and ran her fingers through it. When she stood upright she retied it, not meeting either of their eyes. Biting her lip. When she did look at Josh, he could see her eyes were wide. Her breath coming fast.

He stepped between her and Sal, shifting so she had to move with him toward the door. "We'll check in with Talia and see if she has anything new."

Dakota strode to the door and out to the hallway. She waited until he shut the door behind them and then set her hands on her thighs to lean forward.

"What is it?"

She said nothing, sucking in breaths.

"Walk with me." He tugged on her arm and led her down the hall to the elevator.

"I don't—" She gasped. "—want them to see."

But she was okay with him being the one who was with her? Josh didn't have time to truly appreciate what it meant that she would rely on him instead of her own team.

He hit the button for their floor. She handed over the card to her room, and he let them in. Talia was at the table. She looked up from her computer and saw Dakota.

"Give us a minute?"

She glanced at him, then took her laptop and shut the bedroom door behind her.

"Sit down." He led Dakota to the couch.

She wrung her hands between her knees. Josh knelt in front of her. "What is it?"

She blew out a breath. "I don't even know."

He guessed all of her emotions were crashing down on her after having been pushed aside for too long. She was wrung out physically and now emotionally as well. "Having feelings isn't a bad thing."

"Well, it's never been a good thing either."

"It is now." He planted a kiss on her forehead. "It's cleansing to get it out."

"It's exhausting. And now I have a headache again."

He moved to kiss her. She waved her hand and then grabbed a tissue from the box on the coffee table. Blew her nose first. "I'm all gross and puffy."

Josh thought it was cute. "I don't know how this will all shake out, but I know I'd rather be with you than without. I want it all. The job—the career—I had dreamed of. The one where I'm making a real difference. I want that. But I also want a relationship with you. The best kind of relationship."

Dakota stared at him. A little bit of shock, a little bit of hope.

"What do you want?"

The door lock clicked. From behind him, Talia said, "Sorry. I couldn't make them wait."

Victoria strode in. She caught sight of them and immediately a gleam birthed in her eyes. Josh hadn't figured any of them were confused about what was happening between him and Dakota.

And it wasn't a job interview for the open spot on this team.

But there wasn't time to talk about any of that right now.

The director said, "We found Clare."

Chapter 26

Victoria used a key in the elevator control panel, then hit two buttons. Eight was the floor for the senator's suite. And the basement.

The motor whirred and they descended. Dakota tried to shove off the embarrassment at being caught in the middle of an intense conversation with Josh. One she wished they could have finished. Especially considering he seemed to think the conversation needed to involve kissing.

She wanted to answer his question. Not that she knew exactly what she was going to say to him. What she "wanted" and what she actually got were usually two different things.

Maybe this break was good. The chance to think it through. To get it right, when they finally did finish that important conversation.

Was this going to be the one time that would be different?

Hope swelled, like the rest of her emotions had. So hard and fast it threatened to choke her they were so overwhelming, like life had caught up with her. Though it was more like it had crashed down on her.

She wanted to trust the hope she had in God and in what she knew of Josh. To believe that maybe, for once, there would be something good in her life.

She understood salvation and the grace she'd been given. The wonderful gift of redemption. But that didn't mean she wasn't lonely. That she didn't want to belong to someone. To find a family that had nothing to do with work.

Though, if it did turn out to be Josh, then it would be partly about work. If he joined the team.

Victoria tipped her head to the side. With Josh behind her, she caught Dakota's attention and then motioned to him with her eyes. Without moving her head. What was this, junior high? The woman seemed to think it was noteworthy that she'd caught Dakota and Josh having an emotion-laden conversation.

Dakota rolled her eyes. Victoria might be all business most of the time, but she was also a hopeless romantic. Dakota still remembered the disappointed look on her face when she'd explained to the director that there was nothing happening between her and Sal. And that nothing was *ever* going to happen. When she'd explained it, Victoria had understood.

Evidently she had her heart set on Dakota and Josh now.

Would she wind up being disappointed?

It might not be the normal environment for a lot of federal agencies, with their rules about employee fraternization. They would have to fill out the change of relationship paperwork. Make it official—if it happened. But also Victoria had determined to establish a close team. One that was a family. In her mind, this meant couples. Teams who supported each other, who worked in pairs, watching each other's backs.

Never mind the fighting. The distraction. The divorces. How did Victoria know it would all work out perfectly? If she wanted relationships in the team so badly, then maybe she should find one herself.

The elevator doors slid open on eight and Sal stepped in. "She's downstairs?"

Victoria nodded. "In the laundry facility."

A huge hotel like this probably had massive machines. Multiple rooms. "How are we supposed to find her?" Both of them looked at her. Josh shifted to stand closer, a welcome solidarity.

"Split up." Victoria pulled a paper from her pocket and handed it over. "I'll go with Sal, you stick with Josh. Work your way, room to room."

The paper was a map. The layout of the hotel basement—laundry facilities and storage closets.

"We'll work our way back to the middle and hopefully flush her out along the way."

"Sounds good," Josh said.

The unspoken hung between Dakota and her boss. Given what the woman had pulled—or attempted to pull—with trying to send Josh to speak to her father, she wasn't sure how she felt about Victoria. It had been messed up and ended with Dakota shooting her father. They were going to have to talk about that, just like she and Josh needed to talk.

And then there was the whole team meeting they needed.

Not to mention all the paperwork there would be after this weekend.

The elevator sped down to the basement. "What is happening with Niall?"

Victoria said, "The agents at his house, watching his family, said he showed up there. They're going to detain him until I can take over."

"Will he get fired?"

"There will be a full investigation into what happened."

He hadn't pulled a gun on her and Josh. But he had attempted to stall them so Clare had a better chance to kill yet more people. They had been fully aware of what he'd been attempting to do. Yes, his family had been in danger, but that would never excuse his actions.

If he continued with the team, there would be legitimate trust issues. A definite disrupt to their team dynamics.

"Look, it's been a long weekend," Victoria said, "for all of us. Right now we need to bring in Clare Norton. When it's done and the paperwork is submitted and we've all had a solid week of sleeping ten hours a night, then we can have a meeting. Hash everything out." She paused. "Okay?"

Dakota nodded.

"Good," Sal said. "Cause we're here."

The elevator doors slid open. Victoria removed her overcoat, revealing a bullet proof vest that matched Josh's—giving no specific designation of federal agency, just the word POLICE. She dropped the coat in the elevator while Dakota gaped. She hadn't noticed.

Victoria wasn't wearing a skirt.

She was wearing *pants*.

"We take west." The director stepped out after Sal and glanced back at the two of them. "Watch each other's backs."

Dakota nodded, still stunned.

Josh said, "We will."

He nudged her out of the elevator. They headed in the other direction, down a long hall of concrete floor. Pipes lined the ceiling, and Dakota heard rushing water.

She pulled her gun and lifted the map with one hand. She shook out the paper and checked the layout. "Dryer facilities are in front of us, end of the hall. Washers are in the room to the left."

"And the direction they went?" Josh dipped his head close, looking at the map.

"Supply rooms. And the kitchen."

He nodded, then stepped past her. Gun out. Leading the way. The sight of him made her heart swell. None of her teammates would ever presume to stand between her and the bullets. She was strong and capable. Many times she'd met the threat ahead while no one stood beside her. She'd been alone, no back up.

Interestingly enough, she thought she liked it. But now she could admit there was a sense of camaraderie, having a partner.

As long as he wasn't hanging out with her just to buy time before he went to speak to her father. But she didn't have to worry about that now.

Harlem was dead.

"I'm glad I killed him."

Josh kept moving, but she saw the hitch in his stride when she said quietly, "I'm glad he's dead."

They continued down the hallway.

"Maybe that makes me a horrible person. I'm not sure that I care." She paused. "Should I care?"

"I think it makes you a human being," he replied, equally as quietly. "What counts is what you do now."

"Like ask for forgiveness?" Did she want to do that?

"Maybe."

"Maybe," she repeated, not sure there was much to say about that. She needed to think more.

Victoria had been right about one thing.

It was time to find Clare.

• • •

Josh kept going, headed for the door in front of him. The sign next to the door read "Washing Room." In a hotel like this, it was probably running all day. The door was ajar.

He had to keep his focus. Not get distracted by what was going on with Dakota. This definitely wasn't the time for relationship stuff. She probably needed to talk to a professional. Someone who could give her the tools to process her pain.

Her life had been affected by major trauma—some of it just yesterday, when she'd faced down her father. There was likely a lot more emotion to work through before she could find an even keel again.

Josh would like to help her. But half the time he wasn't perfectly sane, given everything he'd seen and done. He was definitely not perfect. Nor did he have all the answers for her.

He would have to leave that stuff up to God.

Funny that it had taken something like this to get him to face the fact there were things he couldn't do himself. *Is that what being with Dakota is going to be like, Lord?* Maybe she was put in his life so that he would grow. To show him where he needed God even more. A relationship that actually spurred him on to grow spiritually wasn't something he'd ever considered.

Evidently when he'd said he wanted "it all," even he hadn't realized the extent of what that could look like.

Help us find Clare, Lord. Help us keep everyone safe.

Then they could work out all those other things.

Josh paused at the door and listened. He could hear the whir of washing machines. The circular rotation that made the sound go around and around in a rush.

He couldn't see anyone inside, staff or Clare Norton. Was she in there hiding out, up to something?

"Come on."

He nudged the door open and stepped inside. Dakota stuck close, and they quickly fell into the rhythm of partners working together. So much had changed in his life in just a couple of days. He could hardly believe how different he felt.

How different his life was after such a short time.

A short, round woman in a maid's uniform scurried around a corner carrying a stack of towels. She froze and gaped at them.

"Is anyone else in here?" Josh asked in a low voice.

She nodded vigorously and shifted the towels so she could point a shaky finger at the corner. She mouthed, "Over there."

"Get to the hall and go upstairs."

She rushed past them.

He looked at Dakota. She used hand signals to communicate. He nodded, and they split up.

Came at the corner from two different directions.

Clare Norton had her back to them, doing something.

Dakota called out, "Turn around, put your hands up."

Josh held aim on her while she jerked at the sound of Dakota's voice. *Busted.* Clare whipped her head around, and then turned. Sweat lined her forehead and upper lip. Her dirty clothes hung on her, and in her hand she held…

"Drop—

Dakota yelled at the same time he did.

But Clare only lifted it higher. Neither of them fired.

It was—

"A dead man's switch." Josh said it even before he realized they were in a much tougher position here than he'd imagined.

Clare shifted, and he saw what she'd been working on. Attached to the wall behind her she had been arming a bomb. A vial of amber colored liquid was wired into the circuit.

In her hand was a switch. If she released it, the bomb would detonate.

"You didn't kill the senator, so now you're going to destroy the building?" By releasing the last of the VX.

"My finger even twitches," she said, "and this whole building falls in on itself. If that doesn't kill everyone, the VX will."

They were about center in the basement. The elevator was on the south side, and they'd walked to about the middle of the hotel.

Was she right? Could the hotel come crashing down on top of them?

Dakota said, "Another task from whoever you're working for?"

Good question. Was Clare acting alone now or still under orders?

"He has the money to provide all kinds of toys," Clare said. "Now, the two of you are going to back up and let me walk out of here, or we all die."

The minute she was gone she would detonate the bomb—with them still inside. There was no way to give the order to evacuate and have everyone leave in time to save lives. And if he found a fire alarm—and pulled it— would she let go of that switch?

"Kill me, and the hotel falls on all of us," she said. "I'm walking out of here. No one is going to stop me. You're going to make sure of that. But either way, I will make my mark. In life, or in death."

They weren't going to dissuade her on the basis of ideology. They would never be able to convince her that what she believed was wrong.

Austin had been different. A young man would have doubts about the worldview he'd been taught, just like every other young man. Learning the world. Figuring out for himself what he believed, apart from what he'd been taught.

Josh had hit a point in his life where it'd been necessary for him to choose whether or not he agreed with his parent's faith. He'd had to decide to take it on board for himself.

With Clare he tried a different tactic instead. "Whatever he's paying you, I'll give you more. Name your price. We can guarantee you'll get out of here alive to collect what you earned."

They could catch her later, when she was comfortable in her riches, leaving a trail of spending behind her. Not that he had a pile of money or anything, but he could hopefully get her to comply anyway.

Maybe Victoria could use her government contacts to help him out.

While he spoke, Dakota moved closer to Clare, picking something up off a dryer as she went. What was her plan? The woman's attention was fixated on him, and he kept it by moving slightly to the left. Enough to make Clare twist around toward him, determined to keep him in her sights.

Clare laughed. "Good one. Like feds have money." She shot him an incredulous look, full of mirth. "You guys don't make that much."

"I have an inheritance. But if you don't want it…" She could decide whether he was telling the truth.

Clare narrowed her eyes. She spun around, and the realization that she'd been distracted flashed upon her face before she turned away. Toward Dakota.

But it was too late.

Dakota lunged at Clare and grabbed the hand holding the dead man's switch. In her other hand she held a roll of duct tape she'd swiped from the table.

Dakota held the end of the tape and wound it around their clenched hands so fast his brain had to catch up with what was happening.

Clare moved. He saw her hand reach for Dakota's gun. What was about to happen played out in his mind. She would pull the trigger and Dakota would die.

Josh didn't hesitate.

He aimed, tugged on the trigger and put a bullet in her thigh.

She turned the gun on him and fired.

Dakota screamed his name.

Sparks of light set off like fireworks at the edges of his vision. He fell back and hit the ground.

Everything went black.

Chapter 27

Dakota caught Clare's gun hand before she got off another shot. Her other hand was useless, taped around Clare's grip on the dead man's switch. She shoved the older, heavier woman back and then kept going. Their momentum shoved Clare's head against the breezeblock wall and knocked her out.

She slumped in front of Dakota and tugged her down so Dakota fell to her knees with the woman.

"Josh!" His name was a wail. A scream that seemed to split her head open it was so loud. So painful.

Hot tears ran down her face.

She'd seen him fall. That close, his vest would work. But there were so many other things that could go wrong. Was he okay? She clambered to her feet and ran to him.

Got two steps, then felt the pull of the unconscious woman.

Dakota fell to her knees again, one hand still attached to Clare's body.

Sal appeared in front of her.

She tried to speak. All that came from her mouth was a whimper. A wordless cry.

He sank to his knees. "Oh-kay." He ran his hands down her arm to the tape that was wrapped around two hands and a switch that would level the building on top of them. "Oh-kay."

He spoke the way she would've done to Neema, hurt and wanting to know where Josh was. When the pain would stop.

Victoria called out, "Ambulance is on its way," her voice strained.

Dakota didn't see her.

"We need the bomb squad, too!" Sal called back. Looking down at Dakota, he said, "She's with Josh. But don't worry about him. Our job is to worry about you." He answered the question she hadn't asked yet.

"Bomb."

"Yes, the bomb." He slid out his phone and called the local police for SWAT. Past that, her ears just quit working.

He jostled her so she could lie down.

Someone walked close to her face. Dakota tried to focus. She was shifted into someone's arms and then lifted. The world spun.

"Clare..."

"She's cuffed. They're dealing with the bomb." He walked.

Dakota blinked some more but couldn't see clearly. "Josh." He would know what she meant.

Sal walked past a bustle of people. She opened her eyes to see them crouched over something. Moving. Talking.

They all sat back.

"Clear."

The man between them lifted off the ground, then flopped back down.

An electronic voice said, "Pulse detected."

"Let's get him out of here."

"See." Sal spoke close to her ear. "He's going to be fine."

Dakota shook her head. Pain reverberated through her skull, threatening unconsciousness at the edge of her vision.

"Does she need a doctor?" She thought maybe that was Victoria.

"She needs to get out of here."

He kept moving. Being in motion wasn't helping. Sal needed to put her down, but she was pretty sure her legs would simply collapse under her.

She knew what she needed. "Josh."

He'd been too close. Those people. *Clear.* The bullet's impact into his vest must have stopped his heart. It would've kept the bullet from cutting straight through the middle of that all-important organ, but it also would've impacted with such force…

Enough it had stopped his heart.

"Josh." His name was a moan from her lips.

"Seems like you have a soft spot for him."

Maybe. That was the word she'd said to Josh. "Yes."

Sal knew and that was enough for now. Would she get the chance to tell Josh her answer? *God, I don't want him to die. I want life. With him.* And yet, just yesterday she had murdered someone.

No, not murder.

She'd killed an escaped prisoner who had been about to kill her. It was justified, no matter who the parties were.

She had pulled the trigger. Part of her screaming, wanting it all to end. The rest of her burning in rage at what he'd done. *I killed someone.*

Would she ever be free of it? He was gone from this world now. Her father was answering for his life. The same way she would have to answer for hers.

What counted in the end was what she did with the time she had left.

Time she wanted to spend with Josh.

More tears ran down her face. Had she stopped crying? "Doesn't make sense."

"What doesn't?"

"Not going to call me Cupcake?" Did she want him to? She hardly knew what she was saying right now.

"Don't joke." He said, "Just tell me what doesn't make sense."

Had she been joking?

"Dakota." He stepped out of the elevator, still carrying her. "Tell me what doesn't make sense."

Josh. "Met him on Friday." How could there possibly already be so much between them? It had been only a weekend. Three days, given it was Monday now. "Monday," she said. "Right?"

"Payday."

Dakota shook her head. Like she cared about that? All her bills were automated. If she needed something, she used the cash she kept in an envelope in her sock drawer. The rest of it was for a rainy day.

"Your sock drawer?" He jostled her, but got the door open.

"Put me—"

Talia wailed. "Is she okay? I heard about Josh. Did he seriously *die*?"

Dakota sucked in a breath. Coughed. Gasped.

Sal lowered her to the couch in the suite she shared with Talia. "Easy. Catch your breath. Big inhale."

It was choppy and ended too soon, but she got air in.

"Blow it out like you're blowing through a straw."

She frowned but gave it a try.

"Good. Keep going." Sal's frown started to smooth out. "Suck in, like through a straw. Then blow out."

"How do you know this stuff?" Talia asked him.

Dakota kept quiet because she wanted to know the answer to that as well.

"My little brother had asthma."

Had?

Sal got up and strode across the room. He came back with a cup of tepid water from the bathroom sink. "Sip it."

Dakota held the cup with both hands. It wasn't much, but she managed to get more water in her mouth than on the hotel carpet, her hands were shaking so badly. "I need to get to the hospital."

"Good idea." Talia nodded. "Get yourself checked out. Who knows what's wrong with you under the surface that we don't see." Then she made a face and ruined all the compassion that had been in her tone.

"I'll throw this water at you." Her voice cracked in the middle, but she got all the words out. Most of the communication happened in her facial expression though. She thought.

"Ah, yes. And check on *Josh*. Of course." She said his name with a *tone*.

"I have to get back for English class so I can turn in my late homework."

Sal actually laughed.

Dakota pushed out a breath. All her energy dissipated like the plug being pulled out of a drain. Enough of the jokes. Besides, there had been *nothing* funny about middle school.

"Talk. Then hospital." She was fading fast. They needed to just hurry up and say it.

"I can't find any trace of the person who sold Clare Norton the contagion."

"And a bomb."

Talia's head jerked. "Wha…"

Sal said, "Continue."

Talia complied. "The server I was in on the dark web is gone now. It's not just missing; it's like it was never there in the first place. There's nothing to find. Like whoever it was simply doesn't exist."

Dakota frowned and started to get up. "That doesn't—"

Her eyes rolled back in her head.

Sal caught her before she hit the floor.

. . .

Josh watched the door until it opened. Blond hair swayed as the woman entered. He didn't want to be disappointed, but…

"Don't look so sad to see me, okay?" Victoria didn't smile. There was something in her eyes. He didn't know what it meant. Something she had to say that he wasn't going to like.

"Where's Dakota?"

She shifted the chair, even though it was in a perfectly fine position, angled toward his hospital bed. Then she sat. Knees together, purse on her lap. She smiled.

He didn't like it. "Vic—"

She lifted a hand. "She's here."

"She's okay?"

"Not exactly." A frown drew her brows together.

Her phone rang. He heard it vibrate. But she didn't reach for it. She kept all of her attention on him. "She's unconscious. They said there might be a bleed on her brain. Possibly from the concussion." She pushed out a slow breath. "They said if the swelling doesn't go down soon they might have to do surgery. Right now she's in a medically induced coma."

She held her hands on her lap again. Josh noticed a white line on her finger. Tan, and the lighter skin where a ring had been. A mark of her history. Of a life lived, loved ones she'd shared that life with. However it had ended, good or bad, Victoria had lived.

Josh shut his eyes. He'd been shot—again. They'd patched up the first, and helped him recover from the impact of the other one. He'd woken up *hours* ago. Had anyone been able to tell him where Dakota was, and what happened to Clare? No.

Until he'd demanded to see Victoria.

He hadn't stopped thanking God that Clare had been captured and everyone else was all right. When she got out of the hospital, Clare would be headed to prison. And Dakota? *God help her heal.*

He needed her to be all right.

He needed *her.*

"Your boss at the DEA called me. He was asking after you."

Josh said, "Yeah?"

She gave him a small smile. "I told him you'll make a full recovery. He said you have promise. That whatever was going on here that you'd gotten involved in, I should seriously consider you for my open position."

"He said that?"

"Guess he figured if I'd come fishing he shouldn't stand in my way." Her smile widened. "Smart man."

"What does that mean?" He wanted to know about Dakota. Josh wasn't interested in a riddle that would, on any other day, have been just another conversation.

"When you get out of here, we'll talk. Okay?"

And he was supposed to know what *that* meant? "If you get me in to see Dakota."

Victoria smiled. "I have an orderly bringing a wheelchair right now."

"Thank you."

"No, Josh. Thank *you*." She leaned her hip against the side of the bed. "I've seen a difference in Dakota the past few days. Something I've never seen in all the years I've known her. Even back when I only knew her from afar and admired the direction her career was going." She paused. "Thank you for that."

Something good?

She smiled, "I was aware of you as well, back when you were in J-bad. The work you and Neema did in Afghanistan was exemplary. Those are the kind of team members I need. You might not always work inside the lines, but you're the ones who sit out in the woods on a Friday night just to save your teammates the hassle of having to show up in a dinky little town to follow some chatter Talia picked up."

"Dakota?"

She nodded. "The past few days…it's like she opened. I don't know any other way to put it than that. She *opened*. To you." She placed a hand on his arm. "So when you're out of here, I'll expect you to call in."

It sounded like she was asking him to report for duty. Which he was entirely fine with.

The orderly came in before he could say anything. Victoria squeezed his arm and quietly left. This exchange with Victoria was nothing like he'd experienced with his boss at the DEA. He decided then that even after working for her for years, he'd probably still be surprised by her.

That thought distracted him from the extremely difficult task of getting from the bed to the wheelchair, without crying a little bit at least. His chest was on fire, and he didn't know what hurt worse.

But he needed to see Dakota. He needed to hold her hand while he prayed for her.

The orderly wheeled him to her room. Josh's heart sank. She was so pale. The orderly hit the brake on the wheelchair, locking the wheels in place, and then he was alone with her.

Hooked up to machines while her body healed.

Was she on a knife's edge?

He squeezed his eyes shut and prayed for her. When he opened them, a tear rolled down his face. There was so much he wanted to tell her. So much he wanted to say.

"I love you."

The words were a whisper from his lips. Josh lifted her hand and placed a kiss on the back of it.

He wanted to know the answer to his question. To know if she could handle them being more than friends and working together on the same team. It wouldn't be easy but no relationship was. He couldn't think of anything that could be better than working so closely with the person who would be his best friend.

If she agreed.

Epilogue

Six months later

"You've got that look in your eye, Weber."

Josh held the door for an FBI agent escorting one of the suspects outside. Wind blew the trees, sending the smell of smoke for miles. Thankfully they'd gotten inside and taken down every suspect in time for the local fire department to come in and put the blaze out.

He trotted to catch up with Dakota, shifting his shoulders to try and ease the tension in his muscles. All it did was remind him how gritty he was with sweat. They'd been running hard for days, working on the takedown for this case.

"What look?"

She stopped in the middle of a sea of people. Flashing blue and red lights. Fire hoses. Mud. But despite the smile, she didn't look at him. She leaned to the side and said, "Neema, heir!" In the low tone he'd taught her to use. One full of command.

His dog trotted up and sat beside her, leaning her weight against Dakota's leg. Taking the pressure off her hip.

Josh bit his lip.

Dakota grinned. "The one that means you're going to make me talk about my feelings."

"Would I do that?"

She'd at least given him the chance to tell her he was falling in love with her, back when she'd first woken up at the hospital. They'd fallen into a rhythm since then. Friendship and…more.

But he was ready to turn that "more" into something that would be a gift from God. The full experience of what a relationship between them would mean, instead of going home at the end of the day to his empty apartment.

"Out with it."

Josh shook his head. She'd learned to read him. He had to give her credit for that.

"Now."

He laughed and reached into his jeans pocket. He should have known she would do this. That she would call him out, and he'd have to ditch all his plans.

They could have that dinner later. It would still be special.

Josh pulled on the drawstring and used two fingers to retrieve what was inside.

"Are you going to make me wear a dress?"

Oh. He'd never thought about that part. "Traditionally, yes. I suppose you would." Unless she really didn't want to. He hadn't wanted to freak her out with where this was going, so it wasn't like he'd brought up the subject of a white gown and a giant cake.

She looked at the ring.

Looked at him.

Looked at the ring again.

"Fine."

"Excuse me?"

She grinned up at him. "I suppose, just once, I could wear a dress."

Good. But that better not have been an answer to the question he hadn't even asked yet. "Dakota."

"What?"

He still held the ring up between them. A few people had stopped, and the noise level of their immediate vicinity had lowered considerably. He took a breath.

"Will you marry me?"

Dakota said, "Yes."

The crowd around them cheered. Josh slid the ring on her finger and spun her in his arms before he set her back on the ground. Then, he kissed her.

Neema barked.

DID YOU ENJOY THIS BOOK?

Would you consider leaving a review at the online store where you purchased it?

Reviews (good and bad) help prospective readers decide whether or not to click that "buy" button. I know I love to see what other people thought about a book.

Want to read more LISA PHILLIPS books?

Check out www.authorlisaphillips.com and sign up for the mailing list, where you'll be the first to hear about Lisa's newest books.

Also by

Lisa

Phillips

Denver FBI
- Target
- Bait
- Prey

WITSEC Town Series
- Sanctuary Lost
- Sanctuary Buried
- Sanctuary Breached
- Sanctuary Deceived
- Sanctuary Forever

Novellas
- Sanctuary Hidden
- A Sanctuary Christmas Tale

Double Down
- Deadly Exposure
- Deadly Secrets

- Deadly Agenda
- Deadly Holiday

Love Inspired Suspense
- Double Agent
- Star Witness
- Manhunt
- Easy Prey
- Sudden Recall
- Dead End
- Security Detail
- Homefront Defenders
- Yuletide Suspect
- Witness in Hiding
- Defense Breach
- Murder Mix-Up

Northwest
Counter-Terrorism Taskforce
- First Wave
- Second Chance
- Third Hour
- Fourth Day
- Final Stand

615 - 767 - 1407

Made in the USA
San Bernardino, CA
11 July 2019